Divided Nation

Part One: Divine Destiny

NaCo

DIVINE ROYALTY PUBLISHING
Johnson City, Tennessee 37602

Unless otherwise noted, all scriptures are taken from the King James Version of the Holy Bible.

Copyright by Divine Royalty Publishing and Divine Royalty Ministry
Johnson City, TN 37602
www.dividednation.org

Cover Design by The Writing Shop, Ventura CA

Preface

Since the 1600's to the present time, the African American presence in America has been one success story after another. We have witnessed African Americans making impressive progress from the basement of America as slaves, ascending to the greatest heights of this country, fulfilling almost every department office and position America has to offer.

The stories behind such progress have been told by authors, poets, playwrights, movie producers and others who were able to capture the drama and trauma that accompanied African Americans' struggles to survive and achieve in a very hostile environment. As their great story unfolded in the African American history, we can't help but celebrate such great heroes and sheroes like Jupiter Hammon, Phyllis Wheatly, David Walker, Joseph Cinque of Amistad, Harriet Tubman, Frederick Douglass, Oscar Dunn, Booker T. Washington, W.E.B DuBois, Thurgood Marshall, Marcus Garvey, Rosa Parks, Martin Luther King, Jr., and Malcolm X, just to name a few. Not to mention the countless others who helped the progress in the areas of politics, employment, entertainment, religion, literature, law, media, film, TV, music, visual and applied arts, science, technology, sports and military.

It could be easily said African Americans are the most progressive people on the planet, because of how fast and far they have advanced.

Today one can't help but wonder why a people whose entire existence appears to be based on progress, has slowed their momentum. Some would argue that African American progress and achievement has come to a complete stop.

Divided Nation came into existence as I stepped out of the world of reality and entered a world of fantasy in my quest to find answers to some questions that I believe lie dormant beneath the surface of the African American community. Questions such as:

Where does a formerly progressive people go from here? What is the next conceivable level? Not only where would they go, but also how would they go? Who would dare to go? What would the mainstream say about their attempt to go? Who or what would be the power behind the forces that would try to stop them from going? The most important question of all is who would go before them as their courageous leader? Many African Americans have been seeking and longing for charismatic, messianic leadership since the glorious 1960's when great African American leaders were plentiful.

The African American community has a legacy of great leaders, who beat astronomical political odds that were staked against them. I wanted to create a leader who could rekindle the dreams and recharge the morale of black people, inspiring them to pick up the momentum of former years while stepping out of the shadow of yesterday's accomplishments. This leader would inspire African Americans to make one more great move -- maybe the greatest move in the history of America.

As this story and character developed I found myself giving today's generation a little more than I bargained for when I began writing Divided Nation. I created Raymond Jackson to expose today's generation to a kind of moral and political leader the previous generation had the privilege of knowing. I hope that Raymond and his mission will be meaningful to today's generation even if they could only experience him on paper as a manifestation of my creative imagination.

I also wanted to contribute, something more than hustling, guns, sex, money, murder or dirty success at the expense of another person's downfall to the literary fiction of our time. Divided Nation is not totally free of such elements, but they are presented in the context of our times to communicate a greater lesson than the drama itself.

From the outset because of its storyline or subject one may assume Divided Nation is a racist, anti-American and controversial book. But if one reads it with an open mind they will see the plot is used to convey a message about destiny's call to a person and to people who are spiritual enough to use democracy as a passport to advance to another political level.

My prayer is that Divided Nation will become an American and African American classic, inspiring many generations to dream and to move away from mediocrity by understanding that, "All things are possible to them who believe," Mark 9:23

Now let's take a journey back to the future!

Dedication

I dedicate this book to the Joseph generation.
You know who you are.
Get ready for the palace.

Picture 1: ***First Time Ever***

It is the year 2024 and a crowd gathers in anticipation of hearing from one of the presidential candidates. Tempers are running high and tension is in the air. There are two marching bands. One is an all-white band playing a political campaign song; the other is an all-African American band playing the same song but with a jazzy, soulful infusion.

In the shadows, Congressman John Newton, a white male in his mid 50's with plans of becoming the next president, is reviewing his campaign speech. Youthful in manner, but versed in the rough and tumble of politics Newton is now approaching the platform with a confident, bright smile. He raises his hand in a friendly gesture to the crowd who is chanting, *"Change America for the better."* He begins to move his fist in rhythm to the chant as he joins in with the crowd. *"Change America for the better," "Change America for the better."*

"We want to thank you for coming out so early this morning. I can see a lot of you have your coffee and muffins," John says to the crowd.

"I made you some Mr. President," a young lady in the crowd shouts.

"Well, thank you dear. If it is good then we might get you to replace the person who makes the coffee back at headquarters," Newton responds.

John Newton was good at blending with the crowd, making them feel that he was a part of them, unlike some of the other candidates who set themselves above the people. He gives his audience a chance to know and like him before he starts his speech.

Even though he is the one running for President he is not the keynote speaker. He is just warming the crowd up for the man who he chose to run as Vice President. Raymond Jackson is a 40 year-old man who looks to be in his 30's, very stylish, conservative, but in a subtle way. Why is Jackson the focal point? For one reason: he is an African American. Raymond's entire value to the campaign is based on his talent to speak, motivate and inspire the crowd. Many people call him the three "M's": Martin, Malcolm and Mandela all in one.

As Newton nears the end of his speech he prepares the crowd for his running mate. "Well, this morning I want to give you the person who you came out to hear. Every time I hear him speak I wonder what he is going to say next. This is the man who is going to help me change America for the better. He is "Mr. Change" himself, and come this November he will be America's first male African American Vice President: Mr. Raymond Jackson.

The crowd cheers as Raymond approaches the podium. The all-African American band is playing a jazzed up version of "A Change is going to Come." Raymond throws his hand up with the peace sign, "Peace! It has been a long time coming, but a change is about to come!" The crowd is hyped up, hollering, clapping and cheering. After they calm down Raymond coolly steps up to the microphone and speaks. "They say a people can change a society, but society can't change a people. Well, we're not here to change a people, especially those who are stuck in their ways. But we as a people can change America for the better. And this can only be done through our collective efforts. No one person, neither John Newton, nor I can change anything without the involvement of the people. I know you are the kind of people who love change, because your presence here today is a change within itself."

The crowd claps and cheers. "But right now time is working against us because we are running out of time. Our sons are running out of time, our businesses are running out of time, and our daughters are running out of time. But if you get us in the White House I believe it will be a time in history when time will stop and stand still." The crowd is clapping and cheering with even more excitement. "But when we get there we are not just concerned about time stopping from that point, I promise you are going to turn back the hands of time. Back to when there were low crime rates; back to when there were enough jobs for everyone; back to when parents could send their children to safe schools; back to when there was justice and equality for everyone. We will turn back the hands of time."

"I love you Raymond," a lady in the crowd screams out.

"Talk to us son," a man's voice also hollers out from the crowd.

"And once we stop time; then turn back the hands of time, it's only one more thing we must do -- and that is get time on our side. See we will no longer have to fight time, we no longer will be working against time, or running out of time, but time will be on our side. Would you tell the person next to you, time is on our side?" The crowd follows Raymond's instructions, turning to each other with a smile on their face as though they were relaying the best news they heard in a long time.

Raymond continues, "This is why we can't lose. This is why we will win in November, because time has already made a conscious decision to vote for John Newton and Raymond Jackson this November. I tell you time is on our side." The crowd waves, stomps feet, pumps fists, claps, whistles and cheers. On that note, Raymond leaves the podium.

Picture 2: *Let's Do Lunch*

After Raymond's inspiring speech the crowd went wild.

As Raymond is led to his limo by his security detail he is kissing babies and shaking hands. People are crowding around him, giving his security men more work than they anticipated. His security is pushing the crowd back while at the same time trying to usher Raymond into the limo.

"We're with you Raymond!" someone from the crowd shouts. Raymond's security finally gets him into the limo as he continues to wave to his supporters who could be easily mistaken for rock and roll fans, and they drive off.

Once inside the limo Raymond's staff informs him of his itinerary for the day. "Sir you have a 3:00 pm appointment with a bank broker and I'm going to call to confirm," Tarisha says in a tone of telling him more than asking. Raymond nods his head OK. Raymond always did what Tarisha suggested.

They have been together since graduate school, where between her and his father Bishop Jackson, Raymond was motivated to go into politics rather than to continue in his promising career as professional singer. He had made numerous accomplishments in the music arena and his performer's confidence played a major role in his ability to communicate to the audience, thus assisting his political career. Tarisha Holiday was Raymond's rock and backbone. She was a tall, light-skinned African American, who often told Raymond if she could give up being a top model for a career in politics, then he could give up singing.

"Sir, were you able to sign those papers I gave you yesterday?" Toni Maybley, Tarisha's assistant, a young white intern asks Raymond. Based on Raymond's lack of a response, Toni shakes her head as she reaches for Raymond's briefcase to retrieve the unsigned papers.

The limo phone rings and everyone reaches for their own cell phones. The phone rings again and everyone smiles. Jackie, Tarisha's other assistant answers the phone. "Yes, yes sir. Can you hold please? It's Mr. Jackson's father," Jackie says to Tarisha.

"Put him on the speakerphone," Raymond says without hesitation. One of his security men moves quickly to push the speaker button.

"Hey Dad," Raymond says like a young boy being picked up from daycare by his father.

"How are things going son?" Bishop Jackson asks.

"Well, you know the political life, there's never a dull moment."

"I just finished watching you on TV, it sounds like you got what it takes," his father says.

"You think so?" *Raymond has always sought his father's approval and sometimes it slips out in his conversation.*

"Either you do, or you're putting on a great act," his father jokes, causing the staff to laugh.

"Hey dad, say something to the staff," Raymond tells his father.

"Good morning Mr. Jackson, Raymond's staff says.

"I pray you all have a blessed day," Bishop Jackson replies.

"Thank you sir we will need it," Tarisha says humorously.

"So what can I help you with Dad?"

"Well, son I really need to see you today." Tarisha, Toni and Jackie shake their heads no, all at once.

"Is there a problem?" Raymond asks anxiously.

"Yes and no, it's very important that I talk to you face to face," Bishop Jackson says as he places a little more emphasis on seeing Raymond.

"What time?"

"How about at lunchtime?" his dad replies.

"Are we meeting at our usual place?"

"Yes, I'll see you there son,"

"Love you Dad, bye."

Raymond's staff closed their planners and shook their heads. Raymond reclines in the chair with a confused expression on his face that he made no attempt to hide. He wondered what could be of such importance that his father wanted to interrupt the flow of his political campaign. Raymond could tell that this unexpected appointment upset his staff, but he never could refuse his father. Tarisha has been with Raymond for over ten years, but couldn't understand how Raymond could be so highly accomplished but to mention his father's name would reduce him to abject humility instantly. Was it fear, honor, a deep sense of respect, or was it pure love? Whatever it was, it caused Raymond to drop everything he was doing and everything his staff planned for him to do. What could be so important?

Picture 3: *Out to Lunch*

Sitting at a table in their favorite restaurant, waiting for his son's arrival Bishop Jackson looks at his watch as a waiter comes to his table. "Would you like to order now or wait for your company?" the waiter asks. "I'll wait, thank you," Mr. Jackson replies.

As soon as the waiter leaves Raymond enters with three of his security men. Other diners recognize him and inform others of who he is. When Raymond reaches his father's table, they shake hands and hug as if they haven't seen each other in years. Raymond reintroduces his three top security men to his father. "Dad you remember Max, Brad and Jack don't you?"

"Oh, yes," Bishop Jackson warmly shakes their hands.

"We will be right over there if you need us sir," Max indicates to Raymond. Raymond nods his head in acknowledgment as he takes a seat at his father's table.

"Did you order yet?" Raymond asks.

"No, I'm not concerned about eating. Maybe I'll get something later," his father says.

"Wow this sounds serious. Are you OK?"

"I'm fine."

"How is mom doing?"

"Everything is fine at home and at the Church," Bishop Jackson reassures him."

"Well, I'm glad to hear that," Raymond says, breathing a sigh of relief. "I'm all ears you got my attention," Raymond says with a little smile on his face.

"Son, I want you to know how proud you've made me."

Raymond sips on his water and smiles to the compliment that was like sweet music to his ears.

"You have accomplished everything I wanted you to with your school, your outstanding achievements and the many other things you've accomplished. You have done more than I would ever be able to do. And now my son has the chance to be the first male African American Vice President of America. I can hardly believe it," Mr. Jackson says with a "how about that?" undertone.

Raymond's security man steps over to give him a message. "Excuse me sir," Max says. "Sir I hate to interrupt, but there is a couple who would like to take a picture with you," Max says.

Raymond looks at his father and his father shakes his head "Yes." As soon as he does a middle-aged white couple comes over.

Raymond is about to stand. "You don't have to get up Raymond, we can sit with you," the lady suggests pushily. Her husband seems to be following along, enjoying the trip.

"You are an outstanding speaker," the husband says to Raymond as he smiles for the camera with his arm around Raymond.

"Stop talking and let the man smile Fred," his wife says. Raymond places a big smile on his face as he finds himself sandwiched between two of his older, aggressive political supporters. "Thank you, thank you very much," they both say as they shake Raymond's hand and then are escorted away by his security.

"I knew it was going to be one of those days," Raymond says to his father.

"It's all part of the job, son. As I was saying I want you to know how proud I am of you. Regardless of what happens from here you have accomplished more than I could have ever prayed for," his father says.

"Thanks dad."

"Son, I want to take you to meet someone tonight. This person is very important to both of us."

"Who is he?"

"Well, I'll wait and let him introduce himself.

"What time can we do this? My staff is going to kill me," Raymond says as he consults his digital planner.

"At 7:00 pm and we should be finished by 8:00 pm."

"Where are we going?" Raymond asks as he looks up from his planner.

"You know the Hotel Plaza downtown."

"Is it a couple of blocks from the courthouse?" Raymond asks.

"Exactly, I'll meet you in the lobby at 7:00 pm.

Raymond notices two more couples waiting and signals them over. One asks for an autograph and the other wants to take a picture. Then all of them gather and ask Bishop Jackson to take the picture for them. This was the sign that his son had the support of the people. During the short time he sat at the table with Raymond, he witnessed people of all ages, classes, ethnicities and cultures asking for pictures, autographs and handshakes. This was also a clear indication his son was ready for the meeting at 7:00 pm. *But was he ready to meet the person who arranged the meeting? What if he was ready for the meeting, but not ready to meet the person who the meeting was about?*

The couple who asked to take the picture didn't have any idea they were being used to bring about events that would be remembered for along time. Some would remember it for the good and others would not. But these moments would be remembered, and this picture was proof.

"1,2,3, say 'Cheese'," Bishop Jackson says and snaps the picture.

Picture 4: *Political Science*

Since Raymond was selected to run for Vice President more young people, especially college students, have become very interested in politics. The political science class at Morehouse University just watched a video of one of Raymond's speeches, and the Professor is conducting an open discussion. "So class what do you think of Mr. Raymond Jackson?" Professor DuBois asks.

"I think he is as fine as ever," one female student answers to the class' laughter.

"Let's limit our comments to his suitability as a candidate please. Thank you," Professor DuBois says. "Steve what do you think about Mr. Jackson?" Professor DuBois asks.

"I believe he could be the first black President and that would be cool," Steve says.

"I need something more than 'Would be cool,' Professor DuBois replies. Lena raises her hand and Professor DuBois acknowledges her immediately.

"Well, to be honest, I think that's what his entire campaign is built on. He is taking the cool approach rather than the normal conservative political approach," Lena explains.

"Do you mean he is taking the liberal approach like Clinton did in the 90's when he went on the Arsenio Hall Show and played the saxophone and his approval rating went through the roof?" the Professor interprets for Lena.

"Who is Arsenio Hall?" Lena asks and the class laughs.

"I don't think he is anything like Clinton," James, another student comments.

"OK why would you say that?" the Professor asks.

"Clinton wasn't cool. He knew how to do some cool things to appear to be cool, but Raymond is naturally cool. See you know about politics, but I'm the teacher of the school of cool," James explains. The class laughs. "No, no let me put you down with the cool demonstration," James says as he stands up and walks in front of the class. "The reason Raymond is going to win is only because it's in his nature to be cool and when you got it like that, you don't have to do cool things to be cool. Whatever you do is going to be cool, and people are going to want to be around you because you make them feel what you are naturally -- cool. So Raymond don't have to go on any show and play the sax, all he has to do is show up in November and its over." The class claps and James takes a bow and walks to his seat.

"That was well put Mr. James, from the 'School of Cool'," the Professor says sarcastically. "But you are overlooking the fact Raymond Jackson is going on the television shows, hanging out with celebrities, embracing the Hip-Hop Culture and these things may be the main factors in winning this election," Professor DuBois says.

"I heard someone offered him a movie deal," a female student says.

"I'm not talking about getting our information about Mr. Jackson from a gossip magazine," Professor DuBois says.

"I don't see what all the fuss is for over this Tom. He's a Tom like all the rest of the house niggers; he's just a cool popular Tom house nigger. All of them are the same to me. When it comes down to it, they are not going to do anything but get rich at the expense of the poor people," stated Scott a more radical student.

"My militant friend, I would think you'd be happy you're getting your first male black Vice President," the professor fired back.

"Happy we are getting a token to pimp our people, causing them to think we have something when we have zip," Scott countered.

"So what are you looking for in an African American Vice President?" the professor asks.

"I'm not looking for anything. Now what I want is a new script. What I want is to go back to the beginning, go back to our homeland and start from the beginning. Our own land, leaders, laws and liberty, the way we define it to be, not what they want to give us," Scott says.

"That's not going to happen. Think realistically," a female student states.

"It can happen if we really want it to, but we're not thinking on that level," says James.

"I don't think anyone is," James states supporting Scott's viewpoint.

"Maybe someone is thinking on that level as we speak, but it has not been manifested yet," Lena says.

The bell rings. "Do a five page report on Mr. Newton and the role he is playing in this race. Due on Monday. Thanks and have a good weekend everybody," Professor DuBois says.

Picture 5: *Give It Up*

Raymond meets up with his father who is taking him to meet Paul Goodson. They step off the elevator and walk up to Suite 108. Bishop Jackson knocks on the door. Mr. Goodson opens the door. He is 5'10", 190 lbs, in his mid 70's (but looks to be in his 60's), bald, clean shaven, attractive and appears to be in good physical shape.

"My son, come in. And you are on time as always," Goodson says. As they enter the room, Raymond is impressed by the grandeur of the suite.

"I didn't know it was this big in here," Raymond says.

"Your first time at the Plaza?" Goodson asks?

"Yeah, and if I had known it was this nice I would have stayed here a few times myself," Raymond replies.

"There's a first time for everything, and who knows you maybe staying sooner than you think," Goodson responds.

Raymond walks over and shakes his hand. "Excuse my manners, my name is..." Raymond begins to say, but Mr. Goodson smoothly interrupts.

"Raymond Jackson. You were born February 12, 1968, in Atlanta, Georgia. You attended Benson Elementary School, Polo Middle School, and Towson High. You graduated on the Dean's List from Harvard University, and you have a scar on your right arm from playing football. Your favorite ice cream is Butter Pecan. You've been married to a lovely lady named Diamond Jackson for 15 years, and for five of those years you have been having an affair with a young lady named Nicole Jones."

Raymond is astonished by Goodson's knowledge of his background. He looks at him and then at his father. His father shakes his head to suggest he didn't tell him anything. "Hold, hold, did my father tell..." Raymond begins to ask.

"No son, no one told me anything about you, I'm your Godfather." Raymond looks at his father in bewilderment as if to ask, "Is this true?" "I was the one who stood at your christening, but stayed anonymous until the time was right," Goodson explains.

"I guess this means the time is right?" Raymond asks as he stuffs his hands in his pockets. "OK, you're my Godfather. You could have revealed this to me at our family reunion. I'm a busy man Mr. Goodson, so what is all this about? Why am I here?" Raymond says with annoyance.

"You are here to give up the Vice Presidency," says his Godfather. Raymond's laughter fills the room until he notices the serious expressions on his father and Goodson's faces. "This is a joke right," Raymond asks his father again, "Right dad?"

"Just listen son," his father responds.

"Raymond where you are in life right now was planned by your father and me. We selected the schools, the people and the places you would encounter to prepare you for this very important time. You are not destined to be Vice President," his Godfather states.

"This is crazy. Man you are crazy," Raymond responds.

"Watch your manners son," Bishop Jackson says.

"That's all right, this is a little too much for him to take in right now," his Godfather says in Raymond's defense.

"Right now, I'm not taking this in right now or ever. You say you both prepared me for this time, but yet you want me to give up everything I've been working so hard for. Then what am I supposed to do? What is it I'm supposed to be if not Vice President?" Raymond asks.

"I can't tell you that yet," his Godfather says.

"This is a game and I'm not playing," Raymond says, and begins to move towards the door.

"I can't give you more information until you are willing to give up everything you have," his Godfather replies.

"What?" Raymond stops and turns to him.

"Sometimes you can't get what is on another level until you are ready to give up what you have," his Godfather explains.

Raymond had heard and had enough. He opened the door and looked at both his father and Godfather. "Do you know who I am? I am the first male African American Vice President. Not I will be, or it 'may' happen, but it's already a done deal. We are living in the future right now and no one can stop it, not even my father and Godfather," Raymond says.

"Son you have nine days to decide what you are going to do," his Godfather calmly states.

"I already know what my answer will be and it goes something like this…" Raymond walks out and slams the door behind him.

Picture 6: *Never Good Enough*

Raymond walks out of the hotel room with his security detail ahead of him and with his father trailing close behind.

"Raymond, wait son, you must think this through," his father begged as he reached for Raymond's arm.

Raymond pulls his arm away from his father and tells him, "No I don't have to think anything through, because you have already done that for me once again. What do you want from me? Is there anything good enough for you? I went to the schools you wanted me to. I got on the Dean's List. Never mind the fact I didn't have any friends. I married the girl you wanted me to, even though I didn't love her, but because you said she would make the perfect wife, so I married her anyway," Raymond says.

"Son I never told you to marry Diamond," his father says in a quiet voice, trying to get Raymond to calm down. But Raymond ignores the hint and raises his voice,

"Yes, you did in your own manipulative way, and if I didn't make the right choice, I would have had to live with the regret of not getting your approval," Raymond says.

"You asked me what I thought, you always ask me what I think," his father replied in his own defense.

"Yes and I wanted you to say for once, 'You make the decision son. Your choice will be the right one. I trust you to make the correct choice'," Raymond explained.

"You don't understand son," his father says.

Raymond walks closer to his father and says in a whisper, but firmly, "Yes I do understand, I am about to become the first male black Vice President in the history of the United States and this is still not good enough for my father."

"Yes it is son, but…"

"No but, no more buts dad. 'It's good you got an A, but you can get an A plus. You spoke well, but you cleared your throat too many times. Your suit looks nice, but it doesn't match your socks.'

I'm tired of these 'buts'. Nothing will ever be good enough for you," Raymond raises his voice again as he backs up from his father.

Bishop Jackson reaches out his hand, "Then what do you want me to say son?"

Raymond pushes the elevator button and the door opens. He walks in with his security in front of him, but Raymond and his father can still see and hear each other. "Say it now dad, say it now. Say 'It's your choice son. I trust your decision son. You will make the right choice.'" Raymond said with tears in his eyes, but his father just stared as the elevator doors began to close. "I didn't think you could say it," Raymond said with disappointment. Bishop Jackson stood looking at the closed elevator doors, seeing the numbers light up as it went to the ground floor.

Picture 7: *On the Run*

The next day Raymond is at his campaign headquarters having a meeting with his staff. "OK people we have been delayed too long and too often. We are about to pick up the pace. It's time to show them how Raymond Jackson breaks the mold -- political style. I want to be at every superstar party. If there is a party and a superstar is there and the drinks are flowing and the action is hot, I want my face in that place. Make it happen! Let's go!" Raymond says as he encourages all his aides to get on their phones. They immediately execute his command, trying to find out who is who and where is the place to be.

Later Raymond stepped out of his limo to walk the red carpet at the Academy Awards. He is shaking celebrities' hands and greeting the cream of the entertainment industry elite. An interviewer, Shirley Turner pulls Raymond to her microphone.

"We have Mr. Raymond Jackson who is about to become the first male African American Vice President. Wow! It's surprising to see you here."

"Well, I'm here to support my friends in the entertainment industry and to put a little twist in this political game," Raymond says with his golden boy smile. He then moves on to make his rounds, meeting and greeting some of the most important attendees at the Oscars.

The next week Raymond is at the ZET Awards taking pictures with the ZET owner. A young black female reporter, Vela Martin stands between the two for a quick interview. "I'm here with two powerful men, one is the man who signs my check, Mr. Zane Armstrong, and the other is Mr. V.P. himself, our political hero Raymond Jackson. It's good to see you out with the people. Many say you brought style back to politics. What do you say about that?"

"Well, I don't know about that," Raymond laughs, "But I can say this, man, right here is my inspiration, because he put the black face in the place, which motivates me to run this political race."

Through the weeks as Raymond makes the rounds of all of the award ceremonies his campaign begin to progress and his popularity grows among young people and the Hip-Hop Culture. At the Source Awards Raymond shows up with two well-known rappers, Big Q and LL. They are interviewed by Alex Morrison, a popular black TV reporter who asks "Raymond-Vice President-Jackson! As I live and breathe! What are you doing here?"

"I'm here having fun, but doing my work like I work it. I'm hanging out with the Big Q and LL, they are showing me mad love. I want us to take it back to the hood in November and let's do something off the chain," Raymond says.

As Raymond winds up his tour of award shows, one of his staff suggests he dig deeper into the church community. What better way to do this than to make an appearance at the Stellar Awards. His staff contacts the topflight gospel singers and he shows up at the Awards with Kirk Franklin and Reverend T.D. Jakes. An interviewer, Janette Waves speaks to Raymond, "We are here at the Stellar Awards with Mr. soon-to-be-Vice-President, Raymond Jackson. Is it true your father is Bishop A.L. Jackson?"

"Yes it is," Raymond replies.

"He has done God's work all his life. How does he feel about your campaign style?" she asks.

"Well, we have two different communication styles as you can see. He respects me and I honor him, but we must do what is best for ourselves and the work we have been called to fulfill," Raymond says. He could feel himself moving to use the TV interview to berate his father, but he resists the urge.

After leaving the Stellar Awards Raymond gets on his tour bus to return home. His campaign team believes that his tour of awards ceremonies was a very successful campaign tactic, and the political projection polls concur. If the election were held on that day Raymond and Newton would win by a landslide.

Raymond's team is ready to have a little downtime. They are drinking and smoking, and acting silly. They offer Raymond a drink and a smoke, but he shakes his head "No." One would think he was already high, because of the spaced out, look he had on his face, but he wasn't. Nothing could help him escape the reality of what was taking place in his life right now. At a time he should be 100 percent sure of himself, he was full of doubt and anger.

Just when things seemed to be going well for Raymond and his campaign, he was dealt a stunning blow by his Godfather who asked him to give up running for Vice President. Raymond was stunned by this request, especially by someone who seemed to have so much influence over his life. So much so that his Godfather knew about him cheating on Diamond with Nicky. How he obtained this knowledge really stirred his curiosity, but more alarming was why he wanted him to give up the chance for the Vice Presidency. *Was he jealous? Or did he feel that he wasn't fit for the job?*

Why was he really running for office? For the status, for the fame or was he really running for the people's interests? He wrestled with these questions.

Even more perplexing was the fact that his father, who seemed to be so earnestly in his corner at first, now flipped the script on him. Had he not done all the things that his father wanted him to do? He finished his schooling, got his degree, was on the Dean's List and was now running for the Vice Presidency. What more could a father ask for? Well, one thing was for sure, and two things for certain, he would stick with his campaign for Vice President regardless of his father and Godfather's agendas.

All of these thoughts were running through Raymond's head as he heard his staff laughing and playing in the background and as he headed home. *Was Raymond in a political race or was he running another race? Was he running away from what his father and Godfather had told him about this entire situation? How long could he run, and where could he run without it coming back to confront him? Maybe he was facing something he could never escape from, even if he tried.*

Picture 8: *Girlfriends*

The media loves Raymond's political style in the era of reality TV. Raymond is giving the media the political show they always wanted. He is conservative, but flashy and very stylish. He has all the ingredients of a great story. Everywhere he is at, they are there with their cameras and microphones ready to record any action or words from Raymond. The media's love for Raymond makes his campaign staffs' jobs very easy. They don't have to sell Raymond to voters, all they have to do is simply have him make appearances like in the past few weeks, and if Raymond just shows up the media will do the rest. The media will play and replay those few weeks over and over again causing Raymond to get free publicity, which means more votes for Raymond. When the media gets finished playing those award appearances, showing Raymond hanging out with celebrities, rappers, gospel singers, actors and actresses, everybody and their momma will know who Raymond is, if they don't know already. So the media is loving Raymond and Raymond's campaign team is loving the way they are loving him.

This type of campaign has had a profound affect on a great number of people, especially two young African American females who just finished watching one of the many videos of Raymond's award appearances. Kim Austin and Whitney Denmark are throwing a small basketball back and forth to each other in very high spirits.

"I would love to shake his hand," Kim says as she throws the ball to Whitney.

"And slip your number into his hand at the same time," Whitney says throwing the ball back to Kim. They both laugh.

"It's a shame the way you know me," Kim replied throwing the ball back.

"Too well my sister, just too well, just like the pot knows the kettle."

Just as Kim is about to throw the ball, their supervisor, an attractive white man dressed in a conservative suit walks into their office, causing Kim to be holding the ball in mid air.

"Hey ladies I just wanted to congratulate you both on a job well done. The investment was a success and both of you are the employees of the month for the third consecutive time," their supervisor, Dan Smith compliments them.

"Thank you sir," Kim and Whitney both say.

"In addition, the bonus you will be receiving this year is two tickets for the John Newton and Raymond Jackson Dinner Ball," Smith says as he comes in and sits on the couch.

"What? You've got to be joking," Kim says.

"No, here they are." Smith takes out two tickets from his suit jacket pocket and hands them to the ladies.

"What's the catch?" Whitney says with a suspicious look on her face.

"Stop playing, these are $1,000 a plate tickets, how did you get them? I thought they were excusive," Kim exclaims.

"They are, but for you two I called in a couple of favors," Smith says with a big smile.

"So no work, you mean there are no potential clients there or anything like that?" Whitney asks.

"No not at all, I want you to enjoy yourselves. The only thing I want you to do is tell Mr. Jackson he's got my vote," Smith says.

"I will do that for you sir," Kim pledges excitedly.

Smith gets up and walks towards the door. "Ladies keep up the good work, because your future here is very promising."

"Thank you Mr. Smith," they both respond.

Before he could get out of the door Whitney calls for him. "Oh Mr. Smith can I have a word with you?" Whitney says as she moves towards him. "

Yes Whitney," Smith replies.

"Sir, the next time you want to pay a $1,000 for a plate, I can fix a mean macaroni and cheese with fried chicken and greens and a nice slice of sweet potato pie," Whitney explained.

"Oh I think I got it. You would rather have the money next time," Smith replied.

"Now we are talking! See that's why you are the big man in charge, you catch on quick."

"Thank you," Smith says.

"No thank you, sir."

Mr. Smith walks out the door, Whitney closes it behind him and when she turns around Kim hits her lightly in her head with the ball. "Ouch, girl I'm going to get you," Whitney says playfully as she chases Kim around the office.

Picture 9: *The Great Ball*

Raymond is easily the most popular person in America at this moment. He is gaining strong support from all segments of society.

The black votes seem to be secured and his appearances at the Awards have demonstrated his ability to relate to celebrities as well as everyday folks.

Now he must find a way to appeal to the mainstream white Americans, whose support is skittish, highly sensitive and capable of flipping at any moment.

His next strategy is to appear at the Great Ball, where many celebrities, the moneyed elite, politicians and others in power have gathered. Many high-profile African Americans are present along with some prominent white Americans.

"I can't believe I'm going to meet him in person," enthuses Kim.

"Please don't get ghetto fabulous up in here. Keep it classy, keep it all classy," Whitney teases before she picks up her cocktail. As soon as she takes a sip a voice is heard all over the room.

"Ladies and gentlemen and all of our distinguished guests, I want to present to you the soon-to-be-first male African American Vice President of the United States of America -- Mr. Raymond Jackson." The gathering gives a standing ovation as Raymond walks into the room with his security. He is shaking hands and kissing ladies on the cheek as his security moves him towards the podium.

"Thank you all for your support; John Newton, my campaign partner and soon-to-be-President sends his greetings and love. He is working hard on the campaign trail in Iowa. You all look so beautiful and it feels good to be in the same room with people who believe in change. So please enjoy yourselves tonight; dance, drink and dream, for tomorrow our dream will be a reality. I promise you. Thank you," Raymond states with confidence. He steps off the podium and begin to shake the men's' hands and kiss the ladies' hands. He goes from table to table following the same pattern until he reaches Kim and Whitney's table.

"Are you having a good time?" Raymond asks the white couple who are sharing the table with Kim and Whitney. "Yes and you look even more handsome in person," the lady bubbles.

"Thank you," Raymond replies.

"We are voting for you and Newton and all of our friends are too," the lady's husband states as he shakes Raymond's hand.

"Well, I'm glad to hear that," Raymond smiles.

"Here is my card, we are big supporters. If you need anything don't hesitate to call," the husband emphasizes. One of Raymond's aides intercepts the business card.

"Thank you for all of your support and contributions. What is your name sir?" Raymond asks.

"Judge Benjamin Williams and my wife, Dr. Lily Williams. We've been following you for years," stated Judge Williams.

"You are a credit to America," Dr. Lily Williams interjects excitedly.

"Thank you very much, and have a nice night," Raymond shakes their hands as his aide urges him on.

"Hi Mr. President, I mean Mr. soon-to-be President, I mean," Kim says, too flustered to speak sensibly.

Whitney takes Raymond's hand, "Mr. soon-to-be Vice President, you must forgive my friend. She is having a nervous breakdown right now, because she is your biggest fan," Whitney says smoothly to earn a laugh from Raymond.

"Can I get a picture with you sir," Kim says as she finally gets her words together.

"Take this and give it to the staff and we will get you that picture before you leave tonight," Raymond responds.

"Thank you very much. My boss said he is voting for you and I am too and all of my family is voting for you," Kim says as Raymond walked to the next table.

"I told you don't get ghetto in here, but it's all in your blood. You just can't help yourself can you," Whitney says as she sips on her drink.

Picture 10: *Let's Dance*

Despite his popularity and how well the campaign is going, Raymond proves not to be an exception to an experience that most powerful black men have endured. Raymond also has a skeleton in his closet. This skeleton is 5'10" - with a creamy complexion, long hair, a shapely toned figure, a dazzling smile and a style of soft elegance that graces the presence of everyone she encounters. Her name is Nicole Jones, but to Raymond she is Nicky, a 25 year old graduate of Harvard University. Her intellect is equal to her beauty and she lets no one mistake her for just a pretty face. Any man would be trapped under her spell without her even trying. Raymond's nose was opened the first day they laid eyes on each other. For the past five years; Nicky has been Raymond's mistress.

As Raymond moves towards the ballroom floor Tarisha comes over to him and whispers something in his ear. At the same time Nicky walks over to meet Raymond. She looks at Tarisha and his security, and then at Raymond. The security moves in to shield Raymond, but Raymond holds his hand up and says, "Give us a little space guys."

"Yes sir," his security says and then quickly complies with his request.

"We will be close if you need us," says Tarisha, Tarisha is very protective of Raymond. She is like his little big sister. She understands Raymond is not in the time of Martin and Malcolm where a politician's extramarital affair could eliminate him from politics. These days, people seem to have accepted the weakness of powerful men, and to have accepted the fact they will have a woman in their life other than their wife. Even though everyone knows about Nicky and Raymond's relationship, it is overlooked as though people are blind to the fact. That is all well and good as far as Tarisha is concerned, but it is still her job to look out for the best interests of Raymond and for his political future. She tells Raymond over and over again, "Just because everyone accepts it does not mean its right. Maybe that is a clear sign that it is wrong."

Tarisha walks past Nicky and nods. "Good evening Ms. Tarisha," Nicky says. Tarisha doesn't respond, but continues to walk. "I don't like her at all," Nicky tells Raymond.

"Can I have this dance?" Raymond says in response.

She comes close to Raymond with a smile that brightens every time she is near him. "I thought you forgot about a sister," Nicky says.

"We were just together last week," Raymond responds.

"I know, but it seems like last month. I miss you."

"Well you know how politics is, we had to really bump and grind for these last few days."

"Um, I like the sound of that," Nicky says very sexily.

"I'm talking politics, not sex."

"Oh that's too bad," Nicky counters.

"You look so good I want to kiss you right now,"

"Then why don't you."

"Come on, you know the media already thinks something is going on between us. We don't want to give them ammunition," Raymond chides Nicky.

"Just a sneaky suspicion?" Nicky asks.

"I wouldn't put it like that."

"What about a dip then," Nicky asks.

"Oh there goes that corporate lawyer coming to surface. There's always a negotiated backup plan," Raymond says.

Nicky laughs a little. "Well, I can't help it, I graduated at the top of my class."

"You sure did in many ways than one." Raymond stares in her eyes.

"Thank you Mr. Vice President," Nicky coos.

"Does the beautiful, high minded and intellectual Ms. Jones really want me to really dip her in public? What would that do to your image?" Raymond speculates.

"It may improve it."

"All right Ms. Beautiful get ready on the count of three,"

"How is the family?" Nicky asks Raymond.

"One - They are fine."

"Your wife?"

"She is doing well also, Two."

"I saw her the other day in the store, I don't think she saw me, but then again I think not," Nicky pauses. "Ray please keep your promise," Nicky says in her little girl voice.

Raymond was always amazed of the fact she could be so smart and strong in every area of her life, but when it came to him, she became like a little girl, letting down her guard that she was trained to put up and keep up. Only Raymond got a pass to enter an area of her emotions that most people never saw. "And Three," Raymond whispers in her hear then deeply dips Nicky. She can't help but burst out in laughter. The song comes to an end and the crowd claps. Raymond and Nicky are not sure if the applause is for them or for the band, but it really doesn't matter, because they are in their own private world. He will always be the star and she the leading lady, even if others only see her as a supporting cast member.

Picture 11: *First Degrees*

One of the reasons Raymond finds it hard to except Mr. Goodson's proposal to abandon the Vice Presidency is because a lot of people will be affected by his decision, some that he know, and some that he does not know, people like Tee and Keith, Tar, Kevin and Loretta Gaither.

Tee goes upstairs while Keith stays in the living room watching a DVD of the movie *P's K's*. Tee returns wearing a big T-shirt and sits next to Keith. She begins to kiss him on the side of his neck. He turns around and they kiss on the lips.

Keith stops. "Are you sure your mom is out of town?"

"I told you that over and over again, she went to a convention and will not be back until Monday. You'd better be worried about where your dad is," Tee says.

"I'm straight. I told him I'd be staying over Alex's for the weekend. Besides, his construction business has him working so much he won't even miss me," Keith says as he moves to the other end of the couch.

"Keith we have been playing this game for over two weeks now and you're still acting like you're not sure."

"No, I'm not saying that, it's just that I don't want your mom to bust up in here while we are in the middle…"

Tee gets up and goes over to the phone, picks it up and dials some numbers and then hangs up the phone. "What are you doing?" Keith asks.

"Just wait a minute," Tee snaps back at him, then she begins to count down; 5,4,3,2,1. The phone rings and she answers it like a smooth operator who orchestrated a plan. "Hi mom… nothing is wrong I was just bored and I thought I'd call you," Tee says while looking at Keith with a sarcastic expression. "Oh yeah, what are you having for dinner? That sounds good, OK I'll let you get back to your lobster tail. I'll talk to you tomorrow, and mom call about ten, all right? Bye," Tee says. Before putting the phone on the charger she hands it to Keith, "What is the area code?" Tee asks.

"213," Keith answers sheepishly.

"And what area code is 213? What area code is 213?" Tee repeats like she is his teacher.

"Somewhere in LA," Keith answers like a student who doesn't want to give the answer to an obvious question.

"Do you feel better now little Keith?" Tee teases.

Keith puts his arm around Tee, "OK you proved your point. My bad. I should have believed you. I just want things to go right."

Tee begins to kiss him but Keith pulls back.

"What's wrong now?"

"You don't have anything on under your shirt," Keith says with a hint of delight in his voice.

"That's what I've been trying to get you to notice for the last 20 minutes. Tee lies back on the couch and open her legs. "Keith are you ready for this?" she asks.

Keith doesn't answer; he just starts taking his shirt and pants off. He then goes over to Tee and help her slip the T-shirt over her head. He began to kiss her neck, then down to her breasts, kissing all over them.

"Do you have on the …" Tee starts to ask.

"Yeah" Keith replies huskily and continues his soft kisses. Keith stops and notices Tee is trembling a little. She is getting cold feet.

Keith gazes at Tee's eyes. "We don't have to do this tonight."

"I'm fine, just some butterflies," Tee reassures.

"Me too, but we are going to lose our virginity to each other, we are going into this new world together," Keith says to reassure Tee.

Tee smiles. "And I'm glad I'm going with you." "Can you hold my hand?" Tee asks like a little girl. Keith takes her hands and they intertwine their fingers. "I'm ready now," Tee says softly.

They both close their eyes as Keith moves in closer and pushes; they both let out uncontrollable sounds mixed of pleasure, pain and surprise.

ꟼ ꟼ ꟼ

The members of the Westside gang are hanging outside of an apartment building about to "put in some work" on some known drug dealers who are inside.

"All right y'all, let's do this," Shawn the gang leader tells his boys. They all pull out their guns, two move in front of the door and two on each side of the door. Shawn looks at Tar and asks, "Are you ready to be a Westsider?"

"I've been ready," Tar answers back, but it's obvious he doesn't know what he is about to get into as he holds his gun like it's a toy.

"Then let's go!" Shawn commands as he kicks the apartment door in and everyone rushes in.

"Freeze!" Shawn orders the two drug dealers at the table. One of the Westside gang members grabs their guns.

"What's going on?" one of the dealers sputters.

"Shut up!" Shawn shouts, pointing the gun straight at his face. "I'll ask the questions. Anybody else in here?"

"No, but they'll be coming anytime now," the other dealer replies.

"You better hope they don't come anytime soon," Shawn says.

"Let's get outta here man," Tar says.

"It's alright little man. You all start putting the money and drugs in the bags and Tar you get the tape. You two get on the floor," Shawn tells the two dealers. "Tar put them on their stomachs and wrap their hands and feet," Shawn says. Shawn knows Tar is getting nervous and he only has a little time before someone else walks through the door. Tar is not ready to shoot it out even though he tries to act like he could.

A Westside gang member looks under the table. "Man look what I found. It's a bag of money."

"All right that's all we came for, let's get out of here. Tar, you finished?" Shawn asks.

"In a second," Tar responds.

Tar adjusts the tape on them and discretely whispers. "Look, it's not tight. Give us 20 minutes then you can pull it off,"

"Thanks man," the dealer manages to utter.

"Tar come on, we're outta here," Shawn shouts. "Move, move, move" Shawn commands while waving his gun and standing in the door. The gang runs outside except for Shawn. Gunshots are heard inside causing the gang members to draw their guns again. Tar turns around in shock.

Shawn comes running out of the apartment building running straight at Tar with his gun pointed at Tar's face. "The next time you do anything like what you just did, I'm going to do to you what I did to them. Let's go," Shawn shouts.

⚐⚐⚐

Kevin, a 26 year old African American post office worker notices Police lights are flashing and a line of squad cars are headed toward the south side of town. "Somebody's acting the fool again," he says to himself as he stands on the roof of his apartment building.

"Are you talking to yourself Mr. Washington?" a voice asks. The voice catches Kevin by surprise, even though he was expecting her. Michele, a 30-year-old Caucasian registered nurse walks towards Kevin. Kevin is delighted by the flowing summer dress she is wearing.

"You look wonderful, baby" Kevin says as he kisses her.

"Thank you baby, and look what you have done to the roof, I'm really impressed," Michele says.

"Nothing but the best for you my dear, all for you." Kevin replies. They share a more passionate kiss.

"Um, I want to go straight for the dessert -- chocolate pudding," Michele teases.

Kevin pulls away from her and escorts her to her seat. "No Ms. Temptation, we are not going to deviate from the plan tonight." Michele sits down with a little pout but Kevin is determined not to be seduced by Michele like so many times before. "You've got to promise me you will not seduce me until we are finished here," Kevin says.

"Well..." Michele responds.

"No 'well', I want you to promise," Kevin insists.

"OK man, I promise no seduction until we finish eating," Michele says. Michele notices a blanket with a big pillow in the corner of the roof; she smiles and says, "I see you thought of everything."

"You think? Check this out," Kevin says as he reaches for a remote control and points it to the flat screen making a picture of a fireplace appear.

Michele claps and then laughs. "You are amazing, your mind never stops."

"Not when it comes to thinking of ways to see your beautiful smile," Kevin says smoothly. "Do you hear that?" he asks.

"Oh yeah, it's my favorite song," Michele says and immediately begin to sing along, *"I love being in love with you, you're sweeter than a honey comb..."*

"Well get used to it because it is on repeat," Kevin says as he gallantly presents Michele with a dozen roses.

Thank you baby, you are going to make me cry," Michele says, as she inhales the rich, sweet scent of the roses.

"Michele I brought you to our favorite place tonight, the place where we first made love right over there in that corner. I did all of this to make you a proposal you will never forget, and to show you how I'm going to treat you for the rest of your life, if you say you will marry me." Then Kevin gets on one knee, takes out a sparkling diamond ring and solemnly asks, "Michele will you marry me and become my wife?"

Michele is crying but manages to answer, "Yes, yes I love you and I will marry you." Kevin places the diamond engagement ring on her finger. They exchange a long and lusty kiss. "I love you and I will always love you," Michele whispers.

"Oh one more thing: remember when I said this will be a proposal you will never forget? Well I thought I'd help you to remember. Look over there by the candles and smile for the camera," Kevin says.

"Oh boy, I told you, you thought of everything," Michele says while laughing and crying for joy at the same time.

At Atlanta High School, Loretta is busy on her laptop computer finishing next week's pop quiz when the Vice Principal, Mr. Hammond, enters the classroom to speak with her.

"Loretta may I have a word with you before the class starts?" he asks.

"Good morning Mr. Hammond," Loretta replies.

"Excuse my manners this morning, good morning Ms. Gaither," Mr. Hammond says politely.

Loretta stops typing, closes her laptop and turns to Mr. Hammond. "What can I do for you?" she asks.

"I don't know how to put this so I'm going to come right out with it," Hammond says.

"I find that to be the best way," Loretta says with a smile.

Hammond gets a chair and sits down in front of her and takes a deep breath. "OK, a friend of mine who works in the human resources area at the Board told me you didn't get the principal's position at MLK High."

The pleasant expression on Loretta's faces fades as Hammond continues, "I know it comes as a surprise. I thought for sure you would get it, seeing how you helped turn Atlanta High around almost overnight."

Loretta pastes on a smile and says, "That's alright, another position will be opening up soon, as a matter of fact I know…"

Hammond interrupts, "There is one more thing I want to discuss with you.

"Yes, Tom," Loretta says.

"I don't know how true it is, but this same person who gave me this information told me something else. " Hammond pauses.

"I'm waiting Tom."

"My friend said that Mr. Owens gave you a poor recommendation. He basically said he felt you would be more effective as a teacher than a principal," Hammond confides.

Loretta tries to keep her composure, but can't seem to maintain it. "What?" she shouts as she stands up from her chair.

"Loretta please, remember none of this is official or on the record. It is inside information that can't be addressed until we get proof," Hammond reminds her.

She begins to pace the floor. "After all of the work I have done here and after he looked me in my face and told me he would give me a good recommendation, he's a snake!" Loretta mutters.

Hammond steps in front of Loretta and gently places his hands on her shoulders, "Let's think this out. Maybe there is something we can do."

"You don't understand Tom. If I don't get his bad reference out of my file I will never get a chance at another principal position, ever," Loretta says as tears roll down her cheeks.

"I know, I know. Give me a couple, no about 60, days and I'm going to see if I can get it off another way," Hammond says.

Loretta shakes her head in disbelief and tells him, "This is not happening right now."

"Loretta you can't say anything to anyone until I get this out of your file. If you say anything, and I mean anything, I will not be able to help you," Hammond emphasizes.

"I understand. Thank you Tom, you are a blessing."

"I'm just trying to help a person who helps so many others," Hammond says.

"Well, once again, I thank you for everything," Loretta says as she gives him a hug. Two of Loretta girls walk in and notice the hug,

"Silky, silky now," the students say jokingly and then burst in laughter.

Loretta releases Hammond and he walks out the room. "Be quiet girls, and take your seats," Ms. Loretta says.

Picture 12: *The Last Night*

Nicky is lying on the bed flipping through the TV channels looking for news about Raymond. She catches the end of a news commentary. "Many believe the only reason Congressman Newton will win the Presidency is because of Raymond Jackson, who is taking him over the top," the female anchor commented.

Raymond has spent the night with Nicky, but his mind is in two other places: on the campaign trail and in his Godfather's room. Nicky notices that Raymond is distracted, but can't figure out why. She begins to think it's the relationship, and that maybe Raymond is getting tired of their affair and rediscovering his feelings for his wife. As far as Nicky is concerned Diamond will always possess an advantage when it comes to Raymond, because of their history and because of her status as his legal wife.

Raymond comes out of the bathroom putting on his shirt and looking for his socks. "You can't stay?" she asks, knowing the answer, but hoping it will change his mind, since it has worked many times before.

"No, I have some last minute things to complete," Raymond responds smoothly.

"Next week you know we are meeting in..." Nicky starts to remind Raymond.

"Yes, I know, LA," Raymond interrupts her as if they never meet any other place.

"Is something wrong Ray?"

"Not that I know of. I just can't find my other sock. Oh I got it, everything is fine now," Raymond says, but he knows Nicky can read him like a book she's read five times, but he hope she will not be asking too many questions before it's time for him to leave. Why did he have to fall in love with a corporate lawyer who graduated at the top of her class and was not ashamed to use her insight and judgment outside of her profession? She had a way of asking the smallest question that would get a big response. Raymond knows she is probing his state of mind, but he is not ready to talk about something he has not himself understood from the very first time it was presented to him.

"Do you feel the same way you use to when you first met me?" Nicky asks.

"No, I feel more for you than when I first met you," Raymond says. Right then and there a knock came at the door. "Who's there?" Raymond asks.

"Security," one of his men answers.

"What's up?" Raymond asks.

"The car is waiting sir."

"I'll be right out, just give me a minute," Raymond replied.

"So you weren't planning on staying anyway," Nicky said with a little attitude.

"Let me ask you a question," Raymond says. Nicky's little attitude evaporates just as quickly as it came.

"Now we're talking," Nicky says as she sits up in the bed. "What?" she says excitingly.

"Would you give up something if you had a chance to get everything, but you didn't know what the everything was, but you feel like it's something you've wanted all your life?" Raymond asks.

"If you don't go for the everything, you will live with regret and that will make you bitter and miserable. You could never enjoy the present for wondering about what could have happened," Nicky explains eloquently.

"I know. I only wanted someone to confirm what I have been thinking for the last few days."

"Are you feeling conflicted?" Nicky asks, not sure she wants to hear the answer.

"No, not from you baby, I'm going through something that is causing me to search deep inside of myself, areas I never knew existed," Raymond says as he walks to the door. He opens it and gives her a loving look and a smile.

"Ray why does it feel like this is our last night together?" Nicky asks with tears welling up in her eyes, but she will not allow them to fall.

"No, I'll see you in LA next week, right," Raymond reassures her.

"Yeah, LA, right," Nicky says softly.

Raymond closes the door and walks off.

Picture 13: *A Date with Destiny*

Raymond and his father, along with Raymond's security, exit off the elevator and walk to Suite 108 and knock on the door. "Come in, it's open," his Godfather answers. Raymond and his father enter the room and stand in front of him. His Godfather says, "I've been waiting for you. How do you feel?"

"Nervous, like it's my first day of school or something," Raymond replies.

"That's normal. Remember, we are here to help you, not to hurt you," his Godfather says.

"I'm only here because of my love and respect for my father," Raymond says.

"You made the right choice," Mr. Goodson says as he puts his hand on Raymond's head. Raymond falls instantly to the floor and vomits.

The security men start to draw their guns, but Bishop Jackson intervenes and says, "Its OK guys, everything is fine. He's all right. Please put your guns away."

In between bouts of retching Raymond is speaking in both a strange language and in English. "What are you doing to me?" Raymond gasps to his father.

"It will be all right son. I'm here," his father responds.

"I'm sending him to Suite 78 with the Caretaker for a few weeks," his Goodson says to Bishop Jackson.

"Should I contact his wife and campaign staff?" Bishop Jackson asks.

"No, not right now. I want as few people as possible to know," his Godfather explains to Bishop Jackson. Then he turns to Raymond's security men and says, "What happens in this room stays in this room fellows, do you understand."

"Yes sir," the security men respond, as they understand the gravity of the situation.

Raymond is on the floor moaning and groaning like his insides are hurting, still speaking in a strange tongue. "OK, help him up," his Godfather orders.

"You're trying to kill me," Raymond says.

"Just a part of you son. Just a part of you," his Godfather says as he touches Raymond's stomach and Raymond looses consciousness.

Picture 14: *Healing*

Raymond didn't know it, but his soul had just undergone spiritual surgery. His Godfather was the master surgeon, his father was an assistant, and his security men were the nurses, (but they didn't know it.) Lying on the floor Raymond had an internal operation that could never be understood by the natural, because it was a supernatural occurrence that was above the realm of the natural. Raymond's Godfather, who possessed the highest level of spiritual knowledge bestowed the most profound change of all on him - inner change.

But if this operation was going to be a complete success Raymond must go through spiritual rehabilitation. This would be the time for Raymond to discover what his soul was created to do in order for him to complete his soul's purpose in his current life. Spiritual rehabilitation is the hardest part of change. It's painful, it's lonely and it's fearful, because you are not sure where it is leading. It sometimes makes you want to stop the entire process and return to the way things were before.

Raymond's soul is still aching, because it wants to go back to the time when things were so certain. But it was also hurting from the desire to move forward into a tomorrow that is full of potential and promises. Whatever the source of this pain Raymond wants it to stop. The only problem is there is no remedy he can take to stop the pain; he can't drink it away, eat it away, drug it away or sex it away. No, not at all. His Godfather made sure he was locked away until he was completely and totally detoxified of his old consciousness. This is extremely painful, but healing the pain is part of the process.

The Caretaker walks into the Raymond's room. Alita Mendez is an attractive 35-year-old Latina who could be mistaken to be 10 years younger. She has long black hair and a model's striking features. She is wearing a nurse's uniform. She approaches Raymond who is lying on the bed. He had been conscious for about 24 hours, but the only thing he was able to do was lay still and think.

"Mr. Jackson, I'm going to check your vital signs. Can you sit up please?" she says. Raymond sits up and she places a thermometer in his mouth. "I'm going to be your Caretaker for a season," she says.

Raymond removes the thermometer and asks, "What is a season?"

She places the thermometer back in his mouth. "It's the period of time you are supposed to be here, not a day sooner or a second later." Then she takes the stethoscope from around her neck and checks Raymond's heart.

"What are you doing?" Raymond asks.

"Just checking your heart rate."

"I'm fine, I'm good," Raymond assures her.

"Take off your t-shirt please and turn around," she instructs. She notices Raymond is in very good physical shape with a well-toned musculature. One would be surprised at how he maintained his physical fitness, being a politician and all, but Raymond was not a typical politician. "Take a deep breath Mr. Jackson," the Caretaker says. She checks his lungs. "One more please. Thank you. Before you put your shirt back on let me check your blood pressure." The Caretaker says as she wraps the pressure band around his arm.

"When can I leave?" Raymond asks.

"You can leave right now if you choose to," the Caretaker answers.

"Oh yeah," Raymond sneers.

"You sure can, but the question you should ask yourself is where are you going," the Caretaker replies while writing down Raymond's vital signs. "So the question is not can you go, the question is where do you go from here," she says.

The Caretaker is heading for the door as Raymond sits shirtless on the side of the bed thinking about why he was there in the first place. It was to discover this other thing that is so important his father and newfound Godfather have trained him for all of his life, and what was so important that he is expected to drop the Vice Presidency to fulfill this purpose. As good as it sounded to know he could leave at any time -- even right now if he wanted to -- he couldn't because he had come too far to turn around now.

"Well, can you tell me what this is all about, at least tell me that," Raymond pleaded.

"Before you leave here you are going to know that and even more. Your Godfather is very special," the Caretaker assures Raymond.

"I see he got to you too," Raymond sighs as he lies back on the bed with his hands behind his head. "Yeah, he is a special one all right. He's got to be a little special if he expects me to give up the Vice Presidency for something I can't see. "'Special' is not really the word," Raymond says sarcastically.

"Well, Mr. Jackson sometimes you must give up something to get everything. It's called faith. You have a lot of things Mr. Jackson: money, friends, and connections. But do you have faith?" the Caretaker asks as she opens up the door to leave.

"By the way what's your name, what should I call you?" Raymond interjects, to no response. She simply closes the door. "When will you be back?" Raymond yells to her through the closed door, but the only thing he hears is her locking the door. "Oh, so it's like that," Raymond mutters and lies back down.

The Caretaker gave him a lot to think about. Maybe he wasn't there to find out what his Godfather was offering him in exchange for the Vice Presidency. Maybe he was there to discover his faith - not a specific religion, but the kind of faith that helps you discover who you really are and allows you to perform the impossible. Could it be that his Godfather didn't want him to know what he had to gain before he gave up what he had, so he could develop his faith? Because it was going to take great faith to fulfill his true purpose and reach his true destiny.

Picture 15: *Work It Out*

Raymond can't believe he has been locked up in the room for 20 days. There is no calendar, but he started counting the days when he realized he would be there for a while. This is the first time in a long time he has been still and in one room for more than a few hours. Ever since he became a political candidate he has been going nonstop. He began to look at this time as a little vacation. But the only problem is the room has no TV/VCR/DVD, decorative art, or no stereo. The room service is not the best and he does not have a number of things that he is used to having access to. He has a shower, wash cloth and towels, a drawer full of underwear and tops and bottoms sets that look like pajamas, a refrigerator filled with bottled water, wheat bread, a bible, and a writing pad and pens. That was it. 20 days with no radio, no cable TV, no world news, no video games, no computer, no telephone, no expensive suits, shoes, jewelry, or cologne. Nothing. Only himself in the room with himself. All of this just to see what could possibly be more important than fulfilling his dream of being the first male African American Vice President.

What he was about to learn was sometimes you must detach yourself from everything you used to be, in order to become who you should be. It's not enough that he is isolated in a room going through a spiritual metamorphosis; but he must find a sure and secure place in his mind if he is to fly to the heights of his destiny.

Raymond is doing his daily workout: push-ups, sit-ups, bends and reaches, and jumping jacks. The Caretaker enters his room dressed in a sweat suit. She shuts the door and stands near the wall watching Raymond do his stretches. "You know there's no food in here, you left me in here with only bread and water. You have to get on your job," Raymond says without missing a beat or breath.

"You are a big boy, I doubt you will die," the Caretakers says.

"I won't be for long; I think I'm losing weight here," Raymond says and stops. "Where's the steak, bacon, chicken, and macaroni and cheese? Man I'll even settle for a bag of popcorn right now," Raymond exclaims.

"My instructions were not to give you anything that you didn't already have in the room," the Caretaker answers.

"Are you all trying to starve me?"

"Mr. Jackson, I assure you, you will not be harmed in any way. Besides you must clean out your system," the Caretaker says.

"Oh yeah," Raymond says as he lies on the floor to start his sit-ups.

"Before you can put new things in, you must get the old out of you. You are a preacher's son. I know you understand about putting new wine into an old bottle, and what the results would be," the Caretaker says.

"Oh there you go," Raymond answers.

"That's right Mr. Jackson, the new wine will blow out the old bottles and both will be destroyed, the new with the old," says the Caretaker. Raymond flips over and starts doing push-ups. To his surprise the Caretaker gets on the floor with him and starts doing push-ups right along with him, turning her head and looking Raymond in the eye as they both lift up and down. She is not even breathing hard. Raymond wonders, "How can this slender female be in better shape than me?" He starts to focus on his strength, but the Caretaker is still looking at him. Raymond is straining to keep up with her, his muscles are burning so he slows down and then stops completely. "Because you are strong in one area of your life doesn't mean you are strong in every area. But where you are about to go, you can't afford to have any weaknesses, because if you bring your old weaknesses with you your new will suffer," the Caretaker explains.

Raymond starts to do his sit-ups and the Caretaker anchors his feet. "I'm going to be honest, I don't think I'm up to what is expected of me," Raymond confesses.

"Well, Mr. Jackson you can't think right now because your mind is still being renewed, you can't say what you can or can't do until you are completely spiritually developed," the Caretaker says. Then she takes her hand and pushes Raymond further to the floor. "Go all the way down. Don't cheat yourself," she says with a smile. Then she continues, "It takes more than brains and muscle, you must tap into the strength that you can't currently imagine to complete the task that can't be seen. Determination may get you a lot of things, but it will be your discipline that will help you keep everything you get," she preaches. Just then the alarm sounds on her watch. She looks at the time and then stops the alarm. "Well, our time is up Mr. Jackson. It has been a pleasure as always," she says pleasantly as she gracefully rises from the floor.

"Let me ask you something before you go and answer me honestly," Raymond says.

"If I can't answer you honestly, I won't answer the question."

"That sounds fair. Do you think I will be able to fulfill their expectations of me?"

The Caretaker removes the towel from Raymond's bed, wipes the sweat off his face as she looks him in the eyes and says, "No sweat, Mr. Jackson." She gives Raymond the towel and leaves the room.

Raymond remains seated on the floor not knowing what to think. Every time he talks to the Caretaker she introduces him to a different point of view which he never considered before. The little that she says opens up a world of confusing knowledge that Raymond never learned in all the expensive, high profile schools he attended. Before she made him look at faith in a new light, but now she has him contemplating getting rid of his old way of thinking to tap into another level of potential. Maybe he would now be able to get rid of his low self-esteem when it came to meeting his father's expectations.

Picture 16: *Stay Out Of It!*

The couple who met Raymond at the Great Ball, Judge Benjamin and Dr. Lily Williams, had been following Raymond's political career since he ran for city council. It was actually Dr. Lily Williams who discovered Raymond at a political fundraiser dinner. Raymond was the keynote speaker and it seemed to her that he spoke with the same passion and eloquence of the great Martin Luther King, Jr. She couldn't wait to tell her husband about Raymond and how excited he made her feel when he spoke of the changes that must and would take place as America fulfilled its potential. That night she contributed more than any person who attended the dinner and from that point on Judge Benjamin and Dr. Lily Williams had been some of Raymond's largest political contributors. To see Raymond's political ascension over the years made them feel they contributed to his success. They have never flaunted their contributions to him, and they support him whenever they can by showing up at rallies, dinners, luncheons, whenever the time allows. And when it comes to financial support money was never an obstacle for them. So Judge Benjamin and Dr. Lily Williams have not only invested their money, but they are also emotionally invested in Raymond, because they watched his career take off to great heights. Now that word has surfaced that Raymond is missing from his campaign trail, they can't hide their concern. But what can they do?

Should they call in favors from some of their powerful friends to look into Raymond's disappearance? It would be worth calling in favors and pulling strings if it meant getting some answers. The Williams's really believe Raymond can contribute more to this country at this time than any other candidate, even the current party in office. Raymond possesses what they lack: passion and purpose. With these two qualities they believe Raymond can raise the vision of this country to an all time high. But they are perplexed about his unplanned absence.

Benjamin is looking at the newspaper while drinking his morning coffee in the kitchen. He calls for his wife, Lily who is getting ready for work. "Did you hear anything about Raymond yet?"

"What did you say dear," Lily asks as she walks into the kitchen putting on her earring.

"I was just reading something about the news interview John Newton had about Raymond's disappearance and I was wondering did you hear anything," Benjamin explains.

"No, I can't say I have. I thought his family said everything was fine," his wife replied.

"No, I think Mr. Newton said his family was 'not concerned right now'," the Judge clarifies.

"Well, there you have it," Lily insists.

"Have what?" Benjamin says innocently.

"Don't 'what' me, I know what you're thinking," Dr. Lily replies.

"I was just going to get a friend to look into it that's all," Benjamin suggests.

Lily drinks some of Benjamin's coffee, and then says, "No, I think you should leave it alone and let it work itself out. He probably had to get away from all the pressure for a while. This is a very big step for him. He may feel the entire country is on his shoulders right now."

"Taking a break in the middle of the biggest campaign in America history -- that doesn't sound like the Raymond we know," Benjamin says.

"Because you don't know when to take a break doesn't mean others don't."

Benjamin smiles, looks at his watch and says as he folds the paper, "Maybe you're right, I'll give it a week or two to see how it plays out." They both head for the door. "It's just that he is perfect and I wouldn't want anything to happen to him. You know there are some crazy people out there who don't want him in office," the Judge says.

"I know dear, but if he made it this far, I'm sure his security can keep him safe," Lily insists as they both leave for work.

Both Lily's parents and Benjamin's parents were involved with the freedom riders in the 1960's during the great civil rights movement. Their parents told them of the horrific ordeals they encountered during those times. The Judge is aware of the possibility of Raymond being targeted by hate groups to stop him from becoming the second most powerful man in America.

Picture 17: *Mother Lover*

While reading the bible (that was intentionally the only book in the room), the Caretaker entered with a baby in her arms. "Good morning Mr. Jackson. And how are you doing this lovely morning?" the Caretaker asks cheerfully.

"I'm fine. What about yourself?" Raymond replies.

"Well, we are doing wonderful. Say hi to my seven-month old niece," the Caretaker says. "Isn't she beautiful?" the Caretaker asks.

"Yes, she is adorable. What is her name?"

"Patience," the Caretaker responds.

"What? What kind of name is Patience? Isn't that an attribute or something? What happened to names like Shanaynay, Shenequa or even Boo?" Raymond jokes.

"That is where you are mistaken. Mr. Jackson those are not names. They sound like dances," the Caretaker says to Raymond's laughter. "Seriously, that's why our children can't sit still because ultimately they become what we name them," the Caretaker asserts.

Then it hits Raymond like a bolt of lightening. It never crossed his mind that you will become what you're being called. This woman was enlightening him on another level once again, so he disclosed what just dawned on him. "So Patience is what you want her to grow up to become," Raymond asked.

"Now you are catching on. See Mr. Jackson, we are the next thing to God to our children. We protect them, provide for them and we should give them peace. We must name them to become what we want them to be. If we call them dumb, don't be surprised if they start doing dumb things," she says.

Raymond is amazed how the Caretaker can discuss profound truths in such simple and basic terms. "I'm going to start calling you the Sunday School Teacher," Raymond blurts.

This caused the Caretaker to laugh aloud. "Now that's a first. I've been called a lot of things, but never a Sunday School Teacher," she giggles. They both laugh together.

The Caretaker walks over and hands Patience to Raymond.

"Oh no! Oh no!" Raymond protests.

"She's not going to bite, I assure you," the Caretaker says as she secures Patience in Raymond's arms and then sits down and crosses her legs and looks at Raymond with a big smile.

"Look at you Mr. Jackson, you are a natural," the Caretaker compliments.

This brought a reluctant blush on Raymond's face as he looked down at Patience who was staring right back at him. The smile evaporated slowly as he thought back to the time when he and Diamond discovered they could not have any children.

"What do you think about breast feeding Mr. Jackson?"

"Do they still do that?"

"Yes." she said in a matter-of-fact tone.

"Did you really think the breast is just for men to play with? Well it's not. It is also used to nurse babies," she said. Before Raymond could respond she makes an even bolder move, uncrossing her legs and exposing her panties to Raymond. Raymond looks in awe, not believing his eyes. The sight brings him to an immediate erection. He is almost certain he is being seduced despite her explanation.

"And maybe you never saw a pretty lady's private parts unless you were about to put your penis in it," the Caretaker says.

Raymond doesn't understand that she is making a point to him. He still has a sneaky suspicion she is trying to seduce him. But he thinks all pretty ladies are trying to seduce him and want to give him sex in one way or another. This is a result of his sex scars. Having sex before truly knowing its purpose has caused him to look at females as objects of sexual desire -- a repository for his semen.

He can't stand the sight of looking at her panties without following up with a sexual activity and abruptly turns away. "Don't turn away Mr. Jackson, you need a reality check. You and other men call them 'tits', and 'pussy', but originally they were for giving birth and nurturing children. Now it is for 'beating that thang up.' I'm quite sure you've heard that term right?" she asks. He has heard it many times, but he is amazed that what appears to be a very innocent, attractive young lady has heard such a term. "Do you believe we live in a corrupted society Mr. Jackson?" the Caretaker asks.

"I never thought about it."

"Do you know whoever has sex or is introduced to sexuality in any way before they are supposed to has been abused," the Caretaker states.

"No, I didn't know that, but it makes sense," Raymond replies.

"Our society molests kids everyday by introducing sex through the media and many other mismanaged tools. Thus we have little boys growing up to fulfill powerful positions, but can't put sex in its proper place, because they have been sexually scarred," the Caretaker declares.

Raymond suspects she is talking about him, instead of to him. Patience starts to cry. "Well, that's our time for today Mr. Jackson," she says and then retrieves Patience from his arms. "Say goodbye to the old man Patience, because Mr. Jackson is being renewed everyday. Mr. Jackson, one more thing. The only way you will be able to appreciate something is to discover its original intent. Once you do that then you will stop beating it up, roughing it up or treating it like a piece of meat. You will begin to cherish and value it. Do you know what I mean?"

"I'm afraid I do," Raymond replies. The Caretaker walks out the door without another word.

The message was too obvious for Raymond to miss. If she wasn't talking about the issues that stemmed from his early sexual encounters, well, then George Washington wasn't America's first President. Once again she had him look at issues that had existed all of his life in a different light. Could this be the reason he looked at females as something to fulfill a sexual desire. He always respected them and worked well with them, but when it came down to it, they all seemed to have some kind of sexual purpose as far as he was really concerned. It was time for Raymond to finally resolve this issue. The Caretaker was making him take a long, hard look inside of the person everyone wanted to elect as the next Vice President.

Picture 18: *Cleaning Up the Mess*

Raymond's Godfather has disclosed to him how he and his father had carefully orchestrated his life for a greater reason than assuming the Vice Presidency of the United States. Even though they had pre-planned his life from Pre-K through college, he still managed to make a mess of things when it came to the sexual affair he had been carrying on for the last five years with Nicky. Now that Raymond had accepted his Godfather's offer and was going through a spiritual cleansing Raymond's Godfather knew there must be some rebuilding in his godson's personal life.

Paul Goodson is not discouraged about all the mess he must sort through when it comes to a gifted man like Raymond. Most gifted people are expected to be perfect, but they know nothing about the principles of perfection and how to exert discipline and resistance in certain areas of their lives. Raymond made fun of the fact the Caretaker identified his Godfather as a special man, but the reality is he was indeed special, because it takes a special man to look beyond the childish mess of a seemingly distinguished man, still see his purpose in life, and still believe this purpose must be fulfilled by any means. Oftentimes a very spiritual and highly respected man must take off the suit jacket of his great reputation, roll up the sleeves of servitude, get down on his knees, and get his elbows deep into some bad smelling mess in order to bring the best out of what God has placed before him. So Mr. Goodson takes advantage of this time while Raymond is being cleansed and purified to arrange a meeting with Nicky.

Bishop Jackson is sitting on the couch reading a book on the other side of the room, somewhat out of view. "Send her in please," Mr. Goodson says.

"Has our guest arrived?" Bishop Jackson asks without looking from the book.

"Yes, I believe so," Goodson replies. Just then the secretary escorts Nicky into the office.

"Good morning Ms. Jones," Mr. Goodson says as he reaches over his desk to shake her hand. "I'm glad you could meet with us," he says as Bishop Jackson walks towards Nicky. "You know Raymond's father, Bishop A.L. Jackson," Mr. Goodson says.

Nicky looks excited to meet Raymond's father. Raymond talks about him all the time, but she never got a chance to meet him in person during their five years together. Nicky shakes his hand. "Mr. Jackson, Raymond has told me so much about you and it's a pleasure to finally meet you," she gushes.

"I wish I could say the same, that is, Raymond has never mentioned you to me at all," Mr. Jackson hints sarcastically. Nicky tries to ignore the edge in his voice.

"Let's take a seat over there," Mr. Goodson directs them. They all walk toward a small conference area. "I'm glad you could meet with us on such a short notice," he says.

"Well, when I received your e-mail you said it was an emergency so I thought to myself Raymond is the only one who has that e-mail address, so I figured he was the only one who could have given it to you. Is he all right?" Nicky asks.

"He's fine," Mr. Goodson answers.

"The news said something about Raymond being missing," Nicky mentions.

"They are exaggerating as usual. Raymond is fine as far as his well being is concerned, but there is another matter. Ms. Jones I want you to know we are aware of you and Raymond's relationship of the last five years," Mr. Goodson says.

Nicky takes a sip of tea while looking at Bishop Jackson. She feels exposed, off balance and cheap right now, and she hopes her discomposure doesn't show.

"I'm not talking about the media's insinuations or rumors, I don't care about what those story hungry bloodsuckers think. I'm talking about what I know and I'm going to get right to the reason I asked to see you today. Raymond's life and career are about to take a turn for the better and we think it's best for you not to see Raymond anymore," Mr. Goodson states flatly.

"Does this 'we' include Raymond?" Nicky deftly counters, her attorney's quick-on-your-feet training coming into play.

"Actually no, this is something we are doing because we love Raymond and we don't want anything like an extramarital affair to ruin his opportunities," Mr. Goodson explains.

Nicky takes another sip of the tea. She is filled with mixed feelings of hurt, anger, fear, and guilt, but you would never know it as she sits with her legs crossed, holding her tea in a most graceful manner. "No disrespect, but who are you sir, and where is Tarisha?" she inquires. Nicky never thought she would ever hear those words come out of her mouth -- her asking for Tarisha. Even though they never liked each other, Tarisha, Raymond's staff supervisor never tried to end their relationship. Sure she talked to Raymond about it, but once she realized Raymond was emotionally committed to Nicky she thought it would be better for them to be together than for the election to suffer because his mind was distracted by a broken heart.

"I'm Raymond's Godfather and I will be directing his political career from this point on. One of my first assignments is to clear out anything and anybody that has the potential of sabotaging his future," Goodson explains. Nicky stares at him as if he were a phantom. The room seems to be spinning and she can't believe the words that are coming out of his mouth. He reaches into his desk and removes a check. "We are prepared to give you five hundred thousand dollars for any inconvenience Raymond may have caused in altering your life in anyway," Mr. Goodson states, looking at Nicky evenly.

Nicky gets herself together enough to set the tea on the table and stand up. "Do you have anything for an 'altered' heart?" Nicky asks sarcastically, peering down at Goodson.

"I'm afraid not," he replies.

"Then you must be implying I can be bought."

"Not at all madam," he replies.

"Then why are you offering me money? Do you expect me to be bought out of Raymond's life?" Nicky asks in full cross-examination mode. She feels as if she is both defending her honor as well as fighting for her relationship.

But she doesn't understand that Raymond's Godfather is not in love with her; he is mercilessly going right for the jugular in the interest of his godson. "Please don't misunderstand me young lady. The money is only to help you get on with your life, maybe take a long trip or relocate or something like that. But one thing is 100 percent for sure, you will not be seeing or contacting Raymond ever again. Take it or leave it," Mr. Goodson avers as he extends the check to her.

Nicky doesn't take it, but turns and looks at Raymond's father and shakes her head with a little smile. She then looks at Mr. Goodson then takes the check out of his hand. She looks at it, then looks into Mr. Goodson's eyes as she slowly and deliberately tears the check up. Nicky walks to the door, opens it, turns and says, "If Raymond didn't put you up to this, can you tell him I did this because I love him. I also want the best for him. Tell him he was the best thing that ever happened to me. Thanks." Nicky then walks out.

Mr. Goodson and Bishop Jackson both look at each other. A part of them couldn't believe she didn't take the check. It would have been easy to accept that their action was the right thing to do if she had accepted the five hundred thousand dollars. But because she didn't, it made it look like she really was in love with Raymond.

The fact is Nicky was totally in love with Raymond. He was her first love and she gave him her virginity. Raymond also made her a promise one night that she has been treasuring in her heart. Nicky walked out of the Godfather's office because she would never let her love for Raymond stand in the way of his progress, even if it meant sacrificing her love.

Picture 19: *Don't Panic*

For the first time in the history of American politics the script has been flipped. The Presidential candidate is riding on the coattails of the Vice President. So if Raymond is missing, for whatever reason, Newton's chances of becoming President are so slim they could hide behind a toothpick.

Newton is in a news studio about to be interviewed. The makeup artist is putting on the finishing touches on his face and on the face of the female interviewer, Denise Waters. "I know you've done this a thousand times Mr. Newton, so just be natural and speak to the cameras," the program producer tells him as he puts the small microphone on his suit jacket. OK people we are on in 5-4-3-2 and --"

"Good evening I'm Denise Waters and you've heard it here first on this news broadcast. Tonight we have a very special report and a very special guest." The cameras enlarge the view to bring Newton into the frame. "Mr. John Newton, a Presidential candidate for the 2008 election. It's good to see you again sir," Denise says.

"Thank you Denise," Newton replies.

"Since you are here this evening, if I can get right to the point, would you please explain what may have happened to your campaign partner Raymond Jackson?"

"Well, for the last couple of weeks Raymond has not appeared for any of his scheduled campaign speeches or meetings. This is not like him, as you know. He is a very professional and efficient individual. I'm here to say I'm concerned about his well being," Newton states.

"Well, Mr. Newton why hasn't the police, or the FBI for that matter, gotten involved or been contacted?" Denise asks.

"This is why I agreed to have this interview. It appears his family members don't believe Raymond is in any danger, so they haven't filed a missing person's report, and the authorities can't officially get involved until this is done."

"I'm sure this is devastating to your campaign right now, because the polls show your team doing very well. Will this affect the votes at all?"

"I'm sure it will if we don't locate him very soon." Newton's face assumes a grave expression as he looks into the camera and says, "This is why I'm appealing to anyone, someone and everyone, if you have seen or heard from Mr. Raymond Jackson or have any information concerning his whereabouts, please call our campaign headquarters. There are hate groups out there who would do everything within their power to prevent Raymond from becoming Vice President, and we need your help," Newton pleads.

"Let's put the number on the screen just in case someone doesn't have it. It's 1-800-CHANGE. That's 1-800-CHANGE. I have one more question for you Mr. Newton. Do you think you can win the election without Raymond as your campaign partner?"

Beneath his make up Newton flushes. He puts on his standard issue political smile and clears his throat. "The race will go on and we will continue to make progress. But right now I'm deeply concerned about Mr. Jackson's whereabouts and his well being. We are a team, and no one man can win an election alone -- it's a collective effort," Newton declares.

"There you have it ladies and gentlemen of America, Mr. Newton believes Raymond Jackson is missing because of foul play. Raymond's family and staff does not think so. Therefore Mr. Newton is seeking your help. Anyone with any information on Mr. Jackson's well being or whereabouts should contact the Change Campaign Headquarters, I'm Denise Waters. Remember you heard it and saw it here first and don't forget it! Good night."

Picture 20: *Toy Soldiers*

Shawn, the head of the Westside gang is in his apartment with his girlfriend Tina, and some of the other gang members. They are playing music, drinking and getting high. It is an unofficial party and the occasion for the celebration is the dividing of the goodies that were taken from the dealers. Everyone laid low for a few days as they were told, and now it was time to get paid. Tina is sitting on Shawn's lap while he counts and divides the money. She is helping him put them in stacks of ten thousands.

There is a knock at the door, one of the gang members pulls out his gun and goes to the window. "It's probably Tar and Jay. They said they would be coming right after school," Shawn says. The gang member looks out the window, "Yeah it's them," he says and opens the door. Tar and Jay come inside.

"What's going on people," Shawn says. Jay hugs Shawn while playing the hand game.

"Much respect," Jay says.

Then Tar follows suit. "Much respect," Tar says to Shawn while giving him a hug.

"What's going on here?" Jay asks. "Well, we are doing it real big and why shouldn't we?" Shawn chuckles.

"That's real. That's real," Jay nods as he gets the blunt from one of the gang members and takes a hit. "Yeah, that's real man!" Jay exhales. Jay was named by his father who smoked so much marijuana, that when Jay was born he would get a contact from being in the same room with him. Jay was getting high at the age of five according to his father, so his father's friends nicknamed him Jay. Back in those days marijuana was called "Js" a.k.a. joints before they were labeled "blunts". Today Jay is living up to his name and reputation. He can't be around a blunt without taking a hit. He once told Tar he can't function in the morning unless he takes two to the head right when he gets up.

"Here you go little soldier," Shawn says as he hands Jay ten thousand dollars in cash. Jay takes the money and smiles, "Yeah this is real, true real," Jay says. "And for you new soldier," Shawn says as he gives Tar ten thousand dollars in cash.

"Thanks man," Tar says trying to keep his composure, because he never had this much money before. As a matter of fact he never seen this much money before, but he didn't want to seem like he was tender.

"We put work in together, we spend together, that's how we roll on the Westside way," Shawn sings.

"This is true, this is real here," Jay says.

Shawn signals Tina to get off his lap, walks over to Tar, puts both of his hands on his shoulders and looks him right in the eyes. "Listen little solder, I want you to know it's no love lost between us. Crazy things like that can happen when it's your first time. But you have to always do what I say if you are going to get out of the situation alive and with a lot more of this," Shawn says nodding at the 10 grand in Tar's hand.

Tar was impressed by Shawn because he was the person everyone talked about in school. All the girls liked him and all the guys respected him. Tar never met his father and his mother was in and out of rehab. The Westside gang was the closet thing he had to a family. So when Shawn pulled off that score, he also scored real big with Tar. Tar was already an official Westsider, but now the Westside was inside of him and he let them in because they got results. Tar was one of those people who was not into a lot of talking. He didn't like to talk about what you could do, should have done, or wanted to do. He was looking for results, and Shawn gave him what he was looking for. So now he is in the Westside gang and the Westside gang is in him.

Shawn sits back at the table and Tina gingerly takes her seat back on his lap like a contented cat. Jay walks over to Tar, shows him the money and says, "Boy we are rich."

"Not quite, but it will do for now," Tar says still trying to play the excitement off.

"Pass the blunt around man. Y'all not keeping it real. Y'all got to stay true," Jay says.

"Before we get drunk and crazy high, I heard something last night at the club," Shawn says.

"Turn that down for a minute," Jay says indicating to one of the other gang members to lower the volume on the CD player.

Shawn continues, "I heard some of the Killer gang members know we hit little Pete and them. Come to find out Pete was the first cousin of one of the Killers. So I think we are going to get some trouble out of them."

"So you know what that means," one of the gang members replies.

"No one walks by himself. We stay together at all times and we stay strapped," Shawn says, then puts the bottle to his mouth and takes a drink. "If you see one of them slipping, you get them before they get you," Shawn finishes.

"Oh we got something real for them right here," Jays says then puts the blunt in his mouth and pulls out his glock. "It looks like you are going to make your first killing sooner than you thought. Are you ready boy?" Jay asks Tar.

Tar looks at Jay and turns away without a word. Tar realizes Jay was just a follower, a wanna-be soldier. He killed before, but only because Shawn pushed him to do it. It was either kill or get out of the gang. Well, when the gang is all you got in life it's easy to take a life to keep that part of your life. Tar wasn't impressed with Jay. He was just tolerating him to get next to Shawn. He acknowledged the fact Jay introduced him to the gang and all. Jay even spoke up for him many times, putting good words in for him to Shawn. Tar will always be indebt to Jay for that. But as far as doing what Jay does or says, no he would not take it that far. Jay asking him was he ready to kill somebody made him feel ready to jump off of Jay's bus.

"Well, little soldier are you ready to kill or be killed?" Shawn piggybacked on Jay's question.

"I'm not ready to be killed, so somebody's got to die," Tar replied.

"Now you're talking like a soldier and that's what killing is all about. I'd rather be judged by 12 than carried by six anytime," Shawn says.

Another gang member chimes in. "That's right, get them or get got."

"That's real, and you don't get any realer than that Tar," Jay says. Tar glances at Jay with a look that says, "I wish you'd stop using the word real and true when you are more fake than a $3 bill. "Drink some of this boy," Jays says as he hands Tar the bottle. Tar puts it to his mouth and drinks some and starts to cough. "What is that?" Tar asks. Everyone starts to laugh at him.

Picture 21: *Temptation*

Raymond has been in the same room for 40 days, only eating bread and water. He came in weighing 230 pounds and now he is down to 190 pounds. He is not upset because this was his original weight before the late dinners, and the fast pace of the political world. He always said he wanted to lose some weight, but every time he managed to do so he gained the weight back and some. This time it felt different. The way he lost the weight was not planned or programmed, it happened by focusing on his spirituality, an area Raymond didn't know existed.

Yes, Raymond grew up in the church like a lot of people, but it's easy to become religious and never become spiritual -- praying religiously, singing religiously, going to church services religiously doing everything religiously--but failing to connect with their spirit within. Raymond's losing weight could very well be an outward sign of what has taken place inside him, shedding unnecessary baggage that held him back from being everything he had been created to be.

Raymond is catching on. He figured out since he had been there the Caretaker has been stopping by every ten days to check on him and to teach him a valuable lesson. She got him so wide open when it comes to her wisdom that he is actually eager to talk with her. He never learned so much from a woman before and it was a little exciting and liberating to him to look at women in a totally different light. Usually with an attractive woman like the Caretaker, Raymond would have set his smooth charm on overdrive and they would be making sweet, sexy love in no time at all. But for some reason he has gained a new level of respect for women during his time away from the campaign. He has gone through a spiritual development process under the instructions of his Godfather and the directions of the Caretaker.

Another thing Raymond notices about himself is his thinking and speech writing are shaper and more insightful than ever before. The last time he was on this writing level with such great clarity was in graduate school, when he received the highest grade among his peers for his thesis. He has written over three speeches a week and his creative juices are still flowing. It is as if his Godfather knew this would happen, so he supplied him with the pens, the pads and unstructured time. There was no TV or any modern technology to distract him, just his raw talent being discovered and recovered. Raymond is learning another powerful lesson: Modern technology is fine, but not at the expense of not realizing your potential. All the energy and time it takes from us is too high a price to pay. Raymond has just decided he can't afford to pay such a price any longer.

Raymond hears someone at the door. He continues to write because he knows it's the Caretaker. She opens the door and pushes a dinner cart inside. Raymond looks up and notices there is a candle on the cart, which adds a very romantic glow to the room. "I see you have been putting the pen and pad to good use," the Caretaker says.

"And I see you are full of surprises," Raymond counters.

"Oh this here, this is nothing compared to the other things I have in store for you," the Caretaker says as she puts the finishing touches on the dinner cart. "Come on over here Mr. Jackson and have a seat. Everything is prepared the way you like it." Raymond gets up from the floor where he was writing and hurries to the chair the Caretaker has pulled out for him. Raymond was like a little boy at his mother's table, ready to eat anything that was under the silver plated cover. The Caretaker takes a seat at the other end of the dinner cart. Raymond reaches over to remove the cover from the plate. "Not so fast Mr. Jackson. There is something we must talk about first," the Caretaker says.

"Do you think we can talk while we eat?" Raymond asks eagerly.

"Mr. Jackson, being disciplined a little longer is not going to hurt you, and after you hear what I have to offer you can eat all you want," the Caretaker purrs in a very sexy voice that was as obvious as Raymond's eagerness to eat.

"Offer? What offer? The last time I accepted an offer from you people I found myself on the hotel floor vomiting and speaking Chinese or something," Raymond says.

"Well, first allow me to say 'Congratulations' to you. You have been here for 40 days and I must say you surprised me, I thought you would be gone by now."

"Why leave this party, I'm having too much fun," Raymond says impatiently.

"Well, I have a graduation gift for you tonight, or should I say proposal," the Caretaker says.

"Does this have anything to do with why you are wearing a big overcoat?"

"Not too fast Mr. Jackson. Your mind is moving faster than your hands."

"I was afraid to ask you why you are dressed like that, because I may have gotten an answer I really didn't want to hear," Raymond says.

"Or maybe an answer you want to hear," the Caretaker says as she takes the cover off Raymond's plate. Raymond can't believe his eyes or his nose, it's his absolute, all-time, favorite foods, savory, well seasoned and piping hot: fried chicken smothered in brown gravy, baked potatoes dripping with butter, greens, candied yams and cornbread. Raymond had been so completely deprived of food that he was prepared to eat anything; but he has in front of him everything he loves to eat. How did she know? He was about to ask her, but then she stopped and gave him that special smile and told him it was all his Godfather's idea.

But right now he didn't care whose idea it was, it was time to get down. Raymond picks up the silverware.

"Slow down Mr. Jackson. You haven't heard the proposal yet," the Caretaker says. Raymond sets the knife and fork down, but can't take his eyes off of the plate. "Mr. Jackson, Mr. Jackson!" the Caretaker raises her voice a little to snap Raymond out of the food trance. Raymond looks at her. "I need your undivided attention for a minute so you can understand the offer," the Caretaker says.

Raymond takes a deep breath, and shakes his head as though he was shaking off a spell. "OK what do you have?" Raymond asks.

"Well, Mr. Jackson I have this," the Caretaker takes off her overcoat and lets it drop to the floor. She is standing before Raymond wearing a white see-through negligee. Raymond snaps back into the spell, this time was because a beautiful lady was in front of him with next to nothing on, revealing everything that a man likes to see in a woman. The Caretaker walks away from Raymond to turn down the lights, giving Raymond a luscious view of her assets from behind. There were no liabilities as far as he could see. The Caretaker comes back and lights more candles on the dinner cart. "Do you like what you see Mr. Jackson?" she asks in a very sexy voice.

"Yes, the food looks delicious," Raymond responds.

"You know you weren't looking at the food Mr. Jackson," the Caretaker replies. Raymond lifts his eyes from the plate and looks back at the Caretaker. She looks into Raymond's eyes, "Do you miss your wife Mr. Jackson?" she asks. Raymond pauses to think about the question; he wants to make sure he gets the answer right if it means a trip into food-and-sex land.

"That's a good question. I stayed gone so much at one time, I don't…," Raymond starts to reply. The Caretaker interrupts him and says, "I'm not talking about missing her presence, but missing her. Maybe I should rephrase the question: Is your wife missing?" the Caretaker asks.

Raymond thinks for a few seconds, and then it hits him. "Oh, I get it. You are good, and you know that?" Raymond says.

"A lot of men and women for that matter cheat on their spouse or partner because they are looking for the person they once were in love with. The only problem is they can't find the missing person in any of the people they have been cheating with. So when the phase wears off they will be cheating on the person they are cheating with and the cycle continues on," the Caretaker says.

"That sounds good and deep and all, but what does this have to do with your proposal?" Raymond asks.

"Well, Mr. Jackson I prepared your favorite meal and I'm dressed like this to offer you me and the meal. That's right Mr. Jackson, I'm prepared to make love to you like you've never had lovemaking before," the Caretaker says to Raymond with raw sexuality. "I'm trained to provide a man exquisite pleasure in every way from head to toe. Personally I would enjoy this assignment, because you are a sexy, smart, strong, powerful man. I can see why the ladies throw themselves at you," she says.

The Caretaker moves over to Raymond and touches his hair, then moves her hand to his face. She comes closer, bending over giving him a kiss on the side of his face close to his ear. He can feel her breath and smell her intoxicating fragrance. "I'm ready to feed you then we can make love for hours; or we can make love for hours then I can feed you; or you can eat the food off of me and enjoy both meals at the same time," she seduces as she moves behind Raymond and begins to kiss his neck.

"What's the catch?" Raymond asks. The Caretaker continues to kiss his neck, and then stops herself. She is enjoying seducing Raymond so much she forgot to give him the downside of the proposal. The truth is she was falling for Raymond herself, this job was getting the best of her. Raymond may have thought it was only an act, but her offer was real.

"Or you can call your wife and begin to locate the missing person you are really looking for," she says as she reaches over Raymond to take the cover off another plate which has a cellular phone on it.

"Are you telling me I must choose between eating and having sex with you, or calling and talking with my wife?" Raymond asks in disbelief. The Caretaker went right back to kissing Raymond's neck, caressing him as much as she could anywhere she could.

"It's a package deal for one night, but it will be a night you will never forget," she says.

Raymond is looking at a plate of his favorite dishes, a plate with a phone on it and feeling this juicy, beautiful, delectable woman touching him all over his body. She smells good enough to eat and the food is calling his name like crack sings out to a crack head. OK Raymond is waiting for the feeling of loose abandonment he usually gets before he turns all logic off and throws caution to the wind. It should be kicking in at anytime now, he says to himself. Raymond closes his eyes to get into the mood and to get the old feelings going. The Caretaker is unbuttoning his shirt. "OK it's about to take place right now," he thinks to himself.

"Oh no," Raymond says out loud.

The Caretaker ignores his sounds and strokes his chest. "Can I tell you something in confidence Raymond," the Caretaker says. "I haven't had a man in years. My job keeps me from getting serious with anyone and you haven't had a woman in weeks. Do you know what we can do together?"

Raymond is thinking, "If she is acting she is really good, maybe she should be an actress or something, because I am totally turned on." The Caretaker is supposed to be irresistible to Raymond, but she is finding Raymond to be irresistible. Raymond can feel her soft, juicy breasts pressed against his back and the heat coming from her body.

But Raymond saw his wife when he closed his eyes. Not that that is a bad thing, but he knows something has changed about him for sure. Any other time he would have used the Caretaker like a biscuit, sopped up the food with her body, and satisfied two hungers at once. Tonight, and perhaps forever something was different. Raymond uses all of his emotional and spiritual strength to pick up the phone.

The Caretaker noticed and reached for the phone, taking it out of Raymond's hand and stopping the call before it could be connected. "I guess you made your choice."

"Yeah, I guess I did," Raymond replies. Where he got the will power to make that choice is totally beyond him.

The Caretaker walks over to turn on the lights, she then puts back on her overcoat, keeping it open for a few seconds and says to Raymond, "Are you sure you don't want to reconsider?"

"No," Raymond says sounding more confident. The Caretaker opens the door and pushes the cart out. Raymond can't believe he had the strength to watch two of the greatest desires in his life right now walk out of his room. The Caretaker stops and pours Raymond a tall cold glass of orange juice and smiles as she hands it to him. Raymond takes a long, thirsty drink; his plan was just to take a sip, but he couldn't stop drinking until it was all gone. He could feel the vitamins rushing to the proper places to fortify his body. "That had to be the best glass of orange juice anybody has ever had," Raymond smiles.

"Well, Mr. Jackson it's because for the last 40 days you've been drinking water. A great man once said if you want to rediscover how sweet the fruit is, you must stop indulging in artificial flavors," the Caretaker says then hands Raymond the cellular phone.

"Who said that?" Raymond asks.

The Caretaker grins at Raymond and says, "Your Godfather."

Picture 22: *Back in Love*

Raymond watches the Caretaker as she exits, but this time she didn't lock the door. That was unusual to Raymond, but the Caretaker had come to realize Raymond had shown much maturity in the last lesson, so now there was no need to keep him locked up like a little child during a timeout. No lock on the door was the sign Raymond was beginning to be free on the inside, developing self-control where no restraints are necessary. Raymond lays down on the bed thinking about what just took place. He looks at the symbol of the choice he made in his hand: the cell phone.

It wasn't hot food or hot sex, but it was the right choice. For the first time in a long time he felt good about the choice he made that would affect his personal life in a positive way. Raymond punched in the numbers to call his wife. "Hello," Diamond answers.

"Hey beautiful," Raymond says.

"Raymond," Diamond cries.

"Your one and only," Raymond says.

"Where are you, where have you been?" Diamond asks anxiously.

"I'm OK. Everything is fine. I had to get away for a little while," Raymond says calmly.

Diamond breathes an audible sigh of relief. "I am so glad that you are OK. A lot of people have been calling here for you."

"Yeah, I thought they would be," Raymond replies.

"Your father told me you had to get away for a while, but then Newton got on TV saying he thought one of the hate groups had something to do with your disappearance."

"Oh yeah," Raymond says nonchalantly. "Are you OK?" he asks Diamond.

"Now I am, now that I know you are fine."

"Have you talked to my mother?" Raymond asks.

"Every Wednesday, you know that," Diamond says.

"How did she react to this?" Raymond asks. "You know your mother; she was like, 'Let's just keep Raymond in prayer.' So we prayed for you many times over the phone," Diamond says.

"Yeah, that's my mom."

"Man, now I can get some rest, I have been tossing and turning since your crazy campaign partner got on the news saying those horrible things," she says.

"Diamond, I don't want to talk about him right now."

"OK that's fine," Diamond says.

"I called you to tell you I really missed you baby."

Diamond is unsure how to respond because Raymond has not told her that in a long while.

"Are you still there?" Raymond asks.

"Yeah, honey I'm here. Have you been drinking Raymond?"

"No, not quite, I haven't had anything for a while. Diamond I want you to know I have a different outlook about you, me and our marriage now. I'm learning to appreciate who you are to me, your true value and worth," Raymond states seriously.

"I like the sound of that, tell me some more," Diamond urges.

"Well, remember how we used to talk on the phone all night when I would go on my trips?" Raymond asks.

"Yeah, I remember thinking to myself, 'If I can't have your body here your voice will just have to do'."

"You're more than word can express, your sweetness is refreshment for my soul," Raymond says.

"I used to love the way you talked to me when we first met -- that is what made me fall in love with you, even though all my girls were telling me I couldn't date a sophomore when I was a senior."

"They just wanted me for themselves," Raymond teases and they both laugh.

"You're probably right," Diamond says.

"I used to love coming home from a convention, running in the house and seeing you in that red negligee. You would have our favorite song playing and all my favorite dishes waiting. Then you would put all of that good loving on me," Raymond reminisces.

"You'd better stop talking like that before you turn me on," Diamond warns Raymond.

"That's what I want, for you to be turned on and never to be turned off again," Raymond says and Diamond falls silent again. "I know after we found out that you were not able to conceive it seemed like things began to change for the worst in our relationship. I know this is why you disassociated yourself from me when it came to public events. But I want us to go back to the way we use to love each other. Do you think it is possible Diamond?" Raymond asks.

"I don't know Raymond, let's talk about it face to face." Diamond loved the sound of Raymond's optimistic words. He had a persuasive style that captivated all who heard him. But when Raymond started talking seriously about their relationship it raised her guard. She had already been hurt too much. She had accepted that a powerful man would have extramarital affairs; it was part of a package deal that came with the territory of being a political wife. Every politician's wife understood their husbands would have some young pretty thing on the side. It was shameful, but it was an open secret. The ladies knew who was seeing whom; no one was stupid about these matters -- every one just played dumb. Diamond had adjusted to this political way of life and one of the ways she did this was by accepting it would never be the way it used to be with her and Raymond when they first got married, when they were in a more innocent state, before the games of the political life began. Diamond had accepted this fact about her marriage in order to help them reach their goals for upward mobility and a better life.

So when Raymond started talking about being serious, she would put up her guard and step back to protect herself from the emotional blow that usually came with such a statement. She had gotten so used to being hurt that any mention of improving their marriage or making it better sent red flags to alert her to not take it seriously, even if it sounded sincere.

"So how was your day?" Raymond asks.

"Things here have been good. Some of the political girls have been talking about social events we are going to have once you are in office," Diamond shares.

"They are really taken a liking to you."

"They only accepted me so fast because of you."

"No, that's not true, with all the great things you got going for you, they should be honored to have you grace their life with your presence," Raymond complimented.

"That's sweet baby, but the fact still remains these were the same groups of females who wouldn't invite me to any of their dinner parties until you announced you became John's running mate," Diamond says.

"You know how people are. It doesn't say anything about you, but everything about them," Raymond assures his wife.

"I guess you're right," Diamond says.

"So go ahead and talk to me," Raymond says.

"Talk about what?"

"Anything, I just want to hear your voice."

"Well, I'm thinking about going shopping tomorrow, I saw this dress I know I would look good in, but only if I get my nails done in one of the colors in the dress. What do you think?"

"I think you would look good in anything,"

"You are full of compliments tonight aren't you," Diamond says. Raymond laughs a little. "I'm thinking about having a dinner party whenever you get home, I think it will be good for the people to see that you are OK," Diamond says.

"Oh man, I just gave her an excuse to throw a party," Raymond says to Diamond's laughter. Her husband knows her well. "That's all right, do whatever you want, whatever makes you happy, because I want to see you smile and I love to hear you laugh," Raymond says. Raymond's charm and persuasion is making it real hard for Diamond to maintain her emotional distance. She feels herself starting to believe what he is saying about their relationship, but she can't afford to be wrong and be jerked around and disappointed again. It took a long time to build protective walls to keep her husband from breaking her heart over and over again as he climbed the political ladder. It would take more than sweet words to cause the demolition process to commence.

Raymond on the other hand is genuinely trying to express overdue love to Diamond, no strings attached, nothing up his sleeves and no mind games -- just love and affection he should have never have stopped giving her, not even for political power and fame. "Don't stop talking honey," Raymond says.

"All right, but remember you asked for it. I don't want you to tell me next week, I'm talking too much," Diamond says.

"I'll never tell you that, I want to listen to you speak," Raymond says. What Diamond didn't understand was her husband hasn't eaten anything but bread and water for 40 days and he had also successfully fought one of the greatest battles of his life. Now her voice was ample nourishment for his soul, because he was being satisfied by just hearing her speak as he ate up her every word.

Picture 23: *Leave Please*

It's 8:00 am and Raymond and Diamond are still on the phone even though they are both half sleep. But they manage to talk to each other all night long, like they used to do when they first met.

The Caretaker opens the door and notices Raymond still on the phone. She envies Diamond right now, not because of Raymond's sex appeal or even the great plan his Godfather has for him, but she secretly envies Diamond because she has a brand new man. The Caretaker knows what this means but Diamond does not have the slightest idea. A brand new man can make a woman feel beautiful, he will start to do the small things that matter: pull out the chair, open the door, listen when she talks, take long walks in the park, create romantic nights at home, go on fantasy trips, send roses just because, call to say "I love you", give gifts and candy, make love in the middle of the day, and talk all night on the phone. "Good morning Mr. Jackson," the Caretaker says.

"Hold on please baby." Raymond places the phone on his lap to cover the receiver so Diamond couldn't hear anything.

"Good morning," Raymond replies.

"Well, Mr. Jackson we have completed our program and you can leave at anytime."

"Would right now be too soon?" Raymond asks.

"Not at all."

Raymond gets on the phone, "Baby I should be home in 45 minutes or less. OK. I love you. Bye," Raymond says as he hangs up the phone. Raymond strides towards the dresser to get his clothes.

"Your Godfather will be contacting you about a meeting he has arranged in two weeks," the Caretaker informs Raymond.

"Will I be seeing you again?" Raymond asks.

"No sir, but I will be seeing you, I'm sure. Thank you for your cooperation, you made my job very easy," the Caretaker says. She shakes Raymond's hand. "Your security and driver are waiting in the lobby. Take care of yourself and keep the faith," the Caretaker says.

"Thank you for teaching me in 40 days more than I never learned in over 20 years of schooling," Raymond says and gives her a hug.

The Caretaker closes her eyes and enjoys the last embrace from Raymond, and then she catches herself and pulls away. "Come on Mr. Jackson your wife is waiting," she says. Raymond smiles and walks out the door.

Picture 24: *The New You*

When you look in the mirror do you like what you see?
Like what you see
When you look in the mirror do you like what you see?
Like what you see
Sometimes in life you're not everything you want to be, but when you look in the mirror be sure you like what you see
Like what you see
When you look in the mirror do you feel complete?
Feel complete
When you look in the mirror do you feel complete?
Feel complete
Sometimes in life you're not where you think you should be, but when you look in the mirror make sure you feel complete
When you look in the mirror do you feel free?
Feel free
When you look in the mirror do you feel free?
Feel free
Sometimes your hair and make up don't make you who you would like to be, but when you look in the mirror make sure you feel free
I love
I love, love me some me
I love, love me some me
When I'm wrong
I love me some me
When I'm right
I love, love me some me
When I'm on top
I love, love me some me

Raymond is sitting in his Jacuzzi listening to this song over and over, as he peers at himself in the mirrors that are all over his bathroom. It appears Raymond is confused about what has taken place in his life. He was a changed person and there was no other way to look at it. Who was this man he found himself staring at in the mirror? Was he a changed man or a man who had been revealed?

Raymond thought about some of the facts he read in the Bible over those 40 days.

He recalls repeatedly when God came to do something for or with a person in those days he changed their name or at least that's how he looked at it when he first read it, but now he was considering another point of view; was he changing their names or was he revealing to them their *real* names? Since Abram's parents brought him up in an idol-worshipping environment teaching him to worship false Gods, this would give Abram a false identity, which means the name he was given was false. So later on in his life he begins to interact with the true and living God who doesn't change his name, but reveals his true name to him, giving him his true identity.

This is logical Raymond thought to himself, and up until now he never thought like that before. He began to wonder where his vibrant new sense of himself is coming from. Maybe the political world had given Raymond a false identity; maybe the prep schools and university education had turned him into something he was never meant to be.

Now the true person is ready to come to the surface and the most frightening thing is he must get to know himself all over again. He wished he could stay in the tub and stare at himself for as long as it took to get to know the "New Raymond." This is why he was listening to the song over and over, programming its message in his mind, emotions and will. He was not the old man, but the new man lived and Raymond loved him. He wanted to live to show others there had been a change in his life.

Diamond walked into the bathroom, "Raymond, Raymond," Diamond says.

"Yes," Raymond answers.

"You've been in here going on two hours and what's up with this song?" Diamond asks as she turns the MP3 player off. "Are you OK?" she asks Raymond. Raymond just smiles and nods his head to indicate "Yes." Diamond kneels down beside the tub, takes the washcloth and soaps it up to a creamy lather. Raymond looks at Diamond as if it is his first time seeing her. Something the Caretaker said popped in his head; sometimes men cheat on their wives because they miss the person they used to be before they got married. Well, Raymond began to see the person he once loved and she was just as beautiful as she was when they first met. Raymond smiled at Diamond and touched her hair. "Come on Raymond, you are going to get my hair all wet and put soap in it," Diamond says playfully. Another profound fact occurred to Raymond; he was rediscovering his wife because he was in the process of discovering who *he* truly was. He couldn't love his wife completely and totally because he didn't know himself to love himself completely and totally. He was noticing something new and exciting about her as he embraced his new self. Diamond began to wash Raymond's body; Raymond was enjoying his wife's touch and the view of her curvaceous shape as he looked at her reflection in the mirrors. Diamond was 5'5", 120lbs with caramel brown-skinned. She had recently turned 43 years-old, but could be easily mistaken for someone in her 30's. There were many times she had to tell teenager boys who tried to flirt with her that she was old enough to be their grandmother. "She has definitely kept herself in good shape," he thought. Raymond was discovering that what he was looking for in Nicky had been in Diamond all the time. Maybe he was just trying to find a younger version of Diamond in Nicky.

"Mrs. Diamond," the maid's voice calls from the intercom. "Where do you want your meal cart?"

"You can take it into the master bedroom," Diamond directs her. Diamond gives the washcloth to Raymond, "You can take it from here, and don't be all day, or your food will get cold," Diamond says as she starts to leave to meet the maid in the bedroom.

"Diamond?" Raymond calls.

"Yes," she answers. "Thank you, baby. Thank you for everything but thank you for being you," Raymond says earnestly. Diamond looks at Raymond strangely and smiles.

"You're welcome," she says and then continues to walk out the door. Her two words could explain all Diamond was feeling about Raymond right now. Even after all he had put her through with his selfish ways, she never gave up on him. She never said anything about Nicky, but Raymond was sure she knew. Knowing Diamond perceptiveness, she knew the first time Raymond met Nicky.

Raymond began to truly understand everything he took her through, because now he got a chance to look at his old man ways with new eyes. What he thought was OK before, he now realizes was not. What he thought was cool, was not. And what was acceptable to the old Raymond can not be tolerated by his new self. The first person who should benefit from this new person was the one who took so much mess from the old Raymond. Often the people we hurt the most are the ones who are the closest to us and the person we protect is the person who does not mean much to us. Raymond used to protect Nicky by not letting her know some of his weaknesses because he wanted her to perceive him as being perfect, but Diamond was witness to Raymond's weakness and imperfection.

Many nights he would come in from out of town he would catch her crying. When he asked if she was OK, she would tell him it was just her allergies bothering her. Raymond would wish it was true, but he knew better. All of this and more caused Raymond to vow to himself that Diamond would get the remainder of his life's devotion, love and total commitment to make her the happiest woman in the world. The old Raymond's focus was on trying to please as many women as he could in his life, but the new Raymond's orientation was to please one woman for her lifetime.

"Thank you" Raymond thought out loud and began to wash himself.

Picture 25: *Stop Cheating Me*

Diamond is sitting across the table from Raymond watching him devour his meal like there is no tomorrow. She had their cook prepare all of his favorite dishes and he couldn't get enough. He looked like he lost a lot of weight to her, so she didn't mind him eating, but he was eating so fast she didn't think he would be able to enjoy the meal. "Raymond slow down before you hurt yourself," Diamond cautions him.

"Oh am I eating too fast again?" She smiles at him and nods her head "Yes."

Diamond senses that something is different about Raymond. At times he seemed so completely removed and at times he seemed so intensely focused, like now. Diamond couldn't get him to start a conversation because his undivided attention was on the plate in front of him. She usually stayed out of Raymond's business and gave him his space. Her mother taught her if you give a man his space he will always come around, but if you nag him he will stop coming around all together. This time it was a little different; she wanted to know where he had been for the last 40 days. Even when he was on the road at conventions or spending time with Nicky he always checked in. This was the first time in 15 years something like this took place and she wanted an explanation.

"Do you want me to bring you dessert?" Diamond asks Raymond.

Raymond continues to chew his food and then swallows in order to answer her. "No, I'm going to finish this. I think this should be enough," Raymond says as he reaches for the glass of water.

"Are you going to eat anything?" he asks Diamond.

"No, I'm enjoying watching you." Raymond smiles and puts another piece of chicken on his plate. "What's on your mind Raymond? You haven't said much since you came into the house, unless..." Diamond pauses.

"Unless what?" Raymond asks.

"Unless you and your girlfriend had a fight, then I don't want to hear about that," Diamond says.

"I'm not seeing her anymore," Raymond announces proudly. Raymond was surprised it was that easy to confess and it made him feel good to say it out loud especially, to his wife.

"So that's it!" Diamond says.

"No, not at all. It's something bigger," Raymond replies.

"Sweetheart, I'm listening," Diamond encourages. Raymond puts down the silverware and looks Diamond in the eyes.

"Diamond I'm pulling out of the race, I'm no longer running for Vice President."

Diamond couldn't believe what she just heard. "What? What happened? I knew they were going to start that dirty politics stuff," Diamond says.

"No, baby no, it's not like that. It's my decision," Raymond says,

"What do you mean it's your decision?"

"I'm pulling out because I want to," Raymond says.

"And they don't have anything on you?"

"No," Raymond answers.

"Then what is going on Raymond?"

"I can't explain everything right now, but what I know is I'm not going to be Vice President." This was hard for Raymond to say and it even hurt to hear it in his own ears. It's ironic that the thing he thought would be hard to confess turned out to be easy and the revelation he thought would be easy to share turned out to be hard.

Diamond stands up from the table and says, "Raymond I don't know what kind of game you are playing here, but it's not funny."

"It's not a game," Raymond says as he looks up at Diamond's face, which was getting more upset by the minute.

"Then what in the hell is it? I bent over backwards to get to this point with you. All of the sacrifices I made and all of the mess I endured to get to this place, and you are just going to take it all away from me with no explanation? It's not fair Raymond, and I'm not taking it anymore," Diamond says and storms off towards her closet.

She had all the right in the world to be angry; she made a lot of sacrifices for Raymond and endured a lot of pain. All she wanted was to be in the inner circle of the political elite. Raymond being Vice President would get her there.

But now that Raymond was talking about pulling out of the race, all of her pain and problems counted for nothing. Diamond pulls out her suitcases and puts them on the bed and walked over to the armoire to take her clothes out, but Raymond stops her.

"Where are you going Diamond?"

"Out of this nightmare you call a marriage," she says as she tries to evade Raymond.

"Honey, please listen," Raymond begs.

"I'm not one of your political groupies. You can't manipulate me to believe everything you say. Whatever I did, I did for you and me. You are not the only person who has dreams Raymond. I have some too, but you just dashed them to pieces for no reason at all. I have nothing now; no husband; no family; no dreams; and no hope. It's time for me to wake up now," Diamond cries.

She was right and there was nothing Raymond could say. He had to let her go. As Diamond begins to pack her clothes, this strange information comes to him from out of nowhere. Raymond thinks to himself at first not to say anything, but she was worth at least one more try. "Diamond look at me. Stop packing and look at me for one minute," Raymond insists. Diamond reluctantly stops her furious grabbing of clothes and looks Raymond in the eyes.

"I can't tell you everything that's going on because it is happening so fast, but I can tell you I'm a changed person. The last 40 days I had to make a lot of major choices in my life and giving up the Vice Presidency and Nicky were two of the hardest. Baby, I don't know where all of this is going, but I need you to go with me. If you don't believe in another word I say ever, you've got to believe this. Since I've been gone I've come to realize your value, wealth and worth to me and I love you more now than ever. Baby I'm on another level and I want you to be on this level with me. Let's love on another level," Raymond says then goes over to Diamond and takes the dress out of her hand and puts his arms around her and kisses her softly on the lips. "Don't leave me now," Raymond says. Then he kisses her again. "Don't leave me ever," Raymond says. They begin to kiss each other passionately. Raymond could feel their love being renewed in each kiss and each touch.

"You are good," Diamond tells Raymond as he kisses her on her neck. She considers all he just said. It didn't sound like the old Raymond. He was more sincere. Most of the time Raymond talked *at* her like he was rehearsing his latest speech on her, but this time Raymond spoke to her. For the first time in a long time Raymond spoke to her and she felt his words as if they were penetrating her very soul.

Raymond starts to take off his wife's clothes, one piece at a time. Then he tenderly lays her on the floor and they make passionate love.

"Oh yes, oh yes, whatever you want to do, I need you, I missed you, yes, yes, yes, yes," Diamond purrs as she enjoys every part of her new husband's new loving and her husband was loving the fact that he was pleasing her.

Picture 26: *Do You Promise?*

Raymond, Diamond and Bishop Jackson have a 9:00 am meeting with Raymond's Godfather. "Would you have a seat here please sir," the receptionist says to Raymond as she pulls out the seat at the head of the conference room table.

"I would prefer for my father to sit there," Raymond replies. "No son you sit there today," his father says.

"Are you sure?" Raymond asks.

"I'm positive," his father responds. Raymond looks at his father and sits down with his wife sitting on one side of him and his father on the other. Ordinarily Bishop Jackson would have usually accepted Raymond's kind gesture to sit at the head of the table, because he feels it keeps his son humble, and with all of his abilities and gifts humility is a therapy Raymond needs to keep the political power from going to his head. But today things were different because Raymond must be in a position to receive the greatest responsibility he or anyone in his family has ever been offered, including his father.

"Mr. Goodson will be right out," the receptionist says and then walks out another door in the boardroom.

"This place amazes me. I never knew any of this was here. I thought it was just a hotel, not even a five star," Raymond comments to his father and wife as he looks around the room.

Bishop Jackson looks at his watch and says, "He should be coming anytime now, he is adamant about being on…"

The door the receptionist went in opens and 12 young men and women dressed in impeccable business attire walk in the room, place their folders on the table, and stand behind their chairs at the table. There are six females on the right side of the table, and six males on the left. Mr. Goodson walks into the room, Bishop Jackson stands up, Raymond looks at his father and rises up and then Diamond stands as well.

"Thank you, you may be seated," Mr. Goodson says. Raymond sits down and begins to get that first-day-at-school feeling again, but this time it's not that strong, Raymond recalls each time he meets this person he feels something is about to happen, and he is tired of the suspense. Today he was going to find out what is up with this Godfather, and what he could be offering him that could possibly be a greater position than the Vice Presidency of the United States.

Mr. Goodson remains standing after everyone else is seated and says, "Good morning everyone. Thank you Raymond and Diamond for coming. I want to first congratulate you on your excellent spiritual rehabilitation. The Caretaker, Ms. Mendez, informed me that you passed with flying colors. She suggests you be placed on record as one of our best students," his Godfather says.

Raymond didn't have any idea he was being tested during those 40 days, so to him this meant he had passed something he didn't know was an exam and that made him feel good and very confident. This made him sit up in the chair a little straighter.

This doesn't come to any surprise to his father because Raymond has always done well when it came to examinations. His father always received compliments from his teachers on how well he did with his schoolwork. Neither did it come to any surprise to his wife, because ever since she met Raymond she noticed whatever he set his mind to, he accomplished in an excellent manner. All of these facts made Raymond an excellent candidate for the job his Godfather was about to offer him.

Mr. Goodson continues, "There is a lot of ground I must cover with you Raymond. You have been our subject for the last five years, so most of us know you. But you don't know anything about us."

"They say a picture is worth a thousand words, so I'm going to direct your attention to some pictures and hope that saying is correct." A projection screen drops slowly from the ceiling in front of the room. A picture of four older men with a little boy appears on the screen.

"The first picture I want to bring to your attention is this one. The little boy in this picture is me when I was three years of age. This is my father, my grandfather, great-grandfather and your great-great-grandfather," Mr. Goodson using a red laser beam to point them out as he identifies them. Raymond looks at his father who continues to look straight ahead. Mr. Goodson continues, "Algeria was once one of the riches Kingdoms in the world." (A picture of Algeria appears on the screen), "But then the Europeans came and began the colonization process. During this time my great-grandfather and your great-great grandfather were best of friends. Also at this time they both were captured and sold into slavery. My great-grandfather was sold to Europe and your great-great grandfather was sold to America. After years in slavery my great-grandfather worked to buy his freedom and returned to Algeria. But life wasn't the same without his dear friend. At times he would be awakened from his dreams by the voice of your great-great grandfather calling for him in America. Many times he wanted to go to America to see could he locate him and buy his freedom like he bought his own, but there was one thing stopping him -- courage! One night while praying to the God of Abraham, Isaac, Jacob, and our Lord Jesus Christ, he promised he would create a way for anyone who wanted to come back to their original home in Africa to do so. Well, my great-grandfather died before he could see this promise fulfilled, but not before passing this promise to his son, his son's son, and his son's sons," Mr. Goodson says.

A portrait appears on the screen of well-dressed African families and then another picture of a modern Algeria where high rise buildings and commercial activity are seen. "From this promise we have managed to become one of the most influential and wealthiest families in Africa, and maybe even the world. My family profited from the mining of gold and diamonds. Once I inherited the family fortune I invested in the gold and diamond trade all over the world. We have bought land all over the continent, and we have been building for the last 50 years. We have built schools, houses, banks, hospitals, universities, courthouses, office buildings and everything you can think of that any other Nation might have. We have the backing of over 40 nations in Africa to recognize us politically and trade with us economically. We are about to make history by an action that has been a long time coming and will be appreciated by many people all over the world. Raymond, we want you to be one of the founders of the New Nation of Africa," Mr. Goodson completes his statement on a vigorous note.

Raymond looks around the table as if everyone in the room were crazy (aside from his wife). "Let me get this right. You are planning to start a New Nation in Africa and you want African Americans to leave America to go live in Africa," Raymond says in disbelief. No one responds. Raymond looks at his wife and smiles, then looks at his Godfather, "Are you crazy or something?" Raymond says.

"Ask questions son, but do not be cynical. We don't have time for that," his Godfather warns.

"OK, allow me to put it in a more professional way. I believe the adventure you are planning to make is causing you all to seem like you are out of your mind," Raymond says sarcastically. Raymond rises from his seat as if to leave.

"Please don't think this is something we thought of overnight son. This has been in development before your political career ever existed. As a matter of fact we shaped and molded your political career for this time. This is bigger than you and I and everyone in this room. It started with our ancestors. We only have the honor to see it materialize in our time," his Godfather says.

This is the second time Raymond heard him say his political career was shaped for this, and he wanted to know for sure what exactly he meant by that statement.

"So why me? There are so many other people who can and would love doing something like this. What about the leader of the Nation of Islam? What about Naji Muhammad or Mwamba Sussan. It seems something like this would be right up their alley," Raymond says.

"Sir, can I address that?" one of the six men sitting at the table asks. "My name is Bryant Washington. You can call me Bryant. I am the head of Public Relations. Right now you are the most popular person in America. Not only do African Americans trust you, but everyone likes you: celebrities, politicians, judges and even the Hip-Hop generation. Regarding those other people you named, no offense, but in light of 911 this move wouldn't last a week, once it gets out. You have a charisma that allows you the ability to introduce the most complicated issues to people and make it seem possible. This is why *you* were chosen and not *them*. I have studied you for years and I can say your gift is amazing. You possess an art beyond the natural. No one will take offense to you and will give what you say a fair hearing," Bryant says.

"It looks like you have a fan Raymond," his Godfather smiles and everyone in the room laughs a little.

As flattering as that sounds it did not answer the question Raymond was looking for as to why his Godfather kept mentioning that he shaped Raymond's political career.

"What exactly do you want from me? I don't know anything about starting a Nation." Raymond was about to be the first male African American Vice President of the United States, but he ruefully made this very revealing statement. One may have thought his words were spoken to evade the responsibility that was being offered to him, but this was not so. Raymond didn't know anything about building a Nation; he was only taught how to navigate in a Nation that has been running for years on its own. The system that now exist is based on shuffling, stomping, smiling and slow dancing around issues that have a way of resolving themselves one way or another. To break a sweat by digging deep into the political crust and core for the groundbreaking event of building a Nation was totally out of Raymond's league.

"Everything is in place and nothing has been overlooked. The New Nation of Africa is prepared to run on its own for the next 20 years with all the proper people in place. 20 years from now we will have our first election. The people will elect persons from the lowest to the highest offices," Mr. Goodson says.

"So the New Nation will be a democracy?" Raymond asks.

"Absolutely," his Godfather replies.

"I'm still not sure," Raymond starts to say, but is interrupted by his Godfather.

"We need you to do what you do best -- motivate and inspire the generations. This time you will be using your power of persuasion to convince people to consider going back to the beginning, to Africa," his Godfather says.

Raymond looks around the room, only he and his Godfather are standing, but at opposite ends of the table. Raymond looks at his father and then at Diamond. "When is all of this supposed to take place?" Diamond speaks up.

"Between now and Election Day," Mr. Goodson says.

"But that's less than ten months away," Diamond protests.

"That's why we don't have time to take all day explaining to you every detail. These men and women are the most talented and gifted people in this world; they all graduated at the top of their classes from the best universities all over the globe. If you accept this offer they will be your new staff -- the people who will make it happen. They will head each operation and department, and they will explain everything there is to know about the New Nation," his Godfather says.

Mr. Goodson is very confident in these young men and women, because like Raymond he handpicked them before they were born, before their parents conceived them and planned their schooling they would receive and in what part of the world they would receive it. Because of their role their parents have been able to live very wealthy lives. They too are very wealthy and have been before they even graduated from grade school, that's how Mr. Goodson was able to be sure about their loyalties and motives.

"Would you please introduce yourselves to Raymond and Diamond," his Godfather says. Each one begins to introduce themselves in order around the table.

"I am Louise Witherspoon, head of Administration."

"I am Gwendolyn Vaughan, head of Marketing."

"I am Ethel Neale, head of Research and Evaluation."

"I am Harriet Pickett, head of Policies."

"I am Sadie Mollison, head of Public Affairs and Communications."

"I am Patricia Grant, head of Programs and Services."

"I am Jesse Hall, head of Business Operations."

"I am Bush Marshall, head of Finance and Business."

"I am Hank Elder, head of Field Operations."

"I am Quincy Morton, head of Demographics Operations."

"I am Delbert Wolf, head of Strategic Planning and Innovations."

"And you know Bryant Washington, head of Public Relations, and of your fan club," his Godfather says playfully. Everyone laughs a little once again. "As you can see everything is well planned and ready to go. We are only waiting for you."

"All of this for a promise?" Raymond asks.

His Godfather smiles, showing his patience and understanding of the fact Raymond is not only being asked to drop his dream and leave a world he has come to master, but he is also being asked to enter a world he knows nothing about, and yet will be expected to perform at the same high level -- just with a different agenda. So Mr. Goodson walks over to the on screen image of Raymond's great-great grandfather and Mr. Goodson's great-grandfather. "Raymond you are a PK, a Preacher's Kid right? How many times have you read the Bible?" he asks.

"A few," Raymond answers.

"Do you now what 98% of the Bible is about?" his Godfather asks.

"I can't say that I do," Raymond responds.

"Well, it's about one promise God made to one man. The promise was, "Your seed would be great and through your seed all nations will be blessed." Did you know that all of the wars, struggles, failures, triumphs, ups, downs, conquests and victories that are recorded in the Bible took place so that one promise could be fulfilled? It said that God sent His Son to make sure the promise God made to Abraham would be kept. "Through your seed all nations will be blessed," and make no mistake about it Raymond, everyone in this room has been born, handpicked and well prepared to see this promise come to pass. But you must believe in the promise in order to see it manifest in your lifetime," his Godfather says.

"Keeping a promise is possible," Patricia Grant head of Programs and Services says to Raymond. Out of everything that was said it was her words that resonated with Raymond. One particularly disgusting heap of mess that floated in the cesspool of politics is the frequent habit of making empty promises. Raymond has done his share of telling people what they wanted to hear, and not what he could deliver. This practice seeped into Raymond's personal life, because he found himself telling people all around him, on and off the job, things he didn't have any intentions of fulfilling. He began to think everyone told white lies that come in the form of making a promise, but not keeping them. This young lady sparked something in Raymond that made him ask himself a question of hope. *Can someone keep their promise in this day and time especially when it comes to politics and public service*? Maybe he should take this project on just for that reason, to see if what Ms. Grant just stated could be indeed true.

This decision was the most perplexing situation he ever found himself in. Millions are depending on him now, including a dozen people in the room that are expecting an answer that will affect their futures. He must give up something that already exists for something that has not been in existence for long, and no one could truly say it would still be in existence five years from now. He must let a job go that he knows 100% he can do without breaking a sweat, for something he's never done in his life. All of this came down to one thing: breaking a promise, to make a promise.

"So son, what is your decision? It's your call and whatever you decide will be the right decision," his Godfather says.

Raymond takes another look around the room, and then reaches for Diamond's hand. She places hers in his, and Raymond pulls her up to her feet giving everyone the impression he is going to take his wife and leave the room, never to look back. They briefly look into each other's eyes. Diamond nods slightly and smiles. Raymond looks at the assembled group and says "Let's change history by keeping a promise." Everyone in the room claps and cheers loudly. His Godfather sits down and looks at him with a big smile on his face as though he was a mother just giving birth after ten hours of labor.

STATION BREAK!!! This is an announcement from the New Nation Campaign Headquarters

IT IS NOW
280 DAYS
UNTIL
DEPARTURE
ARE YOU
READY?

Log onto
www.newnation.org
to register today and see
the layout of the
New Nation of Africa.

Picture 27: *Look At The Past*

Everyone in the boardroom was delighted that Raymond accepted the proposal to be a founder and leader of the New Nation of Africa. The 12 staff members rise to shake hands with Raymond, Diamond and Bishop Jackson. All are smiling from ear to ear.

Raymond doesn't have any idea how all of their lives have been shaped around this; if he had declined the offer, it would have been a major setback for all of them. All of them had been trained in different parts of the world, but yet their destiny is intertwined with each other to the point if one fails to live up to their training and purpose it would upset the entire organization. The system Mr. Goodson set up was ingenious; every part worked in harmony with one body to achieve and accomplish the goal. Raymond didn't understand this but his new staff understood it clearly as they embraced Raymond as their leader who would help bring everything they had been working so hard for into fruition.

"All right people lets get back to work, we have a lot of things to do in a short amount of time," Mr. Goodson says. The remaining staff shakes Raymond's hand as they leave the boardroom.

"Raymond this is the New Nation constitution and an outline of the B2B Tour. I'll explain it to you later in more detail. Thank you for saying 'Yes'," Bryant, Raymond's biggest fan says.

Mr. Goodson goes over to Bishop Jackson, "I know you have to go, I'll see you later, thanks for everything," Mr. Goodson says. "Raymond I want you to go back to your political campaign and I will tell you when you should make the announcement. Act like nothing has changed until I give you the signal. Timing is very important for something like this, we can't do anything prematurely. Do you understand?"

"I think so," Raymond replies.

"May I have a few private minutes with you, Diamond?" his Godfather asks.

Raymond looks at Diamond, who shakes her head "Yes." "Sure," Raymond says then turns back to his wife and says, "I'll send the car back for you." Raymond moves in as if to kiss Diamond on the side of her face, but whispers in her ear, "Watch his right hand," Raymond says and then leaves.

Goodson smiles and escorts Diamond into his personal office, pulls out a seat for her then he takes a seat behind the desk.

"This is a very interesting operation you have here and a very advanced plan. Do you really think it can be accomplished?" Diamond asks. This was a crucial question coming from Diamond, because she has unlimited potential to influence Raymond's decisions. She doesn't mind the fact he made the decision without discussing it with her. Raymond has always made decisions independently. But she is concerned whether the potential of the New Nation of Africa really exists. If Raymond gives up the Vice Presidency what could guarantee that the New Nation was going to work? And if it didn't work, where would that leave her and Raymond? Where would that leave them socially, financially and politically? For Diamond this move was more risky than she was used to assuming.

"Everything can be accomplished if everyone plays their part," Mr. Goodson says. He then goes into his desk, takes out a folder and hands it across the desk to Diamond. She opens it and sees some disturbing pictures.

"Where did you get these from?" Diamond asks.

"That's not important right now. What is important is what is going on in these pictures," Mr. Goodson says calmly.

Diamond is obviously disturbed about what she sees in the pictures. It's her and a young man who is giving her flowers. "He was my pool person. We only talked, and he kept me company. One day he gave me flowers and the next day I fired him because I didn't want anything to happen to Raymond's political career," Diamond says as she fights back tears.

"Well, I know you are being honest with me because we had a little talk with your former pool man, Mr. Matthew Duke, and he told us the exact same thing you just said. Just to make sure we gave him a million dollars to leave the country and not be seen again," Mr. Goodson explains.

"Does Raymond know?" Diamond asks.

"No, I haven't told him, I think that's your job when you feel the time is right."

Mr. Goodson understands the pressure Diamond has been under for the last ten years of Raymond's political career and since Nicky entered the picture. In this double standard society it's OK for the husband to have someone on the side, however, it is still unacceptable for a wife to return the favor. Mr. Goodson sympathizes with Diamond, but he did not show her those pictures or sent Matthew Duke away for that reason. It was something more than Diamond feeling the need to act out the part of the "desperate housewife." Mr. Goodson's total concern was on making sure Diamond or Raymond's pasts did not come back to look them in the face like the Ghost of Christmas past. He had already cleaned up Raymond's mess, and now he wanted to make sure Diamond's mess -- as small and innocent as it might have been -- be wiped completely clean even in her heart and mind.

"So you have no feelings towards him?" Mr. Goodson asks.

"No! No, it was never like that with me. And I didn't want to give him an idea to develop anymore than what he had so I fired him," Diamond said simply and convincingly.

Mr. Goodson sat up and leaned on his desk to get a good look into Diamond's eyes. "I know Diamond, but I had to be 100 percent sure." Diamond makes a noticeable sigh of relief. "Listen to me very carefully Mrs. Jackson, this may be one of the most important conversations you will ever have in your life," Mr. Goodson says. Then he gets up and goes around and sits on the corner of the desk in front of Diamond, positioning himself to have her slightly looking up to him. "I realize it wasn't easy for you being with a man who loves his gifts more than he loves his wife. It takes a strong woman to endure what you have been through. Now it is time to change all of that. I am giving you your power back. Today when you walk out of this room you will no longer sit on the sidelines of Raymond's life cheering him on as he makes offensive foul after foul against you and your marriage. You will posses the power to protect your family and marriage. This power is not going to come by way of thunder and lightning. I'm speaking this life into you right now."

"No one knows Raymond better than you. All of the studies, searches or investigations would never have come up with the data you have collected about him over the 15 years you've been together.

You know his strengths and weaknesses; use this information to protect him, not hurt him. He needs you to protect him from himself and from others. I'm reinforcing your power as I speak, but it is going to be up to you to maintain this power by getting up early in the morning and praying for your husband. Your prayers can prevent these tricks, tramps and traps from stopping him from reaching his destiny. He needs you desperately right now, more than ever."

"One more thing: from this point on Raymond will be a one-woman man. We have given him something in the last 40 days he didn't get in the last 15 years, and that is self-control. Other things were given, but as far as your marriage is concerned he never had self-control. A gifted man without self-control is very dangerous to everyone. Now you have his undivided attention. The question is can you handle a faithful man after getting used to living with an unfaithful one? Don't answer the question, just listen for now. He needs you to be everything he was looking for in those other tricks, tramps and traps. He needs you to be a sister, friend, soul mate, wife, mother, student and prayer partner. You are no longer this positive political puppet the political system created you to be. Today I am cutting your strings and you will be the woman God created you to be before the foundation of the world, before Raymond, before politics, and before your heart and dreams were crushed. I speak this in you now. Let it be and receive it my daughter."

Immediately Diamond felt a refreshing coolness throughout the room, but an invigorating warmth inside her body. Tears was streaming down her face as Mr. Goodson spoke words she had known and felt but were buried deep in her heart. How did he get the key to unlock her thoughts that lay in the treasure of her soul for years?

He had these pictures and didn't threaten to use them against her nor did he try to control her in anyway. Diamond initially had thought he was just another politician trying to use her husband's power and position for his own political interests. But what kind of politician had the goods on someone and did not use them for leverage? He not only did not use this information to blackmail her, but he went so far as to loosen her from other baggage that had been weighing her heart down for years. As he spoke to Diamond it was as he was breathing life into her, a new life she hadn't felt in years. The political life had made her shoot herself with a dose of emotional medicine to numb the pain that comes with political life. She knew if she didn't harden herself emotionally, she would become like a lot of political wives -- alcoholics, pill poppers, addicts or worse. Not caring was the only way she could help her husband reach his political goals and yet still remain able to enjoy some of the benefits. That was the plan until Raymond's Godfather spoke into her very soul. She could sense her long-buried feelings rushing back and her tears were a sign she could have pleasure, hope, idealism and optimism again. She felt the power she once felt when she was 18 years old. This was a time when she knew her purpose in life, and understood she was created to contribute to the world in a unique way. She was alive again, no longer the "walking dead" whose existence was like that of a zombie. She wanted to stop crying in Mr. Goodson's office, but every time she tried to stop another flow of cleansing, healing emotions would wash over her. Maybe the tears were long overdue, for she had held back so many for so long them.

Mr. Goodson understood exactly what Diamond was feeling. Raymond had to go through his cleansing process and as his partner and soul mate Diamond also needed to go through her own cleansing process. But hers would not take 40 days. It was occurring right now in Mr. Goodson's office.

Mr. Goodson walked out to allow her to be alone; he dared not interrupt the healing and growth in anyway by asking her anything. He decided to let her have a good cry. This cry had no negativity. She was not depressed, she was not hurt, she was not sad, and she was not being oppressed. Every tear testified of the good news that Diamond, who once was dead, a victim of the game of politics, was alive again!

Picture 28: *When Change, Change*

John Newton's campaign staff is trying to maintain their momentum despite Raymond's disappearance.

Newton and his staff attend a fundraising luncheon where Raymond was scheduled as the keynote speaker. Newton is planning to fill in for Raymond, because the way he sees it, he can't afford to cancel another event, because it is costing him votes each time he does.

Newton is sitting beside his top aide Skip Bradley at the table on the platform eating lunch. "I can't believe there is no word about him or from him yet," Newton complains.

"The police still insist they can't do anything until the family files a missing person report," Bradley says.

"Well, after today I'm going to see about that even if I have to sit his wife down and convince her myself," Newton says.

"What time do you want to address the crowd? They should be finished eating soon." Bradley asks.

"Give me a few seconds. I have to think of another excuse as to why Raymond is not here. I'm running out of excuses and explanations," Newton sighs. He takes a sip of water. "The media is eating up Raymond's disappearance -- which is a mixed blessing. Did you see this morning's paper?" Newton asks.

"Yeah, the headlines said, 'No show for the show that goes on the road', Bradley quotes.

"It's outrageous I tell you," Newton says as he takes another drink of water, an obvious sign of nervousness.

"This is why I was totally against building our campaign around his ability to speak. Everyone came out to hear him and they are going to be very disappointed. This is exactly what I was afraid of," Bradley says.

"Well we are going to find out if what they use to say still stands true, 'That one monkey don't stop the show,'" Newton says then and approaches the podium. He taps his glass to get everyone's attention. "Thank you ladies and gentlemen for coming out to support us once again. You have been supporting change all over the country and this afternoon we want to give you something back for your support. I know most of you came out to hear my running mate..." Bradley interrupts Newton, holding his cell phone and whispering in Newton's ear while the audience watches and wonders what is going on. Many begin to whisper.

"Are you sure?" Mr. Newton asks. The question causes Bradley to get back on the phone to repeat the question to the person on the other end. They must have assured him of what Newton wanted to hear, because Bradley starts shake his head up and down like it was about to come off. This made Newton smile broadly, which excited the entire room.

"Ladies and gentlemen thank you for your patience, and please excuse the delay. Right now, I introduce to some, and present to others, my running mate, Mr. Raymond Jackson," Newton says.

Raymond enters looking vibrant and shaking hands and waving like he never lost a beat. Everyone stands and gives him a round of applause. The crowd stops clapping and takes their seats. Raymond scans the crowd and immediately becomes saddened, because he will not fulfill their wishes for him. It felt like only yesterday he told everyone in a speech he would be running for the highest office held by any African American, and the country was delighted. Everyone was rallying for change. Raymond now found it hard to look the people in the eye, knowing the change they are supporting would not take place, not by him anyway. But as hard as it was he must go along with the show.

"It is good to see so many of our friends who are ready for a changed America," Raymond says. Raymond often prepares the night before for his speaking engagements, but he had made no plans to speak before this group. Raymond recalled one of his speeches he wrote while going through the cleansing process for those 40 days and begins to speak. "I'm not going to be before you long. I just want to remind you of the process of change. Sometimes ladies and gentlemen, we expect change to come in one way and it actually comes in another form. Or just when you thought change should be surfacing something else happens unexpectedly. Recently I had to come to grips with an aspect of change that I didn't know existed. It forced me to ask a question, a question that I am going to ask you this afternoon. What do you do when change makes a change?"

Raymond paused and his captivated audience went into deep thought, causing many to shake their heads to suggest they were grappling with the question, even if they didn't have the answer itself.

Raymond continued, "I discovered you can be ready to embrace change, and then out of nowhere the process of that very change begins to change. There is only one thing that can be done, and this is what you must do if you are going to participate in true change: We must respect change's decision to change, because no one can control change. No one and nothing can stop change from taking place; no Democrat, no Republican, no black, no white, no rich or no poor," Raymond says and then pulls out a leaf from the inside pocket of his suit jacket.

Raymond continues, "I picked this up on my way in here today, it's a leaf, a wonderful picture of change. Raymond holds the leaf up as he continues to speak. "This leaf was once green, but now it has so many beautiful colors, there is not a power in this world that could have stopped this leaf from changing, not even itself. Thank you," Raymond says then walks off the stage. The audience gives him another standing ovation. They were not disappointed at all; it was one of Raymond's shortest speeches, but still profound and full of powerful substance. To Raymond's listeners he was sending a message that changes will come in America even if those who don't want change try to prevent it.

To Raymond's audience the leaf represented the many colors of cultures and races in this country that would come together in true equality and justice when John and Raymond are elected. This is what they may have concluded as they gave him a standing ovation, but Raymond was speaking of the fact he was ready to make a major change for the entire country as a whole, but the change he was pursuing had suddenly changed its mind and was now going into another direction.

Picture 29: *Don't Get It Twisted*

After Raymond gives his speech about change he and his security plan to exit as soon as possible, but Raymond was stopped by fans, seeking his autograph and photos. The media was compelled to ask him about his absence.

"I had to take a break to strengthen myself," Raymond states confidently.

Newton's aide, Skip Bradley, caught up with him. "Mr. Newton would like to see you sir."

"I'll take you to him sir," Bradley says "That's all for today, I'm sorry, Mr. Jackson has an important meeting," he says as he pushes through the crowd. "Excuse us please," Bradley continues to repeat himself until they entered a room where both staffs were waiting.

Tarisha walks over to Raymond and hugs him, "You are OK, thank God," she says.

Raymond hugs her back and says, "I'm fine. I just had to get away."

"Well, can't you let a sister know what going on?"

"You're right, I'm not going to give you any excuse, it will not happen again," Raymond says.

"I hate when you do that. No, I want an excuse, so I can fuss at you. You know I can't be mad at you when you say stuff like that," Tarisha says.

Newton's and Raymond's other staff members begin to gather around Raymond to greet him, letting him know it's good to see that he is OK and everything is fine. It's as if he just got out of the hospital after a serious operation and everyone wants to let him know they are glad he pulled through. All smiles, hugs, and kisses from the ladies and firm handshakes from the men. "Let's have a party!" somebody shouts out. "Raymond is back!" Then someone begins to chant, "Raymond is back, Raymond is back" and soon everyone in the room is chanting "Raymond is back! Raymond is back! Raymond is back!"

Newton walks into the suite of the excited campaign team and staff. He immediately sees Raymond and walks right to him. The others, seeing Newton's grim expression, stop chanting and go back to drinking coffee and soda and appearing to be busy with campaign duties. Raymond takes a few steps towards Newton. Raymond extends his hand to shake Newton's hand, but Newton hugs Raymond.

"Man it's good to see you alive," he says.

"It's good, everything is good," Raymond says with relief.

"You're not hurt or anything?" Newton asks.

"No, I'm fine," Raymond says.

"So what happened?" Newton asks.

"I just had to get away for a while," Raymond answers.

"For a while? It has been over 40 days," Newton exclaims.

"Lets sit down and talk," Raymond says.

"Raymond, I don't have time for the bull. We are about six weeks behind schedule. We have 20 states to cover and nine months before the election. And you drop out of sight for 40 days with no real explanation, so please excuse me if I don't have time for the small talk. Where in hell have you been?" Newton says raising his voice so all can hear.

Raymond's staff and security detail walk over quietly and stand behind him, "OK man just calm down," Max says.

Newton looks at Bradley, "Can you believe this? Can you believe the nerve of this person? No, the pride of this man," Newton says.

Raymond looks at his staff and security and says, "Come on let's get out of here."

"Alright Mr. Almighty Raymond lets play it your way. Let's play it the nice and cool way. Is that what you want? I'm in your zone now. Tell me what is going on with you," Mr. Newton says sarcastically.

"Nothing, everything is fine Newton," Raymond says coolly.

Bradley takes out his laptop, "Well everything is not fine, because in the last 40 days you were gone we disappointed over 20 thousand people and this may have caused us to lose 10,000 votes," he says.

"Not to mention you gave a very lazy speech with no fire or passion that you usually give in every speech I have heard," Newton says.

"Are you finished, because if you are I have better things to do than to talk about what happened," Raymond says.

"No, I'm not finished. Let me tell you something Raymond, I have worked too long and hard for you to mess up my future. I will be the President of this United States with or without you."

Raymond was trying to take the high road and walk away. Yes, he did owe him an explanation, but not in front of the campaign staff. He didn't want to hurt them any more than he had already and would in the near future once he told them he would not be running for Vice President any longer. He only wanted to get Newton to calm down so they could talk like two adults. But no, Newton is letting his big mouth get him in trouble again, and this time Raymond was going to tell him what was on his mind ever since he introduced himself to Raymond.

"Are you finished?" Raymond asks Newton.

"Yeah, as a matter of fact I am," he replies.

Raymond is standing with his aides and security and Newton is standing with his team, the two campaign staffs forming an unlinked circle around them. The staffs tried to talk over Newton and Raymond's conversation, but Newton became too loud to be ignored as though he wanted to put Raymond on the spot. When it seemed as though Raymond was going to speak everyone became extra quiet to hear what he was going to say.

"You've got me all twisted, as a matter of fact you've got this whole process all twisted, but I'm going to help you straighten it out. See John if you win in November it will be because of me. I know this, you know this, your boys and everyone in this room knows this. You have been using me as a donkey to ride into the White House. I should be President. I know more than you and more people approve of me." Raymond says, glancing at Skip Bradley, Newton's top aide. "Oh, your man here hasn't given you the latest approval rate?" Raymond says with a smile. "Tarisha, what is it?" Raymond asks.

"Since yesterday the people approved of you 90% above everyone in the race," Tarisha states without consulting any notes.

"90% and I haven't even hit my stride yet Newton. See John *you're* winning right now because *I'm* winning right now. The way I look at it is I should be President and you should be Vice President, but we all know the country is not ready for a black president. So I will settle for the Vice President right now, and personally I didn't mind. Up until this time I haven't said one word, like a good little boy I have stayed in my place."

"Then your big mouth had you go on the news after my family told you I was OK and make false accusations about hate groups. Where do you think that puts me and my family right now? You have put a bull's eye target on me and my family's back, all because of your big mouth. Raymond turns to Bradley and taps on his laptop, "But I guess you didn't figure any of that out did you?"

"Calm down Raymond," Newton demands.

"Oh now you want to calm down? No it's too late, because your big mouth put me on the spot in front of all of my staff and you tried to belittle me in front of your people. Isn't it enough that I'm giving you a free ride into the White House? You are pretending that it's your votes and not mine that are getting you there," Raymond says.

"Don't let your imagination outgrow your position Mr. Jackson," Newton counters.

"What position is that? Under you Mr. Newton? No it's your imagination that is getting the best of you if you really think you can win in November without me, and let me tell you this for the record," Raymond says and then looks at Newton's aide. "Make sure you get this down. I'm going to say it slow so you will not lose any of the essential parts," Raymond says to him, then turns back and gets into Newton face. "You have more than an imagination problem, you have a bad case of amnesia if you forgot who they really want. They want a male black Vice President, which means I can get anyone to replace you - you are dispensable, I am not." Raymond looks at Bradley and asks, "Did you get that down?"

Raymond, his security and staff walk out the room.

“Is that what you think Raymond?” Newton bellows.
Raymond continues to walk.
“Can you believe that ingrate?” Newton asks Bradley.
“Unbelievable sir,” Bradley says. “Unbelievable.”

Picture 30: *Don't Play Dumb*

Tar is a full-fledge Westsider, and everyone at school knows it and that is exactly the way he wants it, he wants everyone to know he is down with the Westsiders. In the 60's and 70's you joined a gang because you wanted someone to do wrong with, someone who would encourage you to do the wrong thing as crazy as that might sound. With that generation it was easy for them to transform themselves into successful upstanding citizens, because they outgrew their gangs and the wrongdoing that was associated with the gangs. But today's generation is joining gangs to defend who they are and to obtain a surrogate family structure. The only problem is you can never outgrow a family structure, because this is permanent. Therefore the gang was true, blood in and blood out. No wonder Tar wants everyone to know he is a Westsider. To him he just found two things he has been looking for all his 16 years: an identity and a family.

Tar sticks his head in the classroom to speak to Ms. Gaither. "Ms. G., Monica said you wanted to holler at me," Tar says.

"Not exactly, but I do need to speak with you. Are you busy now?" Ms. Gaither says.

"Yeah, I was going to get something to eat he says," Tar responds.

Ms. Gaither stops working on the computer and motions Tar into the room. "Come on, it's not going to take that long," Ms. Gaither says as she sits Tar down in front her desk.

"What's up?" Tar asks.

"How is your mother doing?" Ms. Gaither asks.

"She's doing," Tar says nonchalantly.

"Is she still attending the outpatient N.A. groups?" Ms. Gaither asks.

"Sometimes, on and off," he says.

"Other than that is anything wrong at home?" Ms. Gaither asks.

"Not that I can think of."

"The reason I ask is because I'm watching my grade "A" student go down to a grade "C" student, and I thought something may be wrong," Ms. Gaither says.

"Naw. I'm good."

"You're good," she repeats.

"Yeah I'm good."

Ms. Gaither pauses and looks at Tar and he looks back at her. She broke the silence, "Then why am I seeing you hanging around the Westside Gang?"

Tar gets up from his seat with a big smile and says, "I knew it, I knew it."

"Yeah, yeah, that's right," Ms. Gaither says.

"I'm good, it's nothing like that. Beside you are the one who told me to get out of the house and give my mother some space," Tar says in his defense.

"Yeah I told you that so you would not be suffocated by an addictive environment, not so you could join a gang," Ms. Gaither says.

"They are friends, if I'm going to be down I have to be all the way down," Tar proudly declares.

"Yeah, you're right, you're being down. You're moving down from an "A" student to a "C" student. That's only the beginning, tomorrow you will be going down even lower." Ms. Gaither says.

Tar walks over to the door, "I'm gone," he says.

"Tar you'd better not walk out that door," Ms. Gaither raises her voice and Tar stops. Ms. Gaither walks over to the door and stands in front of it with her hands folded and says, "Tar I've seen this a thousand times son.

"What's that?"

"I've seen a straight "A" student have problems at home, go to the street for refuge, join a gang and get killed or go to prison for killing."

"What do you want from me? You want me to hide in the house?" Tar asks.

"Whatever you do, don't play dumb to be accepted by anyone. Don't let them pull you down -- you bring them up. Because it's one thing to play dumb with me and your gang members, but it's another thing to play dumb with yourself," Ms. Gaither says then moves from in front of the door. "Go get something to eat," Ms. Gaither says.

Tar wants to respond to her words, but he knows she's right. He was smarter than all of them put together, but yet he felt they were treating him like he was the dumbest one, and he never said anything about it. Tar walked out of the classroom.

Picture 31: *Offensive Foul*

Mr. Lyman the President knows if he is going to win in November, Raymond is the man to beat. Mr. Lyman actually cares about the American people. If it wasn't for the fact America was ripe for a male African American Vice President he would be easily elected to serve another term.

Two of his aides are having lunch in the White House and Raymond is the subject of their conversation. "The Guy is a little nervous about this one. He doesn't think he has a chance of beating Newton with Raymond as his running mate," Mike says.

"Yeah, who would think America was ready for a male African American Vice President," Vince responds.

"This is what I was trying to get across to the team years ago -- that statistics have shown there have been no African American attempting to run for Vice President, only President. So if anyone would focus on the Vice Presidency they would get it for sure."

"I don't think Lyman is ready to lose to Raymond Jackson and I'm not ready to lose to Raymond, we have four more years in us," Mike says as he takes a swallow of his iced tea. "We've got to think of something to stop them," he says.

"What does the Big Guy suggest?"

"He has given us the green light. It's totally up to us," Mike replies.

"What do you have in mind or should we give it a couple more weeks?"

"We don't have a couple more weeks. Have you seen the latest reports," Mike says as he passes some papers across the lunch table.

Vince takes a few seconds to look through them as he takes a couple swallows of his iced tea. "He has these many potential votes in Rhode Island and Iowa" Vince asks.

"So can you imagine what Pennsylvania, Maryland and Louisiana look like?" Mike asks. "So no, we don't have a lot of time at all."

Vince continues to look at the report in amazement. "This is unbelievable. The sad part about it is everyone knows it's Raymond's election," Vince says.

"Which means we have to go after him now," Vince says finishing Mike's thought. "What do you think about Plan A?"

"No, that's a little too much, he's not a terrorist or anything," Mike warns.

"I was thinking about Plan C-2, but he would only use the racial implications to his advantage," Mike says.

"Yeah and if he plays the race card everything would backfire on us and work in his favor."

"Exactly," Mike concurs.

"We need something that would kill his reputation in addition to killing his political career."

"OK, I got it, since you put it like that. In light of the Catholic priest scandal and the Michael Jackson charges, lets implement Plan D-3 and the latter part of F-2," Mike suggests.

Vince thinks for a couple of seconds, "OK, I can see that. Yeah I think it will work."

"When?" Vince asks.

"Yesterday," Mike says.

"Who do you have in mind?"

"I'll take care of all of that," Vince assures Mike.

"Make sure all ends are completely tied and leave no fingerprints on this one," Mike tells him.

"Yes sir."

Mike gets up from the table, "I'll be watching the news," he says on his way out.

Picture 32: *That's Foul*

Raymond and his staff are in the campaign bus returning from a political rally. Tarisha notices Raymond's strained face and knows exactly what to do to help him relax. Tarisha passes her assistant a gospel-jazz CD, "Play this," Tarisha says, then pulls down the TV and hooks up the Play Station. "Somebody is going to get a beat down today," Tarisha says trying to pique Raymond's interest to get his mind off of politics. Then she turns on the other TV to CMM because Raymond likes to feel he is not missing out on anything even if he is not actively paying attention to the news.

Raymond loosens his tie and rolls up his sleeves, "Remember you asked for this," Raymond says.

"You're down two games man. You've got to catch up before you can be a winner," Tarisha says while handing Raymond his controller. The security and staff love to see these two go at it on the Play Station. It's like the boys against the girls, the muscles against the brain, the brawn against the beauty, and Raymond and Tarisha are the ultimate representatives.

"Yeah, I got you baby girl, where do you think you are going?" Raymond asks.

"Right here, you are too slow man," Tarisha responds.

"Go! Go! Go!" The female staff cheers her on.

"Get her, get her!" Raymond's security detail coaches him.

"Yeah, you thought you got away," Raymond says.

"I got a first down and I can live with that," Tarisha says.

"You're about to give that ball up, that's what you are going to do," Raymond teases Tarisha.

"You've got to catch me first," Tarisha says.

"Go! Go! Go!" the girls cheer again.

"She's going to pass it Raymond," one of his security men warns him.

"I'll take that," Raymond says as one of his men intercepts the ball.

"No man you're cheating, they can't help you," Tarisha says.

"They are helping you," Raymond says.

"Tarisha, Tarisha," Toni Maybley calls for her.

"What's up," Tarisha says as she continues to play the game.

"I think you should look at this," Toni urges her. Tarisha continues to play against Raymond. "Ms. Tarisha, this is an important situation," Toni says. Tarisha stops immediately and looks at her assistant like she just cursed at her. Her assistant points at the other TV airing CMM with the closed caption that says, "Mr. Raymond Jackson has been accused of having sex with a 16 and a half year old female." Tarisha reaches for the earphones as fast as she can. She listens to the report as she looks at Raymond still playing the game.

"Raymond I think you should look at this," Tarisha says.

"No, you are in trouble now. There's no getting out of this," Raymond says.

Tarisha raises her voice, "Sir please take a look at this," Tarisha hands Raymond the earphones, Raymond spots his face on TV once he put the earphones on to listen to the reporter, he began to shake his head in disbelief. The closed caption reads: "This 17 year old said in the police report she had consensual sex with Raymond when she was 16 and 1/2. It's not said how they met or where it took place, but it is said her parents took her to the station. We are here at the station and we will be waiting for more of this breaking news, back to you Sam."

Raymond takes off the earphones and all of the staff cell phones began to ring. Raymond can't believe what he just heard, in his entire political career he had never been accused of any scandal.

"No, it's not true and we don't have any comments at this time," Tarisha says to the other person on the phone. Her staff repeats the same message to the callers on the other end of their phones. Raymond sits back to think about his next steps: turn himself in or wait until he is arrested.

"Sir it's your Godfather and he said to meet him in MLK Park," Tarisha says.

"When?" Raymond asks.

"In 20 minutes," Tarisha replies.

"Tell the driver the park is 50 minutes away and we need to be there in 20," Raymond says. Raymond felt a peace come over him. If anybody should know what to do, his Godfather would.

Picture 33: *Regroup*

It seemed like he made it in 15 minutes. Raymond notices his Godfather sitting in a wheelchair, which he only uses in public as a ruse. He is actually a very physically fit man. He is talking to Bishop Jackson as they drive up to the park. Raymond walks over to his father and Godfather, who is being pushed in a wheelchair by a female aide. "Let's take this path that leads around the lake," Mr. Goodson instructs his aide.

"Yes sir," she says.

Raymond was walking to the right of his Godfather and Bishop Jackson on the left. "Raymond I'm not trying to be insensitive to your situation here, but we don't have anytime to waste. I need to know exactly what took place," his Godfather commands.

"I never saw that girl in my life," Raymond says.

"Raymond you know how you and your staff like to party. Could it be possible she was at one of those wild parties?" Bishop Jackson asks.

"It's not impossible, but unlikely. These are exclusive parties and can't just anyone walk off the street to come in," Raymond says.

"Whether you can or not this is exactly what they are going to say happened," his Godfather says.

"You have to believe me, I know I've done a lot of crazy things in the past when it comes to females, but this is not one of them. I think someone is trying to set me up."

"Who?" Raymond's father asks.

"I don't know," Raymond answers.

Mr. Goodson signals his aide to stop and says, "He's right. There are so many people who want a piece of your political behind, it's like open season on you right now. The problem is who would do this? We can take our pick from the supremacy groups to his political rivals," his Godfather says.

"Who Lyman? If I find out he has something to do with this I will break his…" Raymond starts to say and is interrupted by his Godfather.

"Listen son, we can't let our emotions get in the way of destiny. Everything that is happening is supposed to happen. Always remember that," his Godfather says and then gives his aide the signal to continue on the path.

"Is this going to delay the New Nation Project?" Bishop Jackson asks.

"That's what I am afraid of. We have less than nine months to get everything in motion. This has the potential of not only delaying it, but also destroying it all together. Let me think for a minute," his Godfather says as he puts both hands together, raises his elbows on the arms of his chair and places his mouth on his closed hands.

The people who are responsible for this have no idea they are about to destroy the birth of something great, something they didn't even know existed. They are going after Raymond's political career, a career he has already given up, but in their reckless attempt to assassinate Raymond's character they are about to assassinate a move that is greater than Raymond's reputation. Whoever these people are, they know his weakness and they will make him look like the typical politician who has great ideas, but no self-control or willpower when it comes to sex. How can this be happening right now? On the eve of greatness something like this comes to threaten the entire process? This and many other thoughts raced through his Godfather's head 100 mph.

"Help me," his Godfather says.

"Excuse me," Raymond says.

"He is praying," his aide shushes.

"I got it. This is a long shot, but that is all we got right now. I'm going to call a lawyer who specializes in suppression hearings. He's a friend who owes a favor. He is licensed to practice law in the United States, but he moved back to Europe a few years ago. We have to stop this from getting to trial and if it can be done, he is the man to do it. OK we are going to use this problem as a springboard to push us into our destiny. We are focused on getting all charges dropped at the suppression hearing. If we do then everybody and their momma is going to want to talk to you and that will be the perfect time to introduce the New Nation," his Godfather says.

Bishop Jackson smiles and shakes his head and his aide is trying not to smile, but can't control the urge to do so.

Raymond still has a worried look on his face. "What if this lawyer doesn't win at the suppression hearing?" he asks.

"Then the entire project must be aborted, and we will not be able to attempt to do it again for another 30, 40 maybe 50 years. All the work that has been done will be in vain. I would have to train someone to train the leaders of the next generation who would be the great-grandparents of the founder of the New Nation."

"Why is that?" Raymond asks like a little four-year-old looking for every answer to ease his troubled mind.

"Son, when we have this hearing every African American is going to be cheering for you, because deep down inside they know what's really happening. So if you win they are going to be willing to listen to whatever you have to say. This is why I say this problem will have the power to push us to our destiny. On the other hand if you lose, even though they know you were set up, they will not listen to a word you have to say because nobody likes a loser, and nobody wants to follow a loser, even if it is only across the street. So you know across the world will be out of the question," his Godfather says.

"So everything is riding on this hearing?" Raymond asks.

"Yes son. This is why we must get the process going. We are going to go to the station with you to take care of all the formalities. Raymond do you remember some of the verses you saw highlighted in the Bible when you were in the room?"

"Yeah, I memorized them," Raymond answers.

"Good, can you finish this one for me? All things work together…" his Godfather says.

"For good to those who love the Lord and are the called according to his purpose. Romans 8:28," Raymond says to complete the verse.

"Now it's time for you to show me better than you can tell me," his Godfather says.

Picture 34: *What's The Verdict?*

In front of the Atlanta Courthouse is a group of news vans, TV cameras and a lot of telegenic people holding microphones. There is a camera everywhere a camera can be placed. Everyone is waiting for Raymond who is in the courtroom listening to the evidence against him. Raymond managed to get past the irksome reporters, admirers and hangers on by being escorted through a rear entrance of the courthouse. No one has seen or heard from him since he was released on a half million dollars bail. Mr. Jackson's lawyer tried to convince the judge to let him out on his own recognizance, seeing as though everyone in the country knows him and if he would think about running he would not get far. But the prosecutor suggested far is exactly where Mr. Jackson have the ability to go, since his resources would allow him to never be seen again. The prosecutor had a valid point and the judge agreed. From that point Raymond had been semi-hiding.

But this time provided him with the perfect opportunity to familiarize himself with the New Nation staff, government polices, structure, campaign tour and other particulars he must understand in and out if he was going to communicate and sell this idea to the African Americans and others in this country.

It has been hard for Raymond to focus on anything with the accusation hanging over his head and everything hanging on the success of this hearing. Raymond is in a situation where he has nowhere to go and nothing to lose, but this hearing. If he indeed lost this hearing he couldn't go back to focusing his attention on the Vice Presidency because his reputation would be scarred, and he couldn't go forward with the New Nation project, because as his Godfather put it, "No one wants to follow a loser anywhere." So the only thing he could do was stand still and let everything play itself out. Life sometimes places us in a situation where you can't go backwards or forward, but the only thing you can do is stand still and see the salvation of the Lord. This is where Raymond finds himself, at a spiritual standstill. If he makes any sudden moves it could be the downfall of many people's futures -- including his own.

A news reporter looks into the camera and says," This is Diana Pride and we have been out here in front of the Atlanta Federal Courthouse waiting to hear about the results of this morning's proceedings. The prosecution has been introducing the state's evidence against Mr. Jackson in the sexual assault case. The defense will present their case or at least see what evidence should be allowed in the trial that is set for three months from now. This is an important case and we're going to keep you up-to-date with any breaking news. This is Diana Pride signing off for now," she says and then hands the microphone to her cameraman.

"I'm going to go see what I can get," she says and then walks into the courthouse.

Judge Ingram, is presiding over the case. The prosecutor, a young white male is sitting at the table listening to his assistant, cross-examine the 17-year-old victim. Kelly Richardson has been on the stand for the last 20 minutes. She is wiping her tears from her face as the assistant prosecutor says, "That is all the prosecution has your honor."

"Defense do you want to wait until after lunch or do you want to proceed now?" the judge asks.

"Your honor I will only take five minutes, ten at the most," Mr. West says.

Raymond, who is sitting next to his lawyer, looks at him a little strange when he said that. Raymond's family, friends, staff, and campaign team have all filled the courtroom to show support. Even John Newton is present, appearing as a person looking after his investment. Mr. West is an African-European who received his license in the US. He appears to be in his mid 50's, is impeccably dressed, and speaks with a slight British accent.

"Very well Mr. West, but if we go over 15 minutes I'm going to call for a recess and you can finish up after lunch." This is for the best interest of our underage alleged victim," the judge says.

"Very well your honor," Mr. West says. "Hello Miss Richardson, my name is Mr. West," he says to Kelly who is still on the stand.

"Hi," Kelly says.

"Miss Richardson I'm not going to be long at all, I just have about seven questions to ask you, maybe even less. Do you have a favorite TV show Miss Kelly that comes on tonight?"

"Yeah, College Reality TV," Kelly says with a little smile on her face.

"Well, you have my word you will be home to enjoy that show with a little ice cream too," Mr. West says.

Kelly smiles again and says, "OK."

"Miss Richardson, can I call you Kelly?" Mr. West asks.

"Yes," Kelly says.

"We already heard early this morning how you were invited to a party and there you met Raymond. The two of you danced and later went into a bedroom to have sex, right?"

"Yes," Kelly replies.

"It was dark so you wouldn't be able to recognize any marks on his body, etc.?" Mr. West asks.

"Right," Kelly answers.

"You also mentioned you didn't know who he was until you saw him on TV, then you told one of your friends in school what happened and she in turn told the student counselor and she reported it to the police?" Mr. West asks.

"That's right. Well my counselor told my parents and then the police," Kelly says.

"That's right, that's the right order," Mr. West says.

"Kelly I have three more questions out of the seven, OK?" Mr. West says.

"OK," Kelly responds.

"How long have you been having sex?" Mr. West asks.

"Since I was 14," Kelly replies.

"Kelly out of all the questions I have asked this is the most important one. Are you ready?"

"Yes," Kelly says.

"Do you have sex during your menstrual cycle?" Mr. West asks.

Without hesitation Kelly frowns up her face and lets out a, "No, that's nasty!"

"Yes, it is Kelly," Mr. West says and then rises up to his feet. "Kelly this is not a question, I only have one question left and about three minutes to ask it, so I don't want you to confuse this statement with a question. What if I told you I have proof you couldn't have had sex with Mr. Jackson, because the night of the party you were on your second day of a seven day menstrual cycle." Mr. West says.

Kelly looks at her father who is sitting in the back of the courtroom.

"You just turned 17 in January and when you were 16 you had your menstrual cycle on the second week of each month. I have here the invitation of the party in question that tells us the date, place and time, you and Raymond were suppose to have sex," Mr. West says as he presents the invitation to Kelly.

She looks at it and begins to cry.

"Now Kelly, I have only one more question left. I am a man who tries to be honest and stay true to my word. I want you to get out of this cold courtroom, out of the eyes of these people, get into your comfortable jeans, get your ice cream and watch your favorite TV show and put all of this behind you like it never happened. If you answer this question honestly you will be able to do exactly that. Did you have sex with Mr. Jackson at anytime in your life?" Mr. West asks.

Kelly looks down and pauses.

Everyone is holding their breath, waiting for this last question to be addressed. Kelly didn't realize that the fate of an entire generation and an entire Nation was hanging on her words right now. Raymond and his family wanted her to hurry up and answer, but there was another part that wanted her to think about what she was about to say and do.

If she said "Yes", regardless of what the lawyer's proof, they would be going to trial. Even if Raymond wasn't found guilty the New Nation project would be off until 2060, and the November election would pass him by, as he would be caught up in court proceedings and trying clear his name and fight for his freedom.

Everyone was on the edge of their seat watching the mouth of a 17-year-old girl, waiting for something to come out. Kelly lifted up her head, looked into the eyes of Mr. West, who seemed to be friendly, wiped the tears from her face and said, "No, I did not."

A loud sigh swept over the entire courtroom as everyone begins to clap.

"Order please, order," the judge says.

"Thank you Miss Richardson," Mr. West says, then he walks back to the table and Raymond gives him a big hug.

Diana Pride, the young female reporter couldn't wait to run outside to her camera to be the first one to report the verdict. "Benson, Benson set up fast, hurry, hurry," she says breathing hard, because she practically did the 60-yard dash through the courtroom hallway to where her camera was set up. "You're on in 3-2-1," Benson cues her.

"Ladies and gentlemen of America this has been a very exciting morning here at the Atlanta Federal Courthouse, Vice Presidential candidate Mr. Raymond Jackson has been exonerated of all charges."

"What?" another news reporter says overhearing her report. "Set up we're going on," he says to his cameraman.

Diana continues, "That right America, we have witnessed a great turn of events here this morning when Jackson's lawyer Mr. West asked the young lady just seven questions -- I repeat, only seven questions -- which revealed the truth that she never had sexual relations with Mr. Jackson. A big commotion is taking place near the door of the courthouse. It's Raymond Jackson, his lawyer Mr. West, and security coming out the courthouse. I believe he will be taking a few questions. We going to follow him very closely," she says.

When the spectators see Raymond they begin to clap, cheer, and begin to chant "Change America for the better." Raymond is being photographed and questions are being shouted at him. Raymond and Mr. West are directed to stand in front of a podium in the center of a pool of reporters.

Mr. West steps up to the microphone. "Thank you for your support of my client. As you can see he was innocent of the charge against him from the very beginning. Mr. Jackson will only have time to take a few questions.

"Do you think someone put her up to this or was she looking for a way to get money out of you?" a reporter asks. "

Yes, I believe she was put up to it, and I have a good idea of who, but I'm not at liberty to say right now," Raymond answers.

"Mr. Jackson, Mr. Jackson do you think this will have a negative impact on your political career?" another reporter asks.

"I don't think so, it should workout for my good, because this proves I am a winner," Raymond says recalling the comment his Godfather made to him in the park this time last month.

"Raymond, how do you feel right now?" another reporter asks.

"I feel like I'm on a new level of freedom and I'm not going to take anything for granted," Raymond answers.

This was an understatement of how Raymond really felt. The weight of the world was off his shoulders. He was as light as a bird and ready to fly to his destiny. His Godfather was right. All things were working together. This event freed Raymond of his charges and also freed him of the political game he had played so long in the American system.

Today was the eve of announcing that he would be withdrawing from the race for Vice President. His Godfather had already told him if he was exonerated, he must seize the moment and use every second. He was ready like a kid on Christmas Eve.

Raymond was ready to open up the gift of freedom that had been given to him in a different way. Maybe Raymond had to go through this experience to feel the passion and the power of freedom once again. Yes, he was on a new level of freedom and right now he wanted everyone to be evolved on this level. He was ready to inspire and motivate an entire generation to move to this level of freedom with authority and power.

"What is your next political move Mr. Jackson?" a reporter asks.

"I'm going to have a big news conference tomorrow to let everyone in America know where my political future lies. So you will have to wait until then. That's all of the questions I'll take for now, but Mr. West will answer some for you. Thank you," Raymond says and is rushed off by his security men.

The reporters turn their attention to Raymond's lawyer. "Mr. West what made you ask that line of questioning and why were you so sure as to how she would respond to them?" Diana Pride asks.

"Well, I can't tell you all of the secrets of the trade, but I will say when I heard of this situation and how close it was to the election, I could smell something foul," Mr. West says. The reporters laugh. "So my first response was to talk to her best friend since grade school, and to get her six month checkup report. Now if I didn't have either of the two, an innocent man would have gone to prison for a long time," Mr. West concludes.

Picture 35: *It's Time!*

The media and everyone who is interested in Raymond's political career have gathered in the conference room at Raymond's headquarters. Photographers are in front of him taking pictures. Tarisha and Toni are sitting on both sides of Raymond, and his security is standing behind him.

Tarisha pulls the microphone on the table in front of her to speak. "Ladies and gentlemen I know you have a lot of questions for Mr. Jackson and we want to answer your questions in an orderly manner. But first Mr. Jackson has a statement he would like to make." Tarisha says and then moves the microphone in front of Raymond.

"Thank you all for coming out this evening. As you all know I have been running for Vice President of the United States, under the campaign themes of, "Change America for the Better," and "It's About Time." It has been a lot of fun and I have met a lot of wonderful people as I developed great relationships across this country. I've always had America's best interests at heart in all of the decisions I've made. I've always thought of every race, culture, family, business, community, city and state. I've thought of everyone's future individually and collectively. But today I must stop being concerned about everyone else and look after my own interests. As selfish as it might seem, it is something that must be done right now. So this evening this is hard for me to do, but," Raymond says then pauses and look around the room, he looks at Tarisha who has an idea of what he is about to say next, and she shakes her head "No."

Raymond continues, "I am announcing my withdrawal from the race for Vice President of the United States of America," Raymond says.

"Oh no," someone in the crowd gasps. The photographers begin to take Raymond's picture even more furiously now.

At that time Raymond's mother and father were watching Raymond on TV from their home. Raymond's mother Julia, put her hand over her mouth in shock from his decision. Bishop Jackson chose to keep her out of Raymond's political life; she had her hands full enough with being the first lady of a Mega Church. She didn't know anything about the decision to withdraw from the race beforehand, or about the New Nation Project. Bishop Jackson wanted her to find out as things developed, so she would not have any extra burdens.

Thus Raymond's decision surprised Benjamin and Lily. The Williams's were watching Raymond on their computer monitor. "What did he just say?" the judge asked his wife.

"It sounded like he said he was pulling out of the race," Lily responded.

At the same time Kim, the female investment banker was painting her nails and toes watching Raymond on the TV in her bedroom when she heard his announcement, she stared at the TV with her mouth open and somehow managed to mumble, "Oh my word."

Nicky was watching Raymond from her living room as she read a book. "Ray what are you doing!"

Kevin and Michele, the interracial couples are driving in their car listening to Raymond on the radio. "I can't believe that," Kevin says.

"Is he serious?" Michele asks.

President Lyman's, staff is jumping up and down, giving each other high fives after hearing Raymond's announcement.

John Newton was watching Raymond on TV from his office as he was smoking a cigar. When he heard Raymond's announcement he opened his mouth and dropped the cigar in his lap causing him to jump up swearing.

When Raymond's Godfather hears Raymond announce his withdrawal from the race he gets up from his chair and turns off the TV to go to bed.

Back at headquarters Raymond is responding to the multitude of questions from the media. "I know, I know this might come as a shock to all of you, including my staff and campaign team, but it's something I have already made up my mind to do," Raymond says.

"Mr. Jackson, Mr. Jackson," the media shouts trying to get their questions in. "Before you ask any questions I have another announcement to make," Raymond says. This causes the entire room to go silent again; only the clicking of cameras can be heard. "I'm withdrawing from the election to focus my attention on another important project that I feel need my expertise and experience. And that endeavor is to begin a campaign calling all Americans of African descent to return to Africa to become the New Nation of Africa," Raymond says.

Raymond pauses knowing this statement would need a little time to hit home. His staff looks at him like he is crazy. The media is taking even more pictures of Raymond and his staff, and even some of the people in the audience to capture people's reaction to Raymond's statements. An African American male had declined to become the first Vice President of the United States. He declined the position to start his own nation in Africa. Even though Raymond was not going to be starting his own country, this is how the general public would remember the moment.

Raymond's mother, Julia who is still watching from her den says, "What?" as she looks at Raymond's father.

John Newton who is still watching from his office shouts, "What?"

President Lyman's top aides stop giving each other high fives when they heard Raymond's last statement said, "What?"

Benjamin and Lily Williams who were still watching on their computer looked at each other and said, "What?"

Nicky who had closed her book completely and was watching Raymond from her living room said, "What?"

Kevin and Michelle, who were driving home listening to Raymond on their radio looked at each other and said, "What?"

Kim stopped painting her nails and toes, stared at the TV in her bedroom with her mouth still wide open managed to mumble one more word: "What?"

All of these individuals spoke for the millions of people who were following Raymond nationwide. "What" is the one word everyone shared had in common. It could mean different things: What is he doing? What is his problem? What is the matter with him? What, is he crazy or something? What pride? What strength?

What nerve? What time are we going? What is the plan? What is the cost? All of these "What's" could mean different things depending on who said it, but it does mean Raymond owes a lot of people some answers.

"What?" Tarisha, Raymond's top aide for the last ten years says as she looks at Raymond. "I will not be able to explain everything to you in one sitting. Tomorrow I will be starting a B2B campaign and tour across America. B2B stands for Back to the Beginning. This tour will be for everyone who wants to hear more information or has any questions about B2B. Whoever wants to participate will be able to change their citizenship and become a citizen of the New Nation in Africa," Raymond says.

"Mr. Jackson, Mr. Jackson," the reporters are shouting and raising their hands like they are school children trying to get the teacher to pick them for a special assignment.

"It's getting late, but I will take a few questions right now. As I stated I will be commencing a campaign and tour tomorrow to explain this great move in greater detail. So whatever questions I don't answer tonight, hopefully I will answer them during this campaign. I would also like to say to my campaign staff, thank you for everything. I will no longer need your services, this is a project you are not familiar with, so there will be others who will take over your responsibilities from here," Raymond says.

Tarisha looks at Raymond with fire in her eyes and the staff shake their heads in disbelief. After all of their dedication to Raymond this is how he returns their goodness! He couldn't even give them enough respect to tell them in private and to shield them from the embarrassment of being fired on National TV. Two female aides get up and walk out. Tarisha, on the other hand, keeps her poise and stands her ground, even though she was hotter than a firecracker on the 4th of July. She listens as Raymond continues. "So I need for your questions to be brief and to the point. Would you please follow the direction of my new Chief of Staff, Ms. Louise Witherspoon?

Louise is a very pretty, fair skinned, African American lady who was educated in Europe. She speaks 14 languages and is very knowledgeable about global affairs. She could be easily mistaken for a top model, but her strong commanding presence would be a clear indication that she was destined to be more than an advertisement for a product.

Louise steps forward and says, (with a slight British accent), "Mr. Jackson is going to answer only a few questions, so when I select you, you may ask your question.

Tarisha looks at Louise as if to say, "Who in the hell do you think you are?" She then looks at Raymond with eyes that say, "I hate you."

Louise indicates a reporter and says, "You sir."

"Mr. Jackson did you pull out of the race because of the false accusations you just were acquitted of?" the reporter asks. "No sir, I'm familiar with dirty politics, even if I have never been the victim of them, until now. But my decision comes only as a result of my total focus on the New Nation of Africa," Raymond says.

"Madam," Louise says and points.

"Are you saying you are going to build a Nation from scratch?" another reporter asks.

Raymond replies, "I can't get into full details because of security reasons, but I will say nothing is being done from scratch. The country I'm speaking of is already in existence. The government policies, government structure and operation are already in place. The only thing missing is you." The reporters laugh. Raymond continues, "It is my job to get us there, so we can have a global voice and enjoy life on a global level."

"This will be the last question," Louise says as she points to another reporter. A gentleman begins to speak, but Louise says, "No, not you the one next to you. Thank you."

"Sir do you know who set you up?" the reporter asks.

Louise immediately jumps in before Raymond could respond, "We are only answering questions concerning Mr. Jackson's new Back to the Beginning campaign sir," Louise says with a stern attitude. If anyone of these reporters thinks for a second this pretty lady with a beautiful accent is a pushover, they will find out the hard way that Louise's brusque manner can leave a bitter after taste in their mouth.

"Alright the reporter says and begins to ask another question, but Louise interrupts him and says, "You lost your chance sir, this will be the last question and she points to the lady in the red blouse."

"Thank you madam. Mr. Jackson do you expect all African Americans to stop what they are doing, pack up their families and leave? And who are you expecting to respond to this call?" she asks.

"We will contact Americans of African descent in this country to give them the choice. They can take it or leave it, but it's my job to present it so they can never say they didn't have a choice in the matter. Prayerfully there will be many African Americans who are well established economically and socially and are ready to give back by helping the New Nation to get established. I will be going across the United States giving more information on this great move. Thank you," Raymond says. "That will be all of the questions tonight. We will be in contact, I'm sure. Thank you for your cooperation and good night," Louise says.

Picture 36: *You're Tripping*

The next day, early in the morning, Raymond's new staff is busy at work. Some are making calls and others are answering phones. Some are taking down the red, white and blue banner and replacing it with the brown, white, and gold, which are the official colors for the New Nation. Others are taking down the sign that reads, "Newton/Jackson '08" and replacing it with signs that say "Founder of the New Nation", and also putting up B2B posters.

"Make sure I see the B2B logo design for the T-shirts, buttons and hats before you get them printed," Louise says, while giving the staff instructions. Louise is going to every department makings sure everything is being done in accordance with her exact standards. Tarisha walks into the door. She notices the big changes in such a short time. She didn't come to talk to Raymond or to anyone else for that matter. All she wants to do is to clean out her desk, collect her belongings and be gone.

Raymond spots her from the other side of the room, "Give me a minute," Raymond tells his staff. Raymond walks toward Tarisha's office to meet her there. Tarisha goes right to cleaning out her desk. "You are making a lot of changes real fast, Oh I forgot -- that's was how you like to do things," Tarisha says sarcastically.

"I deserve that Tarisha, but look, you don't have to leave, you can stay and help me," Raymond says.

"It's a fine time to ask me now don't you think?" Tarisha says as she continues to gather her belonging.

"Listen I couldn't tell anyone until I was given the go ahead. You know I would have told you if I could."

"I thought it was about more than politics with you and me. Do you know I'm the only lady you've been with for the last ten years and never had sex with?" Tarisha says. Tarisha had a right to be upset, hurt, mad and disappointed. She had protected Raymond from many females who wanted to get his penis at the expense of his career, she was his glass shield. There were times she and Raymond came close to having a sexual relationship, but she successfully battled her own desire to protect his political future. She had contributed a lot of hard work behind the scenes to make Raymond shine in front of the United States citizens, and all she got in return was to be disgraced on national TV.

"I thought I knew you Raymond," Tarisha says.

"You do," Raymond replied.

"I never knew you had a desire to go back to Africa. Where did all of this come from?" Tarisha asks and then stops her packing to hear Raymond's answer.

But Raymond pauses and looks over her head. "Oh, now I *do know* that reaction," Tarisha says.

"What?" Raymond asks as though he is trying to cover up something.

"Whenever Mr. Jackson pauses to respond, something is wrong. I learned that the first year I started working for you at the same time I learned that you like cold pizza rather than a steamy hot pizza," Tarisha says.

Raymond smiles at the fact that Tarisha was amazing, instead of losing a great aide, he was about to lose someone with uncanny astuteness and an ability to read people.

"Yeah, I think it's time for you to go, you know me too well," Raymond teases.

"Seriously, Raymond is someone putting you up to this?" Tarisha asks very concerned.

"No, no I'm doing this because I believe in it."

"Well, I believe all children of the world should never go hungry at any time in their lives, but you don't see me dropping my career and professing to become a missionary," Tarisha replies.

"And why not?"

"Because I can help them better by doing what I do. I was doing a great job until you decided to stop everything to go build a Nation." Tarisha says.

"I'm not building a Nation. I was asked to be the founder," Raymond says.

"So the other individuals involved, did they influence your decision to do this?"

"If you know me so well, why don't you know that I'm not a follower? You should know I'm going to make up my own mind," Raymond says testily.

"You're right, I'm sorry, you're not easily influenced," Tarisha says and continues to gather her things.

Raymond walks over to her and takes both her hands. "Tarisha I never begged anyone for anything, but I'm begging you right now, please come with me, I really need you," Raymond says sincerely.

"It seems like you have all the help you need -- what's her name -- Louise," Tarisha says pronouncing Louise's name using a fake accent.

"This is just until the move is complete. I need someone to help with the entire operation," Raymond says.

"Raymond I'm tired right now. I rearranged my life for you before to get into politics, and now you are asking me to take a permanent trip across the world. I don't know about that. Maybe I need a break from politics for a while. It will give me a chance to think," Tarisha says.

"That good enough, I can't ask for anymore," Raymond says and then hugs Tarisha in a tight embrace.

"Raymond I'm going to let you out of the promise you gave me when you said I would have a job in the White House, but only if you do one thing for me, "Tarisha says.

"What's that?"

Tarisha keeps looking Raymond in the eyes and says, "All I ask is you really know that this is what you want to do. Man, you still don't know how powerful your words are. When you talk you inspire people to believe they can do anything and they will drop everything to follow you to the ends of the earth. You have to do more than believe in this, you have to see it through."

Tarisha was right once again. She had come to know Raymond in a way that his Godfather, his father, Nicky, Diamond or Louise would never know him in 100 years. She knew Raymond was a gifted man with a high calling, who could get bored very easily. If things were not going the way he felt they should go, after he put all of his effort in it, he would walk away and start working on something else. Sometimes everything could go according to plan. Every "i" is dotted and every "t" is crossed. Victory can be in the bag. But then the feeling hits him, the feeling to pack up to leave one project to go to another. Tarisha witnessed Raymond do this many times and right now this change of projects, from the Vice Presidency to this New Nation looked familiar. One thing Raymond must do is be sure this is what he wants, he must finish what he starts. If not a lot of people would feel the emptiness she felt right now. She knew that she would be OK, because she was a beautiful, smart woman with many marketable accomplishments. She could easily find new employment, and move on with her life. But if Raymond was not sure of what he was doing and what he really wanted, hundreds of thousands and -- maybe even millions -- would not be as fortunate as her. Tarisha hugged Raymond for what they didn't know would be the very last time.

Picture 37: *B2B Tour*

There was no more time to waste as far as Raymond's new staff was concerned. Timing is everything in politics and business. You can have an excellent idea or project, but if it's not presented at the right time, you could lose your potential market. The B2B staff knows this to be true, so they are doing everything they can to get Raymond back in sync with the timing of the mission.

When the evil forces see they can't destroy your mission they will do everything in their power to delay it. So if Raymond was going to catch up with time he must get use to another form of transportation. When Raymond was running for the Vice President of the United States he would hit the road by way of tour bus, limo, town car, or truck. But now that his focus is on being a founder of a new nation he must mount up with wings as an eagle in his own private Gulf Stream II jet.

The jet is white, brown and gold, inscribed with "NNA" in green letters on the side. This is another clear sign that Raymond has indeed risen to another level. Don't misunderstand luxury for necessity. Even though Raymond is flying with the big boys, he is not styling and profiling on the clouds. In the next six months this jet will go more places and accomplish more things than any other transportation that was made and manufactured in its time. Raymond has been scheduled for a 25-city tour that has to be completed in 30 days.

These cities are where a great population of African Americans reside, and they must be the first for the presentation of the B2B tour. It has already been arranged for Raymond to appear in arenas and public places where thousands can meet at one time. Raymond has addressed the most popular African American groups and organizations to the most unrecognized ones.

In that short amount of time Raymond has addressed millions of African Americans. Wherever Raymond went and to whomever he was speaking, to small or great crowds alike, his message was profound, but simple. He invited all African Americans to begin to think on a global level by moving to the New Nation of Africa.

Raymond pointed out that we are living at a time when many races, cultures and ethnic groups are expanding the scope of their efforts for the betterment of all people. Churches, businesses and corporations are also taking advantage of new technologies that have been developed to advance their interests. The New Nation provides a chance for African Americans to take a big step into the global world, and maybe get back to where they would have been if slavery had never been a part of their history.

Raymond also emphasized that it was time for professional African Americans who have contributed to this country to extend their gifts and talents beyond America and the Western World. "This is a once in a lifetime chance to give back to the place that gave you life to the very talents you are using." Another time he said, "You will be the first generation of professional African Americans who will put your fingerprints on history in the making." Another outstanding statement was, "The New Nation of Africa gives us a chance to show the world what we have already shown America, that we are survivors, and we are achievers!"

Raymond's staff noticed that Raymond always receives a standing ovation. This surprised Raymond's new staff because their studies showed most of the time when a new idea was presented to the African American community their first reactions was to criticize it, reject it, be defensive or somewhat hesitant. Later they would come back to analyze the subject matter and embrace it wholeheartedly. But for some unexplained reason this was not the case with Raymond and his presentation of the New Nation.

"I told you he had this appeal that everyone liked, and that this would cause a lot of people to bypass all of the political processes and procedures, and go straight to consider the subject at hand," Bryant constantly reminded his colleagues as he gave himself a pat on the back. Bryant was correct from a Public Relations perspective. But what he had not considered, was that African Americans have always been looking for someone to take a tall stand in politics since Martin Luther King Jr. Many men and women have tried and God blessed their efforts, but Raymond is the only one who came close enough to take a people to a place they have been dreaming about for so long.

Even those who would not register to change their citizenship from being a citizen of America to being a citizen of the New Nation of Africa still at least gave him a standing ovation.

Raymond's tour also consisted of going on the top talks shows that reached millions in minutes. His first stop was CMM, where he and President Lyman had a joint interview with the famous Ted Hillman. This interview was the most highly anticipated interview in the history of CMM, and it is only ninety days after Raymond announced his withdrawal from the vice presidential race and the commencement of the B2B Tour. Raymond and President Lyman appear on the split screen on TV.

"Thank you gentlemen for taking time out of your most busy schedules to have this interview. President Lyman you are in the middle of a campaign that will give you another four years in the White House, and Mr. Jackson you are on the B2B or Back to the Beginning Tour. Good morning to you both," Ted says. "Mr. President let me start with you. How do you feel about Mr. Jackson having a campaign across this nation of this sort, and what does this do to our country?" Ted queries.

"Well, the way I feel is great, because he is doing what this country has done more than 200 years ago. I can never be against true progress in any sense. As far as the United States is concerned we are not relying on any one race or culture. We are made of many different peoples and if one goes on to progress politically then I feel good about that," the President says.

"Mr. President, are you saying if over 30 million African Americans leave this country it will not affect us?" Ted asks.

"I'm not saying that Ted. Of course it will shake every part of this country because African Americans play a major part in every area of our nation. But a shaking and a crumbing is not the same thing. We will survive this like we have survived everything else," President Lyman says.

"Mr. Jackson many people think this B2B tour surfaced from the false accusations that were plotted against you by someone who was attempting to assassinate your career," Ted states.

"No Ted, this decision was made before that incident ever took place. All that incident did was push me to act at a certain time," Raymond says.

"Well, what do you say to people who think you are starting a cult and you have no experience to be starting a country?" Ted asks.

"Well, first of all, I'm not trying to start to a cult. Why is it when ethnic groups decide to go back to their homelands they are labeled patriotic, but when I suggest such a thing I'm starting a 'cult'. Secondly, why when I was running for Vice President I was 'very intelligent', and 'the man for the job', but when I want to be a founder of a Nation, I'm 'not qualified' or I'm 'inexperienced'? It's not fair," Raymond says.

"Do you think he is trying to start a cult Mr. President?" Ted asks. "I don't believe so. I met Mr. Jackson many times and he has a very sincere and sound point of view. As a matter of fact before any nation can be accepted in the international community as legitimate another Nation must validate them. I want to go on record as the President of the United States of America as validating the New Nation as an official country in the international community," the President says.

"Are you aware of the import of your words?" Ted asks.

"I see Raymond and all other African Americans as descendants of our country, just as they are a descendant of Africa, and I believe we should help them go home if this is what they want, not hinder them," President Lyman says.

"Mr. Jackson what do you say to that?" Ted asks.

"I'm surprised. I'm just about as surprised as you, Ted. My staff didn't have any idea President Lyman was going to make such a declaration. I thank you Mr. President, and I thank the United States for such a powerful endorsement. But I would like to clear something up. I never suggested 30 million African Americans are going to exchange their citizenship for a New Nation citizenship, as much as I want it to happen it's not going to take place like that. It's going to be a process," Raymond says.

"Good point sir. Mr. President allow me to speak candidly. I think you are embracing Mr. Jackson's idea because Mr. Jackson was winning the election and by him making this decision it removes him as a threat to your re-election. Also, many will suspect your endorsement was also politically motivated, because this may get you more votes. One thing I do know is this is a very brave decision that Mr. Jackson has made, but it is a decision that will split the country right in two. If one African American leaves not only will they be missed, but they will be missing. Thank you gentlemen, that is all the time we have right now, and I know you must leave for other appointments. God bless you both," Ted says they cut to a commercial.

In a matter of minutes after the interview thousands register for the New Nation, the President's approval rate skyrocketed, and CMM had the highest viewers on all morning talk shows for that entire year.

A week after Raymond appeared on CMM he was on the Harry King Show for an interview. "I'm Harry King and I'm here with the one and only Mr. Raymond Jackson. He really doesn't need any introduction, because he has been known by all for years as the one who would become the first male African American Vice President. But these days he is known as the one who is campaigning for the B2B move. It's good to have you here sir," King says.

"It's good to be here," Raymond replies.

"So how is the campaign coming along?"

"Well, it's hard work. We covered over half of the country and we are getting a lot of positive responses. The registration numbers are more than I thought they would be at this time," Raymond says.

"Do you have anyone actually changing their citizenship and registering to leave in November?" King asks.

Raymond smiles and says, "Yes Harry, we have 600,000 so far."

"Whoa! Are you telling me 600,000 have already said 'Yes' to going to Africa?" King asks.

"You sound surprised Harry."

"That I am."

"Well, I can't take all of the credit. My staff is doing a wonderful job and I must say this operation was in place before I started. I'm just fulfilling my part."

"Can you also tell that some people were waiting for a day like this when someone would do what you are doing?"

"I can say yes to that. Many people in our community believe we never had a choice in the matter of being in this country because of the way we were brought here. But today I'm presenting them with a choice they never had before," Raymond says.

"On the other hand there are lots of people who think this is very racist. They believe you are fostering racism in the workplace, schools, and in the home," King says in an accusing voice.

Raymond is used to this type of forum where the interview always start off respectful and pleasant, but then the attack comes from out of nowhere. Raymond knows how to handle these attacks.

"Why? Because I'm thinking global and they are still thinking local in terms of how they will display their talents?

"Well, with all due respect sir, if I said it's a good idea to go to Africa, would you think I'm a racist who wants to get rid of all the less desirables, or would you think I'm supporting a good idea? If I say no, I don't think it's a good idea would you think I'm trying to keep you in your place, or would you think I'm attempting to keep a great important culture in America?" King asks, which was a very good question that only he could state in such a politically correct fashion.

"I'm well aware of the great dilemma this great move brings about, but this is something every individual has to decide for him or herself. You can't allow anyone to convince you of what you should think, feel or do at this special time in history. Every great move has brought controversy such as this," Raymond says.

"Why November? Why have your departure date or the great Exodus a day before the election process this year?"

"Well, it would not be fair for people to vote who will no longer be a part of this country. It's also a time of political evolution. While some will be preparing for the polls, others will be preparing to travel to another political dimension. Both will be voting in their own way," Raymond says.

"I have one more question for you, because I know you must be leaving us soon. You used the word evolution rather revolution, and that is very interesting. How are the Black Caucus and other African leaders taking this evolution in the African American community?" King asks.

"Well, I used that word because in the 50's and 60's the African American community had a revolution. I remember hearing, as a little boy 'The revolution would not be televised." Leaders like Martin Luther King and Malcolm X advanced every area of this country in a big way. Well, today if our community has advanced, and we have, surely we shouldn't be still having the same revolution our previous leaders had. We should be having an evolution into a powerful political economy, to be a social and new global force to be reckoned with in the international community. On that note I don't know how the Black Caucus and the others feel, but I will be having a Town Hall Meeting with them very soon."

"Thank you Mr. Jackson for your time. We will be right back," King says.

"Raymond did it again," his staff says among themselves as the registration rose a total of 300 thousand more people since the interview aired.

Picture 38: *Turn It Up*

While traveling from another gathering, Raymond is getting some well-needed rest. His staff reviews his market and public relations surveys. "I can't believe the reactions we are getting from these talk shows," Louise says.

"They are a real big deal here in America," Bryant responds.

"I thought we were going to get most of our responses during the presentations with the organizations, institutions, groups, etc. I never thought they would come from this source. Look at these numbers," Louise says as she hands Bryant the registration report.

"Louise, we have to get Raymond on the ZET Network."

"I was thinking the same thing."

"But what show?"

"The most popular one of course."

"The only problem is it's the News Story and Raymond was featured there when he was running for Vice President and they were tracking his political career. But there is a political show called Brother J," Bryant says.

"OK that is who we want, lets get him on there," Louise responds.

"And that's where my problem lies. Brother J is a great showcase, but it's not the most popular show on that network."

"OK what is?"

"It's a music video show, '106 and P', that is the next most popular show."

Louise stops and thinks. "I was thinking Raymond should go on that show, but make sure that Brother J orients it toward politics. They can still have the videos but with a political theme," Louise says.

"Hey I like that. Raymond would like that. He already addressed the leaders at the Hip-Hop Summit, and so this will give him a chance to talk to the grass root people of the Hip-Hop Culture," Bryant says.

"I like it, lets do it." It took Raymond's staff no time to get him on 106 and P.

A week later 106 and P host Freedom announces, "As we have been telling you all week long, today we have a very special show. We have Brother J here today because we want him to introduce to us a man who really doesn't need any introduction. He has been moving across this country, in our neighborhoods and communities in a record time," Freedom says. "We bring to our show right now one of the most powerful persons in our nation right now -- Mr. Raymond Jackson," Brother J announces. The studio audience claps and cheers. They are a very mixed crowd today of college students, young adults and adults, and Hip-Hop celebrities. But the crowd was just as excited as most of Raymond's audiences are.

Raymond comes out going into the audience shaking hands and giving hi-fives. The audience was eating it all up. When he gets on the stage and greets Freedom, and Brother J the people begin to chant, "B2B" over and over again. It was not planned, programmed or prepared, it was something that just happened and Raymond was feeling it in a big way and loving every minute of it.

"Have a seat man, have a seat. I know you have to be dead on your feet, you're doing it big across America," Freedom says.

"Yeah, I'm a little beat down, but I'm determined to finish what I started," Raymond says.

"We're going to get right into it. We have our political analyst, Brother J, here with us today and he is going to ask you some questions pertaining to the New Nation and the B2B Tour," Freedom says.

"First Mr. Jackson it is an honor and a pleasure to meet you in person, you are my hero and a lot of peoples' hero in our community today," Brother J says to the crowd's applauds. "I also wanted to say it was big for you to give up the opportunity to be the first male African American Vice President to pursue your dream and vision for African Americans' future in Africa. That's Mega!" says Brother J. The audience claps and cheers in agreement.

Brother J continues, "What made you so sure you were making the right choice?

"Well, when the offer was first presented to me, I thought it was a joke or something. But once it dawned on me that it was real then I had to do some serious math. I had to figure something out and the sum that I came up with was this. If I was about to become the Vice President of the world's super power, then surely I have what it takes to at least be a founder of a Nation that is not presently at the United States' level. That's one. Two is, if this Nation was about to take a chance on me by making me the first male African American Vice President, I believe I should take a chance on myself by giving the African Americans in this country a global option," Raymond says and the audience claps.

"That's truth. Today can you clear up something for our viewers that you cleared up for me when you addressed the Hip-Hop Summit -- that the New Nation of Africa is already built and in tact, and we are not going out to some desert place trying to build with rocks, sticks or bricks," Brother J says.

Raymond laughs. "It's amazing how so many people get that image whenever you talk about Africa, and now the New Nation. This is why we have a website of the New Nation," Raymond says.

"What is it so the people can have it if they don't already," Brother J says.

"It's www.newnationb2b.org. This way you can see the Nation itself. We are not asking anyone to come and build, just expand what is already in existence. I can say we have everything this government has from a structural point of view. This is a well-functioning entity. Go check it out by hitting us on our website," Raymond says.

"So we can get jobs right now in the New Nation if we want to?" Freedom asks. "Not only can you get a job, but we have opportunities for you to open your own business to help the economy to grow in the New Nation. We are looking for the first generation of thinkers, inventors, entrepreneurs, builders, movers and shakers, so we can move to bigger and better things." The audience claps and cheers.

"Before we go to another video, you said something at the Hip-Hop summit that really inspired me and may be the deciding factor in changing my citizenship. Can you repeat what you said?" Freedom asks.

"Well, I'm very impressed with the Hip-Hop culture because I'm from this culture myself and I witnessed this culture beat some great odds. It was said this culture would not last and it would not amount to anything. Well, today the Hip-Hop culture has impacted the world in music, fashion, jewelry, cars, inventions and many other great contributions. We need this kind of talent in the New Nation. Right now you are the culture to be reckoned with. But if you will take this major move to Africa you would be the Nation to be reckoned with. Together we can impact the globe," Raymond says.

The audience gives Raymond a standing ovation, as does Freedom and Brother J. Freedom says, "Now that's whoa! Is it me or is it getting hot up in here? Listen for more information about B2B or log onto their website. Make sure you register to be apart of this great move, be a part of history in the making. Now check out this throw back," Freedom says and the video "I Know A Place" begins to play.

The registration rating went to another level and people were hitting the website more than ever; checking out the New Nation's land, government, structure, constitution, employment, and many other facts.

Louise told the staff they had to do more national syndicated daytime shows before Raymond went to the Town Hall Meeting and to also schedule him for some R&R with his family. Everyone agreed if there must be one more show before the break, then it should be the "Big O Show." She had both black and white viewers. "The Big O Show" had been one of the shows that was on Bryant's list, and he made it happen in no time at all.

"Hey America, we have a very exciting show for you today. I have the honor to have as my guest one of the most popular men in the African American community -- or should I say in the country -- right now, Mr. Raymond Jackson. Would you give him a Big O welcome," Ophelia O'May says. The audience claps and cheers.

"Thank you, thank you," Raymond says with a big smile.

"Well Raymond, where should we begin? For the last few months your life has been one big drama after another. Lets start with why you gave up what most people thought was a sure victory in the 2008 election for Vice President for you?" Ophelia asks.

"Well I don't like running from the ghost of 'what if', and I hate regrets, so when this offer was presented to me I took it. I believe being a founder of a country is a worthier goal than being a Vice President of one." Some of the audience applauds, and others don't.

"As you can see people have mixed feelings and mixed reactions to this subject matter. This is easily one of the hottest topics in America, maybe the world, but yet it's the most controversial one as well. How do you handle such mixed reactions?" Ophelia asks.

"Well, I anticipated this because we live in a mixed, multi-cultural society. Your audience itself reflects the very profile of America, so I expected a mixed reaction from a mixed culture. I have some people who think it's a great idea and give me 100% support. Others don't like it at all and oppose it 100%. These two types can exist in the same household. Some think it's racist, but others don't think so. This is what I expect," Raymond says.

"Is it? Is race a motivating factor in any way?" Ophelia questions.

Raymond looks into the camera. "I can honestly say to the millions of people who watch your show everyday, and to the same people who were about to put me in the White House as Vice President, this has nothing to do with race. I believe this move compliments America. As President Lyman mentioned, this country is in existence today because it made the very same move when the forefathers founded this country. Now one of America's children has grown up and become mature enough to follow in her divine footsteps, just in a more modern manner," Raymond says. Everyone in the audience claps.

"They told me to watch you because you have a way with words," Ophelia says. The audience laughs along with Raymond. "OK tell me about the New Nation. I saw the website, and I've been to Africa myself many times and it's a wonderful place. So it looks like the country is already built," Ophelia says.

"Yes, it is, I get this all the time. There will be no building -- just expansion on the citizens' part. Right now the country can support 12 to 20 million citizens. In the next five years that number will double. Everything is built for expansion," Raymond says.

"Do you expect all African Americans to drop what they are doing and pick up and go to Africa?"

"No, we know better than that. We know all African Americans can't leave right now. Some will opt to stay and go later, but we are expecting a lot to leave now as well. We are also keeping in mind that African Americans didn't all come over at once, so I don't expect everyone to leave at once," Raymond explains.

"So over a million have already registered to leave in November?"

"Yes," Raymond answers.

"I have a few questions on my top five list and this is one of them. Will whites be allowed in the New Nation?"

Raymond begins to laugh a little as he says, "That's like asking Mandela if any whites are allowed in South Africa." The audience laughs. "Yes, all nationalities, races and cultures are welcome to the New Nation of Africa, but African Americans will for the most part be in leadership positions as whites are in this country," Raymond says.

"I'm thinking about getting a vacation home there," Ophelia says.

"You know, I have a lot of celebrities telling me they are going to do the very same thing, making the New Nation a home away from home," Raymond says.

"We must go to commercial break, but before you go I want you to tell us about the promise. I read it on the New Nation website and read articles of you talking about it. Can you explain how all of this, the Nation and this move is based on a promise?"

"Well, it was told to me that there were two best friends who lived in Africa before the slave trade began. When the slave trade began they were split up by slavery. One was sold into the Spanish-European Colony and the other, to America. The one in the Spanish colony bought his freedom and returned back to Africa, but his friend stayed in America under bondage. The friend in Africa was haunted by dreams of his friend calling him for help, but he refused to go back in slavery to rescue his friend. So he made a promise to God and himself that he would build a Nation for the descendants of ex-slaves in America to be able to come back home. This promise has been passed down from one generation to the next and each generation has contributed something to the building of that promise. Thus we have the New Nation of Africa," Raymond says.

"So getting the descendants of the former slaves to go back to Africa will be equal to bringing the spirits of the best friends back together," Mrs. Ophelia says.

"I never looked at it quite like that, but that's a good way to put it," Raymond says and the audience claps.

"We are going to continue our dialogue because I have more. But before I go, I want to say, to some it might not be the right thing to do, to some it's not the right time, but besides all of that to me what you are doing is very powerful. I'm not talking about the move itself. I'm talking about helping your ancestors keep a promise. Now that is powerful." Ophelia continues, "And I believe they all are looking down at you giving you a standing ovation, if for nothing else, for honoring a promise - and so do I," Ophelia says and then stands up and gives Raymond a standing ovation and the audience follows her lead. "We'll be right back," she says.

STATION BREAK!!! This is an announcement from the New Nation Campaign Headquarters

IT IS NOW 250 DAYS UNTIL DEPARTURE HAVE YOU REGISTERED?

Log onto

www.newnation.org

to register today and see the layout of the New Nation of Africa.

Picture 39: *A House Divided*

Judge Benjamin and Dr. Lily Williams decide to eat dinner on their patio as they watch TV to enjoy the beautiful evening in Atlanta. They are laughing and discussing what occurred at their jobs today. Then one of the many B2B commercials comes on the TV.

"Remember it's not another movement, it's a major move," Raymond says in the commercial. "If you would like to be a part of this major move or give a donation to help this move please log onto www.newnationb2b.org. I thank you in advance."

A frown comes over Ben Williams' face as he reaches for the remote to cut the TV off. Lily noticed the change in his expression when Raymond's commercial came on. She has noticed it since the day Raymond resigned as a Vice Presidential candidate. Her husband said nothing about it or mentioned Raymond's name ever again. This was a clear sign he was disappointed. He was not even mad or hurt, because if he were he would be talking until he was blue in the face (or Lily was blue in the face). The fact he had not said one word showed he was disappointed, because when he was, he would simply shut his mouth and clam up.

"Why did you do that?" Lily asks.

"I don't want to hear anything coming from that insane man," Benjamin says.

"Don't call names Ben."

"Lily, who in the world gives up a sure position in the White House, but an insane man?" Ben says.

Lily wants to get him to talk about the matter to get it out of his system, so it will not rot inside of him, making him a bitter man, because the last thing we need is another bitter judge in the courthouse. "So let me get this right. When Raymond was running for Vice President and you donated $100,000 towards his campaign, he was not insane. But now that he decides to not run the race you want him to, he is insane?"

"Don't tell me he got to you?" Ben says.

"No, I'm not saying anything. I just want to understand something. So you were just using him for your own purposes?" Lily asks.

"No."

"That's what it sounds like to me Ben. It sounds like you invested in something, and because you didn't get the return you were expecting you are very disappointed."

"No, I'll tell you what it sounds like Lily, since you want to give me your psychoanalysis. Raymond is just like most of them I see coming in and out of my courtroom everyday. No matter how much you try to help them, they turn right around and bite you in the behind."

"You are comparing an upstanding politician to hardened criminals, now *you* are talking like an insane man. Is it a crime for a man to follow his dreams Ben? Do you remember when I first heard him speak and I came home all excited to tell you about him, how he spoke with so much passion and promise, he inspired me to really believe in our American system again. That night we made love like we hadn't done in a long time, because he spoke to something inside of me that I can't explain. You heard it yourself Ben, that's why you would have given your last dime to get him in the White House. But now I'm beginning to think you only liked Raymond as a person who would stay in his place even if that place was the White House," Lily says then stands up from the table. "Ben you must remember, there is a big world out there that is getting smaller everyday, and America is not the only place you can live out your dreams," Lily says and then starts to walk away.

"Where are you going Lily?"

"To call our accountant and tell him to write the biggest check we can afford to give to the B2B movement," Lilly says then continues to walk. The judge calls for her, but she ignores him.

⚐ ⚐ ⚐

Meanwhile on the upper west part of town Kevin is sitting on the couch flipping through the channels. His fiancée Michelle enters the apartment with her briefcase and a supermarket bag of groceries.

"Oh man you startled me. What are you doing home before me?" Michele asks.

Kevin doesn't say anything, but continues flipping through the channels. Michele puts the bags down on the kitchen counter. "Are you hungry?"

"No," he says as he stares at the TV and continues flipping through the channels. Michele stops and looks at him and notices what he is doing; so she goes over to him and sits down beside him, and orders, "Look at me."

"What?" Kevin says.

"Who made you upset?"

"Why do you say that?"

"Because this is what you do when you get upset," she says. Kevin notices himself flipping through the channels. He stops and tosses the remote on the chair.

"Let's have sex," he says.

She laughs out loud and says, "No, because that's the other thing you do when you are upset."

"So what do you want to do?"

"I want to sit right here and listen to you tell me what's wrong."

"All right," Kevin says, and takes a big breath. "My co-worker and I got into a big fight, and the supervisor threatened to let me go," Kevin says.

"What happened?"

"It all started when we brought up the B2B thing." "So it was a political disagreement. You guys have those all the time."

"No, this was different for some reason. They were actually saying they think it was a good idea for African Americans to have their own country."

Michele sits back in the chair and looks at Kevin strangely. "And what was your response?"

"I told them they were racists and they were showing their true colors."

"Did you allow them a chance to explain themselves?" Michele asks.

"Yeah, and every time they opened up their racist mouths they proved I was right. I knew it was only a matter of time."

"Kevin I can't speak for them, but I don't see anything wrong with African Americans having their own country," Michele says.

"What, you too!" Kevin exclaims as he rises from the chair.

"Kevin, I'm sorry but I don't see that as being racist. If African Americans contributed to this Nation in many ways, I don't see why they can't get a place of their own and contribute on an international level as well."

"Which is translated, 'Now that you help build this country, you can leave now. Your services are no longer needed'," Kevin says.

"No, Kevin *you* are racist if that is how you are thinking. That makes you racist, not us," Michele says.

"'Us'? Who is 'Us'? I thought it was you and me," Kevin accuses. "I don't believe in the B2B gospel this Mr. Jackson is preaching, but one thing's for sure, it's bringing out everybody's true colors," Kevin mutters, then opens the door and walks out.

Michele runs after him, "Kevin, Kevin stopping running all the time!"

Picture 40: *You Miss Me!*

In spite of the fact Raymond pulled out of the Vice Presidential race, and declared his allegiance to the New Nation of Africa, he is still the most popular man in America. You would think people would stay clear of this man who wants to invite all Americans of African descent back to Africa to begin a new nation, but instead everyone wants a piece of him in a positive way. He is booked on talk shows, radio shows, black political events, churches, universities, conferences, seminars, workshops, and panel forums.

Raymond's staff is pushing him to the limits. They want to ride the crest of this wave all the way to departure day, even if it means no sleep for any one, not even Raymond. Raymond, his staff and security are riding in the custom-made 2024 Cadillac Truck. His staff is talking about the great success they are having, and Louise is going over today's scheduled event, which they are on their way to.

"Sir today is an easy day all you have to do is kiss babies, shake hands, take some pictures, eat, drink and be merry," Louise says.

"No speeches?" Raymond asks.

"No sir, not today," Louise replies.

"Good I can lose this tie and jacket?" Raymond says as he begins to undo his tie, take off his jacket and unbutton his shirt. "I'm really impressed how many people responded so fast as though they were waiting for this to take place," Raymond says. Raymond looks down at his feet and takes off his shoes, "Pass me my tennis shoes please," Raymond asks his security man.

"Well, sir not only were a lot of people hoping for something like this, but a lot of people were expecting it to happen sooner or later according to our information," Louise informs Raymond. As he gets himself together, even though it appears he is not paying attention, Louise knows he heard every word and is storing it in his mental files.

"Louise, did you notice how when I asked Max to pass me my tennis shoes he knew exactly where to go to get them?" Raymond asks as he ties his tennis shoes.

"Yes," Louise says.

"And do you know why he knew exactly where to go to get them?"

Louise shakes her head and says, "No, I can't say that I do."

"Would you like to know?" Raymond asks. Louise sees the big smiles on Raymond and Max's faces, and on the other security men.

"Why not sir," Louise plays along.

"I'm going to let Max tell you. Go ahead Max tell the beautiful lady why you know exactly where to go to get my shoes," Raymond says.

"Because..." Max tries to start to explain, but Raymond interrupts.

"No, No say it loud like you're black and you're proud." The other security men laugh.

Max raises his voice a little and says, "Because he beat me at one-on-one in basketball and the bet was the loser had to take off the other person's tennis shoes and carry them around for one day." Everyone in the truck laughs.

"The entire day sir?" Louise asks.

"The entire day and I'm taking on all challengers," Raymond replies.

"I want some payback today," Max says.

"You got that, all of that and more," Raymond says.

Max and Raymond had an easy, brotherly camaraderie. Max had been protecting Raymond since Raymond first began his political career. He had proven his loyalty to him in every area, protecting him at all costs. In truth, he was as much of a friend and a confidante in addition to providing excellent security.

Louise and her assistant shake their heads. "Who is this rally with?" Raymond asks.

"A center for orphans and seniors," Bryant answers.

"That's a good combination," Raymond says.

"Yes, I thought we could show the media what the New Nation has to offer the orphans and the elderly using their facility as a backdrop," Bryant replies.

"Sounds good to me," Raymond responds.

"Sir, that reminds me, we have two give-a-ways for the elderly and orphans," Bryant says.

"Just let me know when you are ready," Raymond replies.
The car slows down and everyone in the truck can see the crowd outside the window. The truck comes to a complete stop. "Let's do it," Max says into his receiver to the other security men outside. The security men open the door and Raymond and his staff step out. The media is taking pictures and the crowd is clapping and cheering. Raymond is waving and shaking hands with a big grin. Raymond understands he has a lot to do in a little bit of time. They would like for him to be there all day and night, but Raymond knows how to get in and out and yet advance the purpose he came there for. He has this timed down to the second and if everything goes as planned he will be out before five.

As far as working a crowd is concerned Raymond is a master at work. Raymond's first stop is the babies; he spends time holding them and kissing them and even feeding a couple of them. Then he moves to the elderly women who are playing checkers. He teams up with another elderly lady to play Spades even though the other team beat the pants off of them. Then Raymond takes it to the baseball diamond where the girls are playing against the boys ranging in ages 5 to 7. Raymond serves as the friendly umpire. That must have worked up a good appetite, because he eats a big plate of barbecue. He has barbecue sauce all over his face and fingers, and the children are laughing at his messiness.

Then Raymond gives his food time to digest as he plays the elderly men in a game of Chess. After winning and losing a few games Louise tells him it would be a good time to present the give-a-ways. So Raymond goes to the stage to uncover the replica of the center, and instead he gives away all expenses paid trips to Africa to anyone who wants to live in the New Nation. There is only one more thing to do then he can exit stage right and call it a day. He must take a group picture with the residents with the replica of the center.

Now it is time for him to wrap it up, or so he thought. "Sir there is a basketball court right over there. I think it would be great publicity if you and Max bring your rivalry here. The teenage orphans would love it," Bryant says. As bad as he wants to leave, as much as he wants to keep his intended schedule, Bryant must have discovered Raymond's kryptonite, which was basketball. Raymond couldn't resist a beautiful, smart lady or basketball, and now that he was a one-woman man, basketball was getting his attention more than ever.

"Alright one game," Raymond says.

"Good I already asked Max and he said he's on if you are," Bryant says. Bryant gets the microphone and says, "Ladies and gentlemen, Mr. Jackson and his Chief of Security, Mr. Maxwell Price have a friendly rival going on. They would like to finish this great day with a competitive game of one-on-one basketball." The crowd whistles, claps and cheers. "So everyone head for the court," Bryant shouts.

The media couldn't get to the court fast enough to get positioned for the best pictures. Raymond walks over with his staff. "Sir we have a long day tomorrow, I think you should get some rest," Louise says.

"This won't take long at all, ten minutes tops," Raymond boasts. Max is already on the court when Raymond walks on, he throws Raymond the ball hard, expecting to catch him off guard, but Raymond deftly catches the ball.

"Oh you are ready today?" Max notices.

"Everyday and twice on Sundays," Raymond says.

"Man that's nice, but I hate to do this to you in front of your fans and all," Max says.

"Stop all the trash talking and take this check," Raymond says giving Max the ball. Max passes the ball back, Raymond doesn't move, but right from the top of the basketball court he shoots all net and the crowd goes wild.

"That was good, but you caught me not looking," Max says.

"Well, maybe you can look at this," Raymond says and shoots again from the top of the basketball court and hits it again. The crowd is loving it.

"Man you are hot today, don't miss and that's all I have to say," Max says.

"Oh I'm not planning on it," Raymond says as he fakes the shot from the top of the basketball court and dribbles, leaving Max behind while going for the easy lay up.

"BAM, BAM," two gunshots are heard. One elderly man is hit everyone else begins to duck, scream, yell and run in every direction. Raymond's security grabs him, and forms a human shield while rushing him to the truck and pushes him in.

"Go, go, go!" Max yells at the driver and the truck pulls off. "Check him! Check him!" Max says to his security team as he looks out the window to make sure they are not being followed. The team lay Raymond across the seat and quickly check him from head-to-toe.

"Turn him over," one security says to the other. They turn Raymond over face down, but don't find a scratch.

"He's OK, he all right," one of the security men says.

"Are you sure?" Max shouts.

"Yes, 100%, Raymond is completely fine," the security man responds.

Raymond turns over and sits up; he can't believe what just happened. "What just... Did someone try to...? Give me your gun," Raymond says to his security man.

"Sir," the security man responds.

"Give me your gun and turn this truck around," Raymond says with a crazed look in his eyes. The security man doesn't know what to do, he doesn't want to disobey a direct order from his employer, but he doesn't want to put the man he is supposed to keep safe in danger.

"What?" the security man says as he looks at his supervisor, Max.

Raymond raises his voice so loud it could have shattered the windows if they weren't bulletproof. "I said give me your gun and turn this car around right now."

"Sir, sir you're not a gang banger, you're a politician," Max says quietly and firmly. Raymond pauses for second, looks around as though he was coming out of a trance and then laid back and began to stare out the window. "It's alright sir, we are going to get you checked out and then take you home," Max says.

In all of his time in politics Raymond had never been caught in a scandal and never was the target of an assassination attempt. His security was only for crowd control and a barrier against lunatics. Now it's time for Max and the team to put on the bulletproof vests and hope for the best, but look for the worst. Raymond never thought in a million years someone would try to kill him. He barely escaped prison only to get shot at. What in the world could be next? Raymond was more upset than anything, and if they would have given him that gun he would have went back there and showed somebody he wasn't the one they were looking for, and if they thought he was, well they still had the wrong one. The only problem was who he would be gunning for? Whoever shot at him had the advantage right now, because they knew who their target was, but he didn't have a clue as to who to shoot.

Picture 41: *Face Off*

Overnight Raymond has moved from the most loved and popular man in America to the Most Wanted Dead man in America. Who would have Raymond on their Most Wanted Dead list? The FBI, CIA, Secret Service, and Interpol, just to name a few of the better known mainstream organizations. Similar to the way everyone knew Raymond was the reason John Newton would get into the White House, but yet no one said anything. Everybody knew these organizations had a good reason to put a couple of bullets in Raymond's head, but kept all thoughts to themselves.

No one has any idea of how much danger Raymond is in right now at this level of politics, and the higher his profile becomes, the more vulnerable he is to anyone who feels they have a right to take a piece of him.

No one knows this better than Nicky. She has been in the political world since she was a little girl. Her father was the top aide of a congresswoman, and he told her many horror stories he encountered before he retired. This is what gave Nicky the courage to go to Raymond's house to share her fears with Diamond.

Nicky knocks on the door and the maid answers it, "Is Mrs. Jackson expecting you?"

"No, but this is an emergency concerning her husband, Mr. Raymond Jackson," Nicky says.

"Come in please." The maid escorts Nicky into the den where Diamond is sitting in a chair with a book in her hand.

"Please come in," Diamond says as she gracefully stands to greet Nicky with a handshake. "Have a seat. May I get you anything to drink?" Diamond says.

"No, I will not be staying long, I only came to give you a message about…" Nicky pauses.

Diamond interrupts, "A message from whom? You look troubled. Are you OK?"

"Yes, I mean no," Nicky says sounding confused. She pauses and takes a deep breath. "Let me start over, my name is…"

Diamond interrupts once again, "I know your name Ms. Jones. Now you're being disrespectful and playing me for the fool. I know you like you know me. We are almost family; you have been my husband's mistress for the last five years and you want to introduce yourself to me? Who do you think I am?"

Diamond asks then sits down crosses her legs, smiles and continues. "I may know you better than you know me. I know where you two met. I know your shade of lipstick and your taste in perfume. I know about L.A. and the trip you both took to celebrate your 25th birthday, let me see am I forgetting anything. Oh yeah, I even know about the three abortions," Diamond says sarcastically.

"I didn't come here to argue with you Mrs. Jackson."

"Then why exactly are you here? I thought Raymond's Godfather made arrangements for you not to see Raymond or talk to him again."

"That's why I'm talking to you about this"

"About what Ms. Jones? You haven't said anything since you've been here. Please state your business," Diamond says.

Nicky pauses again and takes another deep breath. She is obviously nervous and for two reasons. First, because she has never been this close to Diamond and she is not sure if she will be justifiably assaulted. Second, she was standing in the house talking to the wife whose husband she is still very much in love with and she is afraid of saying something that will give that secret away.

"I heard about the assassination attempt. You have to stop Raymond from doing whatever he is doing because..." Nicky is saying when Diamond gives off a derisive laughter that fills the room. "I don't think this is funny at all, they are going to kill him," Nicky says in a soft voice.

"You know Raymond, when he makes up his mind there is nothing that can stop him. Besides he will be alright," Diamond says.

Tears begin to swell up in Nicky's eyes. "He will not be alright. You don't know these people. They will kill Raymond right in your face and then send you flowers the same day," Nicky says.

"You've got some nerve coming in here crying and telling me what to do with my husband," Diamond says.

"If you really love him you will make him stop."

"Stop acting like you know what's best for him. What you two had is over and you must move on. There are plenty of political pimps that are looking for a political ho," Diamond says.

"I deserve everything you are saying right now, and I'll take all of that and more if it means saving your husband's life."

Diamond laughs again, "Oh he's my husband now? Why wasn't he..."

Nicky interrupts Diamond this time, "You've got this all messed up, I don't care about us or the relationship. I don't care if I ever see Raymond again. I'm only concerned about saving his life," Nicky says. Nicky still loved Raymond, with all of her heart; he was the only person she gave herself to totally; mind, body and soul. And this is the reason she got the nerve to ask Diamond to convince him to pull out of the B2B campaign all together. Yes, she lied about not caring about seeing him again, but she felt she had to lie to save his life, and that was the whole truth of the matter.

Diamond rose up from her seat and said, "Listen 'Ms. Concerned', I'm going to tell you something I've been wanting to tell you for years: get out of my life, get out of my family's life, and leave us alone. Live or die Raymond will be with me and I with him. I've won and you've lost. Do you get it?" Diamond says.

Nicky walks towards Diamond and says, "You don't even love him do you?"

"The only reason I won't slap the taste out of your dirty mouth is because I have too much class, but if I ever see you near my husband again it's going to take a little more than class to keep me off of you," Diamond warns.

"You're fighting the wrong person Diamond. Granted you should have fought me last year or even the first time you heard about Raymond and me, but it's too late for all of that. Can't you see it's not about winning or losing, because if these people have their way, we'll both lose in the end," Nicky says.

Diamond reaches in her suit pocket and presses a button on a remote signaler. "Don't you get it girl, we never had him in the first place. Something bigger than both of us had him and we were only going along for the ride. The only difference between you and me is, I know when and where to get off, and you don't. But I'm going to help you. This is your stop darling."

The maid immediately enters. "Ms. Elizabeth, would you show our guest to the door please? Thank you," Diamond says. Both of the ladies leave the room, Diamond in one direction and Nicky in the other.

Picture 42: *U Can't Die Now!*

Raymond is operating in a whole new world, full of new ideas, new outlooks and oppositions, new rewards and repercussions, new pains and problems, new conditions and contradictions. All of this comes by way of a new promise made to give African Americans a new way of life in the New Nation of Africa. We are always looking for new things, but very seldom think about all the new responsibilities that come with them. This is the very new price Raymond must pay if he is going to achieve such a monumental task. Now Raymond has a good idea of what all the great African American forefathers and foremothers, activists, and civil rights leaders learned as they discharged their duties. They must have learned the importance of staying focused on the purpose regardless of what they faced, i.e., cross burnings, church bombings, KKK attacks, lynching, children dying and other inhumane atrocities. They still stayed focused on their purpose. Let's face it Raymond is not like the men and women of old Martin Luther King, Jr., Frederick Douglas, Malcolm X, Thurgood Marshall, Clarence Mitchell, Andrew Young, Harriet Tubman, Rosa Parks, Yvonne B. Burke, Shirley Chisholm, Constance Baker Motley, Patricia Harris or Amayla Kearse. Raymond is the best thing that has happened to American politics in a long time, and the best thing that has happened to African American politics in a very long time, but he has a long way to go to live up to those great men and women. If his Godfather has his way, he will learn what it means to be them, if not in pattern in principles. I'm sure his Godfather senses Raymond must be feeling the pressure of fulfilling his destiny right now. He must be going through what all the great leaders, saints and martyrs felt at one time or another, wanting to just leave everything behind and go back to his convenient, comfortable, glitzy and glamorous life in politics, the way he used to know it. Politics without assassination attempts on his character and life. His Godfather feels an urgent need to speak with him in light of the recent tragic events. So he arranges to meet Raymond at a special place.

Mr. Goodson and his top aide are entering the graveyard early in the morning. His assistant is pushing him in his wheelchair. It had stopped raining about three hours ago, but the clouds are keeping a little moisture in the air.

Mr. Goodson has a lap full of roses. "It sure is a nice morning," Irvin, his assistant says.

"It's a good morning to be alive," Mr. Goodson replies. They stop at a gravesite. Irvin cleans off the tombstone, and they continue to move on. They go a few steps,

"I believe we have one sir," Irvin says. They stop at a tombstone that reads, "Michael Smith 1999-2001." Irvin cleans off the site.

"What do you think?" Mr. Goodson asks.

"I believe a doctor, three kids, enjoyed hiking and poems," Irvin says. Mr. Goodson smiles, shakes his head yes and then hands his assistant a rose to place on the tombstone. They continue to move down the path looking at tombstones as they go.

Raymond and his security walk up to where his Godfather and Irvin are. "Good morning sir," Raymond says.

"Good morning Raymond. I see you got my message," his Godfather says.

"Yes, you said it was urgent that I meet you here," Raymond said.

"How are you doing son?" his Godfather asks.

"I'm good sir," Raymond answers. Mr. Goodson points at a gravesite and Irvin stops. "I didn't know you had family here sir," Raymond says.

"I don't," his Godfather replies.

Then why are we here?" Raymond asks as he watches Irvin clean off a tombstone.

"I come here once a week to visit the place where I must come one day. It helps me appreciate life and it prepares me for the transition," his Godfather says.

"What do you think sir?" the assistant asks. The tombstone reads, "Little Kimberly Smart, 2004-2006."

"Well, a physiology teacher at Howard University, one little girl, loves Chinese food and likes slow dancing," his Godfather says.

"I like her," Irvin says. Mr. Goodson hands Irvin a rose and he places it on Kimberly's gravesite. "Push me for a while Raymond," his Godfather says. Raymond gets behind his Godfather's chair and begins to push him down the path as they talk.

"When I heard about the incident the other day I knew I had to talk with you. I want you to be clear of some things. Don't ever be afraid of passing on to the next level. One of my teachers taught me that once you know your purpose and destiny you can never pass before fulfilling your purpose and reaching your destiny. Now death, on the other hand, you should fear, because death is dying before you fulfill your purpose and reach your destiny. Another reason I come here is to put roses on the graves of little men and women who never got a change to be introduced to their purpose or destiny. I don't feel sorry for them. I celebrate them by envisioning what they could have been if they had lived long enough to know their purpose. On the other hand Raymond there are a lot of men and women in this graveyard who died old, but never discovered or tapped into their purpose. Now those I feel sorry for. My teacher once said the richest place in the world is the graveyard, because the soil contains the wealth of the unwritten books, songs that haven't been sung, business plans and great ideas that have been buried forever with men and women who never discovered or fulfilled their purpose. The reason they missed you, and the reason you are still here is because you found your purpose and you can't die until it's fulfilled. Do you understand?" his Godfather asks.

"Yes sir I do," Raymond replies.

Irvin walks in front of them and stops at a gravesite where the tombstone reads, "Timothy Clark, 1968-1970." Irvin cleans it off. "What do you think Raymond?" Irvin asks.

Raymond looks at the grave for a minute and then says, "A corporate leader, liked fishing and fine wine."

"Why not?" his Godfather responds. Raymond begins to push his Godfather through the path of the sea of tombstones. "Yeah, a good morning to be alive," his Godfather says.

Picture 43: *Political Emotions*

The B2B Tour has been very successful in spite of the assassination attempt on Raymond's life. Raymond is at a point in this project that no matter what happens to him, good or bad, he knows his efforts will help advance the project. Many people are seeing Raymond in a different light than when he was running for Vice President: instead of seeing him as another American politician, he is being looked upon as the founder of a nation. To many young people he is perceived as that cool, crazy, or whatever word you want to use that describes someone doing something that has never been done before. Still there are mixed feelings that produce mixed messages given by people who have mixed ideas of what this all means.

At Morehouse College Professor Tiron DuBois has been using Raymond's career as a case study in his political science class. He wants students (some of whom are future politicians in one way one another), to analyze their ideas in relative to and apart from their emotional outlook of the B2B New Nation of Africa project.

"Good morning class. We have a lot of ground to cover this morning," Professor DuBois says.

"I have been looking forward to our class today, in light of our Mr. Jackson's decision to decline a sure-win for Vice Presidency and opt to be a founder of the New Nation of Africa," Tim says.

"That's right the New Nation of Africa," Professor DuBois says. He walks over and pulls down a map of Africa in front of the board. "I'm sure you have heard something about all of this, unless you are dead, because you can't go anywhere these days without someone saying something or seeing something about it."

"I'm tired of it," a female student says.

"Well, that is what we are going to talk about today. How do you feel about it? What is your take, and what are your questions, if you have any?" the Professor says.

Lena quickly raises her hand but Professor DuBois says, "I'm going to get you girl, but I want to give Scott the honor of speaking first, seeing as though he had his political wish come true.

It appears there is a political fairy that granted your wish to have someone you thought was a Tom and a token to turn out to be the very one who would start a Nation for Americans of African descendants. So I want to say congratulations to you," Professor DuBois says as he claps his hands and the class follows suit.

"It sounds good and all, but I'm watching and waiting," Scott says casually.

"I would think you would be jumping up and down, the way you were preaching about how we need our own Nation," Lena says.

"You can't expect a man to be running out going to get his passport, ready to change his citizenship because somebody says he is starting a Nation like he is opening a barbershop or something," Scott says in his defense, causing some of the students to laugh while others didn't think anything was funny.

"Whether people believe it or not that is exactly what is happening right at this very moment. People all over this country are changing their citizenship to go to the New Nation of Africa," says James.

"Of Africa," the Professor says.

"That's crazy because they don't know if it's true or not. I mean I know the website lets you see the country and all, but still…" Scott says, his trailing statement expressing his doubt.

"How many of you checked out the website?" the Professor asks. Most of the students raise their hands.

"All I hear are haters in here, but I bet if the white man told you all to go to the middle of nowhere, you all would get a ticket, cap and T-shirt," Tim says. Tim's classmates immediately began to boo him.

"Well, Tim it seems like Mr. Jackson has your citizenship," the Professor says.

"I'm thinking about it, if I can transfer my school credits and find a half way decent job, why not?"

"Don't let your emotions make you do something you will regret in the future. Make sure you think this through. A lot of people are going off of the emotions of anger and bitterness of what they feel this country has done and gotten away with in the past.

Sometimes when you act out of emotion, when the emotion subsides, you sometimes regret your actions," the Professor says.

"What I have been thinking the most is Raymond wasn't good enough to be the President of this country even though everyone knew he was more qualified than his presidential candidate running mate. But he was good enough to be Vice President, and now that he is starting his own Nation people are saying he is not good enough to be leader of a country. Maybe this is fate putting him where he should have been in the first place," Tim says.

"That is an excellent spiritual and political analysis Tim," the Professor says and then begins to pass out a book on the life of Marcus Garvey. "Class in light of this turn of political events we are going to study a man named Marcus Garvey. We might discover that Mr. Jackson is not the only one who had such an idea of Americans of African descent moving back to Africa. One thing you must keep in mind about politics -- or anything for that matter -- seasons come and seasons go and seasons come again. History has a way of repeating itself. Sometimes people are not ready to handle great ideas, so I believe the same great idea will come back to revisit another generation who will embrace it and carry it into destiny," the Professor says as he opens the textbook. "Who wants to read the introduction for me?" the Professor asks.

Picture 44: *Family Feud*

Everything his Godfather told Raymond about death and purpose has been playing over again in his head. Since the assassination attempt he has been reading his bible more, and has been thinking about what life after death is going to be like. He never gave it much thought before; he had been so busy trying to find the true meaning of life, he never gave the true meaning of death a second thought until now. He didn't want the assassination attempt to make him so paranoid that he couldn't finish the work he started, and finish with the same passion he started with or greater. He would not be intimidated by evil forces trying to hinder his progress, even if it means beefing up his security. He will not be stopped, especially at this time in the project.

Raymond is scheduled to have one of the most important meetings in his career -- a Town Hall Meeting with most of the influential African American leaders. This meeting is to provide answers to many of the leaders who deserve the respect to be consulted on this issue. Raymond has already made a good impression on the African American community as a whole. He is also pleased that President Lyman endorses this move and recognizes the New Nation as a sovereign state. With the President's endorsement there is not much anyone can say about it, even if it was politically motivated.

Raymond's staff already knows the importance of this meeting and Raymond is prepared to give answers. He is tired and emotionally drained, but this must be well executed. Raymond also understands some of the hardest people to convince of the merit of your idea are your own colleagues. These are people who have the same degrees you have, the same influence you have, the same material wealth you have, the same political struggles you have and the same stubbornness you have. This is the time for him to be the best. More than ever he must be prepared to give the right answers to everyone.

The Town Hall Meeting is being held at Morehouse University. Many African Americans have packed the university auditorium to hear Raymond's remarks. There are many African American groups and organizations who heard Raymond speak during the B2B Tour, they were so impressed with him they wanted to hear him again. Some packed the auditorium to ask questions, while others are there to support their organization's leader on the dais.

Bryant Walker is presiding over the Town Hall Meeting and he brings the meeting to order as he says to the audience. "We are here in wonderful Atlanta, Georgia the resting place of the great Martin Luther King, Jr. This is indeed a great backdrop for the great men and women we have here tonight. It's great to be here and it's a great day. Allow me to introduce our panel to you." Walker proceeds to introduce the august persons representing the wide spectrum of the finest African American organizations. "Thank you all for coming," Walker says. "In the center of the stage we have the man we all have come to talk to or talk about, Mr. Raymond Jackson." As has become customary, the crowd gives Raymond a standing ovation. "Well, it is obvious why we are all here. This Town Hall Meeting was called to see where the African American leaders stand with the B2B move Mr. Jackson is encouraging to the New Nation of Africa. Our format will be basic. I'm going to save my questions until later. Right now I want to give our distinguished guests a chance to make a comment and ask one question that Mr. Jackson must respond to. We are going to start with the representative of the nation of Islam," Walker says.

"Thank you Mr. Walker. Mr. Jackson I want to congratulate you on taking a move that was necessary and overdue. I commend you for your courage and for taking the challenge many have only spoken about, but never had the courage to complete. You are a credit to the African American Community," the representative of the Nation of Islam says. The audience applauds. "The only question I have is in reference to the restitution. As you know this country has promised each former slave 40 acres and a mule. Do you feel we should encourage the government to give us what they didn't give our ancestors before we leave? I believe this is not only politically correct, but it is biblically correct, because the Bible states when the children of Israel made their exodus out of Egypt they left with great substances, substances their captors had given them on the way out. Shouldn't we be entitled to leave that exact way?" the representative for the Nation of Islam asks.

"Mr. Jackson what do you have to say to that?" Walker asks.

"First, thank you for your compliment. It's only by the power of God I am able to fulfill such a great task. In response to your question I don't believe we should be waiting for anyone to give us restitution for two reasons. First, if they haven't given us 40 acres in a mule by now, my educated guess is they are not going to give it to us and we will find ourselves being late for our date with destiny by prolonging a move waiting for such restitution. Secondly, I don't believe this country has enough money to give us to compensate for the many great men and women we lost in the struggles for our freedom and civil rights," Raymond says. The audience applauds. Raymond continues, "See I was taught sir as a little boy, that man handles restitution and it can be withheld for a long period of time or indefinitely, but on the other hand it's God who deals with restoration and He gives that when the time is right. I believe this is what the move is all about, God restoring us back to a place where we can receive all the blessings He has for us on a universal and global level." The audience gives him a great applause.

"Next please," Walker says.

"Thank you, Mr. Jackson I too believe you are doing a very courageous act and you should be commended for such a great demonstration of organization, and for political and corporate efforts that speak of brilliance that is ahead your time. The only question I have is what role does the black woman play in this New Nation?" the representative of the Minority Women Organization asks.

"Thank you for your compliment madam. On our website we have information that gives you the many programs that will assist single mothers to succeed at a very fast pace. We have funds that will help them relocate to the New Nation and we also have other business programs that will help businesswomen make contacts all over the world. The New Nation wants women to know they are the nourishers of the country. We want to grow from the knowledge they learned from the women's liberation movement and the civil rights movement. I believe the greatest thing the New Nation can offer is a new identity for minority women. That is, you will no longer be identified as minority women and in the New Nation, therefore you no longer have two strikes against you. Anyplace that helps you move towards a better idea is a place I believe you should want to be." Once again the audience all applauds heartily. Raymond's staff is standing on the side of the stage with big smiles on their faces. They are amazed and proud of the answers Raymond is giving to these expert leaders.

"We will have the representative from the NAACP next," Walker says as he points to him.

"Thank you Mr. Walker. First, I would like to say I don't have any compliments because I don't believe this is a good idea and it will never be a good idea," he says.

"Boo, Boo, Boo," the crowd begins to shout.

"Please ladies and gentlemen do not boo any of our guests. Everyone is entitled to his or her opinion. Please be considerate. Sir you may finish," Walker interjects.

"Thank you. As I was saying, I don't think this move is a good idea because of the backlash the African American Community is going through in the workplace, the schools and even the homes. Not only that, but the aftermath of 911 makes us targeted as likely terrorists. This is not a good time for this move," the representative from the NAACP states.

Raymond replies, "Sir as you know from the history of the NAACP all advancement of colored people has had a backlash, and this should not be any different. This is true not just for us, but for anyone who wants to progress into territory where they have never been before. Also, America knows we are not terrorists, we are her sons and daughters. This is a very peaceful mature political move into another chapter of African American History. Sometimes sir, people don't want you to start a new chapter, because they know it means the ending and closing of an old chapter, if you know what I mean," Raymond says, and the crowd claps and laughs at the same time.

Louise stands with her arms folded on the side of the stage smiling broadly, shaking her head in amazement at Raymond's powers of persuasion and reasoning. At first she wondered if Mr. Goodson was reading more into Raymond than what was really there. She even at one point thought that he was overrated, until now. But she acknowledges he is at his mentally sharpest out on stage, because she knows how many cities he's been to, how many talk shows, how many radio shows, how late he has been getting to sleep, how many times he missed Diamond's calls, how many speeches he's given, how many questions he had to answer in a fresh way. She knows how the assassination attempt rattled him to his core; he never really had time to get himself together and regroup. So she knows he is dead tired on his feet, but yet still sharp on his toes. She no longer thought of him as being overrated; he was becoming underrated each time she heard him speak.

"United Black Church, your turn sir," Walker indicates.

"I believe you are doing an outstanding work and our prayers are with you and your family. My question is very brief and to the point. "Where does the African American Church fit in your plan?" he asks.

"As you know my father is a pastor of one of the biggest churches in the southeast, and the way I see it is this is a golden opportunity for the African American Church to go to all nations as Christ commanded. This move will give you an international pulpit to spread the Good News to other nations, starting in Africa. There are a lot of churches that already do a lot of missionary work in Africa; so now they will only be moving closer to their work. I see this as a great move of progress for every African American Church," Raymond says. The audience applauds.

The NAACP representative gets up and hollers out, "This is ridiculous, this is not going to work and we should not be involved in such a thing."

"Sir, sir would you please sit down," Mr. Walker shouts.

"Boo," the audience shouts.

"No, I will not sit down. This is not right," the NAACP representative says. Someone from the crowd throws something on stage. The audience in the first three rows begin to push one another and make a big commotion. The people on the stage are trying to get the representative from the NAACP to sit down. Someone else from the crowd throws another object on the stage almost hitting Raymond. Raymond's security runs out on the stage, grabs him and rushes him out of the building.

"Where are you taking him, he is not finished," Louise says to Max.

"Yes he is, they are getting crazy in there."

"No, wait they are going to calm down."

"No, put him in the car," Max tells his men, then stops Louise from following them by grabbing her arm and saying, "Isn't it enough that we almost got him shot, you want him to get trampled over in an uncontrollable Town Hall Meeting?

"You are overstepping your boundaries here Mr. Price, remember you work for me," Louise says.

"I may work for you, but my job is to protect Mr. Jackson from anything close to what happened the other day. Call me overprotective right now, but I would rather be called that, than to be called to say some good words about him in a church full of his family and friends dressed in black," Max says.

"OK I understand your point. Can you let go of my arm now?" Louise says.

"Oh I'm sorry, I was looking into your lovely eyes and I forgot I had you by the arm," Max replies, moving instantly from defensiveness to charm mode.

"Is this your way of coming on to me, Mr. Max? If so I must teach you some subtler techniques," Louise smiles, showing dimples on her face.

"Now that Mr. Jackson is safe do you want to get something to eat?" Max asks.

"Now isn't that much better than grabbing a lady by the arm? Sure I would love to get something to eat with you," Louise coos.

Picture 45: *Mailman*

Raymond's father Bishop A.L. Jackson of the New Direction Church has one of the biggest congregations in Atlanta. He taught Raymond, along with his congregation, the importance of knowing one's purpose and fulfilling it. He oftentimes preached that it's not your purpose, but the Lord's purpose for your life that you should be attentive to.

Right now he couldn't be happier with Raymond because he knows for sure Raymond is fulfilling the Lord's purpose for his life. The love they had for each other is something you would see in the movies, when the father wants the best for the son and the son wants to please the father. Raymond sought to please his father all of his life, and now that he had accepted the total plan for his life Bishop Jackson couldn't be more pleased with him.

The first time Mr. Goodson introduced the plan to Bishop Jackson Raymond wasn't even born. Pastor Jackson was a young minister on fire, teaching and preaching all over Atlanta. He had only been married a year when Paul Goodson told him the entire plan, from the promise, to his son running for Vice President, to becoming a founder of the New Nation. Not once did Bishop Jackson deny or doubt the ability of these events to come to pass, not one time. He didn't doubt, but continued to grow spiritually as he became one of the most powerful pastors in the religious community. He and his wife, Julia have experienced peace and prosperity during the 50 years they've been together. Their son and daughter, Cristal, both have successful lives and Raymond is doing exactly what he is supposed to be doing right now. That explains why Bishop Jackson was so confident in Raymond giving up the Vice Presidency, because he was told by Mr. Goodson that all these things would take place, before they did, and they came to pass exactly the way he said they would.

Bishop Jackson is coming out of Sunday church service, going about his usual routine, shaking hands, saying goodbye to his congregation, and offering benedictions as his aide escorts him to his car. As he is about to enter the car, a truck drives alongside. The driver lowers the tinted window, points a gun, and snarls "Give

Raymond this message for me," as he fires six shots into Bishop Jackson body. The truck speeds off. Women are screaming, babies are crying, Bishop Jackson's aide manages to catch him before he hits the ground.

"Call the ambulance and police," the aide shouts. Those nearby take out their cell phones and make the call.

⚐ ⚐ ⚐

Raymond walks to the nurse's station with his security detail following closely behind him. "I'm looking for the Jackson family," Raymond says. The nurse directs him down the hall. Raymond and his security move fast down the hallway where he spots his mother Julia, his sister Cristal, and some members from the church. Julia and Cristal are sobbing without abandon, and you can hear some of the church members praying in whispers. Raymond kneels down beside the chair of his mother and hugs his mother and sister at the same time.

"Look what you did son," his mother says and continues to weep out of control. "You have to fix this son, you must fix this, his mother cries out.

"I will momma, I will," Raymond says as tears begin to swell up in his eyes. Raymond then gets up to find the doctor who can tell him about his father's condition. He spots one, "Sir!" Raymond calls as he approaches him. "Sir, what is the condition of my father Bishop A.L. Jackson?"

"He is still in surgery. We have the best attending to the situation. But I'm not the head doctor in charge, let me get him sir," the doctor says.

Diamond comes back from getting Julia and Cristal a cold drink, and spots Raymond talking with the doctor and notices his agitation. "Give this to Raymond's family," Diamond says as she gives the drinks to one of Raymond's security men. "Raymond let's go over here," Diamond says grabbing Raymond by the hand.

"Not now honey," Raymond says.

"Please Raymond lets just sit down in one of these rooms," Diamond encourages. She almost pulls him away and they walk into one of the private rooms in the waiting area, as his security stands outside the door. "Can I get you something to drink?" Diamond asks.

"No, I'm good," Raymond says, his face betraying his words.

"Raymond your father is strong, he is going to pull out of this you know that."

"Yeah, you're right," Raymond replies.

"Nicky came to the house the other day…" Diamond starts.

"What did she want? I thought she agreed not to…" Raymond begins to say.

"She wanted me to convince you to stop what you are doing. You two must have really had something special, she really loves you."

"Honey this is not the time or the place."

"This is the perfect time and place Raymond," Diamond says. Raymond leans back in his seat. He knows whenever Diamond calls his name after a statement it means she's got something on her mind that she must express.

"All right, what's on your mind?" Raymond asks.

"She accused me of not loving you enough to stop you from doing this to yourself. Raymond I do love you and I never stood in the way of your career, but I don't want to be in Julia's shoes, in the waiting room praying that my husband will not die," Diamond says.

"Baby, I'm too far in now. I couldn't pull out even if I wanted to," Raymond says.

"At least try to understand how I feel and maybe you can come up with another plan or something," Diamond replies.

"There is no other way. I must face whatever comes head on."

Diamond leans back in the chair and puts a smile on her face. "I told her no one can stop you when your mind is made up, but she insisted I try to reason with you. You know what Raymond, for the first time I was hoping she knew you better than I did."

A horrifying scream is heard outside the room. Raymond rushes out the room and runs towards his mother and sister. The doctor has just told them Bishop Jackson has passed away. Everyone is crying uncontrollably. Raymond runs to hug his mother and sister, trying to be strong for them, but hearing them cry is getting the best of him. Then he looks down the hall at Diamond and their eyes meet. She begins to cry. He knows exactly what she is thinking.

⚐ ⚐ ⚐

The choir is singing. ♪*My soul worships you, my soul exalts your name, my lips sing your praise and my feet will walk in your righteous way*♪. The choir consists of gospel artists and celebrities from all over the United States. Everyone has come to pay their last respects to a great servant of God.

He had built his church from a handful of members to over 100,000 parishioners. The church has rehab programs, employment centers, housing programs, adult education, and college scholarships. He made connections with celebrities, politicians, the elite as well as the everyday common person.

The list of his relationships he had developed through the years was endless, and it is clearly seen by the many people who came out today. The home going service started at 9:00 am in the morning in order for everyone whose life he touched to come and pay their last respects. Mayors, City Councilpersons and Governors felt the same as they gave citations and condolences.

It was now 10:00 pm and Raymond was sitting in between his mother and Diamond and his sister, with rows of family and friends all around them. The choir was singing Bishop Jackson's favorite song "My Soul Worships You," (composed and written by NaCo, who was leading the Georgia Mass Choir.) Many of the church members are in the spirit of worship knowing this can be the only way to be comforted in a time of such a great loss. There is another reason many had packed this church and that reason is the presence of Raymond Jackson.

While this was undoubtedly a sad occasion, but many saw this as a chance to see Raymond up close and shake his hand. Some even came hoping they would hear him speak. As a matter of fact more people than anticipated still packed the church at 10:00 pm because Raymond was scheduled as the final speaker.

The choir completed their song as Raymond approached the pulpit. He looked tired and sad, but he composed a calm face. "I want to take this time to thank everyone on behalf of my family for the cards, gifts and the kind words you had to say about my father. You have made this a joyful day despite the fact one of God's great five star generals has been called to retirement," Raymond says. The crowd claps. Raymond removes his notes from the inside of his jacket pocket. "I remember asking my father one day when we were going on a vacation," he says and then pauses. Everyone watched attentively as he tried to continue, "He said son..." Raymond says, and then stops. He puts the notes back in his pocket, as he shakes his head "No", and then says, "I can't do it, I just can't do this. Ever since I was a child I have seen my father stand behind what he called this 'Sacred desk'. I watched him preach under all types of conditions. I also witnessed him preach to a handful of members until they became hundreds of thousands, sometimes three services a Sunday," Raymond says.

"Amen," some say in the congregation.

"Sometimes he was in pain, but he still preached like nothing was wrong at all. I always wondered how he could do it," Raymond says and then pauses.

"Take your time son," one of the pastors says.

"I tried to *be* him tonight. I attempted to speak like I'm not in pain, and give you the best speech of my life, but I just can't do it. My father is a greater man than I," Raymond says as noticeable tears begin to roll down his face.

He steps from behind the pulpit, walking as he speaks into the cordless microphone. "They killed my father. These weak cowards couldn't get to me, so they killed my father, expecting to stop me from reaching my goal. But you know what?" Raymond says as he takes off his suit jacket and his security man rushes over to take it from him. "The only thing they have done is made me mad. Would you tell somebody next to you, "They done made him mad!"

The crowd begins to tell each other that statement and it appears a fresh energy came sweeping through the entire cathedral. "That's right, whenever you get setup the only way you can strike your enemy back is reverse the 'setup' and you will get 'upset' Raymond says.

The crowd claps and shouts, "Amen."

"I read a book that mentioned whenever you are fighting your enemies you should always give your enemies a way of escape, because you never want to put your enemies' backs up against the wall. Well, my friends somebody has pushed my back against the wall tonight and I'm about to come out fighting." The crowd erupts into applause. "Would you tell three people, 'Come out fighting!'

"Come out fighting, come out fighting, come out fighting," the crowd chants.

"Stop crying and come out fighting. Stop sulking and come out fighting. Stop feeling sorry for yourself and come out fighting, because the Bible says, 'He taught my finger to fight and my hand to war'. Let's come out fighting!" Raymond shouts.

The mourners are standing, some with their hands lifted up in praise, others are dancing in place, while most are watching and waiting for the next words to come out of Raymond's mouth. "This is what I believe my father would have wanted. Everyone who has not registered to move to Africa, I want you to register tonight in honor of my father. This is what he would have wanted for at least one service and I know this is what he would have wanted for you. Come down from where you are, touch my father's casket and go through those doors where my staff will help you fill out the registration form," Raymond says as he positions himself behind his father's casket. "Bring the camera right here I want to give a message to someone." The cameramen rush to get a close up with his father's casket in view.

"I have a message for the person who killed my father. I don't know who you are, or who sent you, but I got the message. What you are about to witness is what happens when you make me upset -- the very thing you tried to stop me from doing! I'm about to turn it up. Watch this," Raymond says as he lifts up both hands as the signal to the people to come and they begin coming from all directions. The choir is singing an old song, ♪*I'm a Soldier in the Army of the Lord*♪.

Thousands of people are registering for the move to Africa. It is as though they don't want Bishop Jackson's death to be in vain. Most people know someone killed him to try and discourage Raymond, so now their aim is to discourage the killer to show him regardless of what you do it is in the African American community to push on. We did it through slavery, Jim Crow, segregation and we will do it now.

Picture 46: *Who Is He?*

It was only a matter of time before the FBI and the CIA came into the picture. The only reason they hadn't made themselves known before now was because of Raymond. They had completed a background check on Raymond the first time he ran for city council and discovered he was squeakier than grandma's window during spring-cleaning. They had always kept their eyes and ears on Raymond. Aside from his affair with Nicky they always looked at him as a hard person to get any dirt on. This is why they didn't get involved with the sexual assault charges Raymond was falsely accused of. They knew he had nothing to do with that girl, because it was not his M.O. If it was they would have discovered it a long time ago and used it to their advantage by now. As far as they were concerned it was politics as usual and they were just going to sit back and let the children sling mud and play a little dirty.

But the B2B, New Nation situation had caught them totally off guard. They would have never thought in a million years Raymond, the good preacher's kid, would ever be thinking on such a large level. "There must be someone else behind this," they were thinking to themselves. "Who could have influenced Raymond to the point where he would give up the Vice Presidency of the United States and start a move to Africa?" The New Nation movement has raised all kinds of strife within the walls of the law enforcement authorities. Since 911 the FBI and the CIA relationship had not been the best because of finger pointing and lack of communication of intelligence information. The emergence of the New Nation situation made an unstable relationship even shakier. Answers must be given as to why no one saw this coming, and who is pulling the strings that caused Raymond to withdraw from the track he has been on all of these years.

A helicopter is flying suspiciously low over Bishop Jackson's burial procession. Raymond looks up and takes off his sunglasses to see if he can see the faces of any of the pilots. He thought maybe whoever is in the helicopter had something to do with his father's death. The two agents communicate to each other as they take pictures from all angles. "Nothing like a funeral to bring out everyone who is connected to each other," Agent Paul says. The agent spots Raymond and Mr. Goodson walking together in the procession. Agent Nicholas begins to take pictures of Mr. Goodson.

"I think I found the puppet master," Agent Nicholas says. He takes pictures of Raymond's new staff. Louise looks up at the helicopter just when her picture is being taken. "Oh, she is a pretty one. Raymond always gets the pretty ones. I envy him," Agent Nicholas says.

Raymond's Godfather and his staff get into the limo. After Agent Nicholas takes the pictures he begins to process the images on his laptop computer, and then e-mails them to headquarters. Agent Nicholas makes a call on his cell phone. "Sir you should have the images in a few seconds. Yes sir. OK, bye," Agent Nicholas says. He places the camera in a bag. "That's it. Let's go home," Agent Nicholas tells Agent Paul.

A picture of Mr. Goodson is transmitted via fax to an office in Langley, Virginia. A secretary removes the picture and takes it into an office, "Sir this just came in," she says.

"Thanks," Mr. Harder says. The picture came right at the time he was getting on his staff about the poor performance when it came to finding out who Mr. Goodson was. "Where was I?" Harder asked his assistant. "Oh yeah, you mean to tell me there is no data on this man right here?" Mr. Harder asks as he pins Mr. Goodson's picture on the board. "Nothing in our computer? No records of any crimes? Nothing in our international database? Nothing about where he got his passport? You are telling me this man just popped out of nowhere? What kind of special intelligence are we running here? I want you to get *something*. He has a mother and a father right? Get me something, anything to give me an idea of where he comes from in Africa, and where is he going from here. A man you can't trace is a dangerous man," Harder shouts, and then storms out of the office with his aide following closely behind him.

Harder was not upset that Raymond was in the process of completing what most great leaders only talked about, but he was upset because this totally blindsided the agency. Harder needed to let his supervisors know he was on top of his job.

STATION BREAK!!! This is an announcement from the New Nation Campaign Headquarters

IT IS NOW 110 DAYS UNTIL DEPARTURE DO YOU BELIEVE?

Log onto

www.newnation.org

to register today and see the layout of the New Nation of Africa.

Picture 47: *Give Us a Break!*

In the limo coming from the funeral everyone was very silent. No one wanted to say anything, for fear of saying the wrong thing. Diamond rested in Raymond's arms while he stared out the limo window. The staff sat next to each other and Mr. Goodson sat by himself at the far end of the stretch limo. Raymond's driver put on a gospel-jazz CD to soothe the group's spirits and prayerfully bring peace to their troubled souls.

Raymond's thoughts were spinning. Who could have done this and why? Maybe they went after his father because they couldn't get him; therefore he was responsible for his father's death. His mother's words echoed in his mind. "Look what you did son - look what you did son - look what you did son," -- this is what he constantly heard in the voice of his mind. He is hurting so badly he feels like running back to Nicky, or maybe starting something with Louise. All of Raymond's past weaknesses were trying to take advantage of his grief, causing Raymond to relapse like a drug addict who has been clean for months until a crisis occurs.

These thoughts were racing through Raymond's head when his Godfather asked, "How are you doing son?"

"I'm OK," Raymond says. "How is everyone else?" Everyone gives a suitable response in their own words.

Mr. Goodson announces, "I made arrangements for us to go to Africa. It will be a much-needed respite for a few days, and the trip will serve to introduce to you your new home. You don't have to be concerned about any clothes or toiletries. Everything will be provided for you on the highest level and you will be well taken care of. You all have done a great job and you have been through a lot in the last few months. We are at the halfway mark and it's time for us to prepare for the last part of our mission. So just as I ordered you to perform at the heights of your abilities, in the same manner I'm ordering you to relax and enjoy yourselves at my expense. Louise, would you please call the airport and tell our pilots and crew that we are on our way," Mr. Goodson says.

⚐ ⚐ ⚐

Bishop Jackson's funeral-turned-B2B registration rally and the hard work of the last six months caught up with everyone, because once they entered the jet, reclined in the comfortable, plush seats, and took off their shoes, that was all it took for them to relax with no cares in the world. Their sleep was peaceful and light. Raymond even had a chance to escape the harsh, grief-stricken words of his mother that had been nagging him. The Lord of the universe made a clear path in the sky for the New Nation jet to reach its intended destination in no time at all.

Picture 48: *This Looks Familiar*

Raymond, Diamond, his Godfather and the B2B staff are getting out of the jet and they notice the red carpet. Many leaders from other nations of Africa are there with their aides and with gifts to welcome Mr. Goodson and his companions.

"I give up one red carpet for another," Raymond says to his Godfather.

"These are just some of my close friends. I'll introduce them to you later," his Godfather says. As they walked to the waiting limo, the leaders and their aides shook their hands, kissed them and presented them with a wealth of gifts, so much so they couldn't hold all of them.

"They are very friendly aren't they?" Raymond asks.

"Forget any preconceptions you may have had about Africa. The first impression is the only impression over here," his Godfather says. Raymond and his staff are enjoying the royal treatment and inhaling its fragrance of love. Back in the states they were treated with much respect and given very professional service, but now Raymond and his staff know the difference between receiving respect and receiving love. They can feel the genuine love in the service these people are giving to them.

Bryant is smiling from ear to ear, he is used to Raymond getting the attention and the VIP treatment, but the staff usually has to fend for themselves. It appears these people are not concerned just about the star, but all who are connected to the star also should have the right to shine. In truth, Raymond is shining from the light of his Godfather's stardom in this part of the world.

Once inside the limo everyone wanted a window seat. Like little kids everyone was getting in a position themselves to look outside. Being in Africa for the first time was bringing the children out of these jaded, seen-it-all, been-there-done-that political professionals. Even though they wanted to get to their accommodations they didn't mind if the driver took the scenic route. They wanted to use this time as an unofficial tour. Mr. Goodson arranged for the driver to take the long route to the estate and even accommodated the group by acting as their personal tour guide, pointing out different sites and special points of interest of the Nation.

They were impressed with how charming, yet progressive and modern everything was. It was just like them being in America but better, cleaner, fresher, newer. "We knew the people who would be coming would be attached to the western way of life, so we created the Nation to have all the modern buildings and technology that America and other countries have. We didn't want African Americans emigrants to suffer from a culture shock," Mr. Goodson says. He was 100% right, the New Nation reflected some of America, Europe, Asia, and Australia. The New Nation reflected an international culture, but it was very stylish, laid back, conservative, light, bright, smooth, fresh and new. From the looks of it the New Nation is the very creation of Mr. Goodson because everything spoke of him. The architecture, public transit, houses, cars, schools, traffic patterns, playgrounds, colleges, parks, museums, churches, landscaping, even the waterfalls. Everything reflected style and class. Mr. Goodson knew that is how God designed everything to be. God's creations are supposed to speak of Him as the brilliant and excellent Creator. Then when man creates something it should speak of his brilliance and excellence, which is only a reflection of God's original brilliance and excellence. This process should continue throughout eternity. What Raymond, Diamond and the staff were looking at was the handy work of a person who received all of his guidance, creativity and vision from the maker of heaven and earth. Mr. Goodson was not ashamed to tell anyone that this Nation's very foundation was built on the wisdom of God and therefore it was created for his glory. And someone would have to be blind not to see the rays of his glory as the backdrop of the New Nation of Africa.

Picture 49: *It's All Yours*

It took the driver 45 minutes to arrive at the estate, a big beautiful 14-room mansion, located on approximately half an acre of vast and precious oceanfront property. When they pulled up to the estate the entire staff was waiting to greet them with a welcome similar to at the airport -- more friendly people who treated them like they knew them all of their lives, and showing them much love with hugs, kisses and more gifts. "I want Raymond's staff and security to follow the estate staff. They will escort you to your rooms and give you anything you need. They will give you a tour of the entire estate, or the entire Nation, if that is what pleases you. Don't be shy to ask for anything, please relax and enjoy this moment. Raymond and Diamond follow me," his Godfather says.

He wanted to make sure he created a relaxed environment so the staff would take their minds off of work all together. Sometimes you can get so involved with working that even when you are not working your mind is still at work, thinking of what you have to do once you get back to work. Mr. Goodson knows it is easy to pull yourself out of the work environment, but the hard part is pulling the work out of you when it's time to rest. He has witnessed many relationships that included marriage and business, fail because the partners didn't know how to take recreation time. Mr. Goodson has taught his staff, recreation is made up of two words re (which means again), and creation (which means create), so in order to continue the process of creation you must recreation; get away from a project, then come back with new and more creative ideas. This is why he is so adamant that Raymond and his staff plays just as hard as they have been working.

Raymond, Diamond and his Godfather walk about two blocks and come to the biggest mansion Diamond and Raymond have ever seen. It was a spectacular Italianate-style 20-room mansion, a rare residence that offered absolute delight in beachside living. An attractive older lady walks briskly toward them with seven staff members. "This is your mansion Raymond it comes with the position," his Godfather says.

Diamond puts her hand over her mouth and looks at Raymond and then at his Godfather. "Oh my Lord," she says.

Raymond looks at his Godfather then looks at the mansion, then looks at his Godfather again. "I've never seen a public speaker at a lost for words before," his Godfather laughs as he motions for the lady to come closer. "This is Ellen, she speaks English, as does as all of your staff, and so you don't have to be concerned about communication. Ellen is the Chief of staff, similar to a majordomo, and she will introduce you to everyone else. She will take care of all of the household duties to ensure that your home is run efficiently. She will also be like a mother to you and Diamond. She will treat you like children, children that pay the bills of course," his Godfather says and they all laugh.

"It's a pleasure to meet you," Diamond says as she extends her hand to greet Ellen.

"Mothers don't shake their children's hands; they give them big hugs," Ellen says as she puts her arms around Diamond and hugs her very tight. Diamond hasn't had a hug like that since her mother died over 10 years ago, so she hugged Ellen back and didn't want to let her go.

"Well, let's go into the house," Raymond's Godfather says very cheerfully. When they walked through the hand-carved mahogany doors they were almost awestruck by the splendid decor.

"Oh my Lord -- you've got to be joking," Diamond says.

"Now this is major," Raymond says as he surveys the entire room without moving out of one spot.

"You can get a tour of the house later. I want you to get some rest and enjoy each other and relax. I'll be back in two days to take you somewhere special," his Godfather says. Then he turns to Diamond, "Are you pleased?" he asks.

"Very much so," she says, her eyes shining.

"Good, that's what I like to hear," his Godfather says as he embraces Raymond and Diamond and walks out the door.

Picture 50: *The Secret Place*

A day before they were to go to the special place Raymond's Godfather sent him a package containing hiking clothes, boots and outdoor gear. Raymond wasn't sure at first what the items were for, but now it was clear. It seemed like they had been walking for hours since they left the driver and Raymond's security at the car. Raymond knew he was in trouble when his Godfather told them if they were not back by nightfall they could leave and come back first thing in the morning.

They had been climbing hills, mountains, and walking through vast tracts of land, all of this to get to this "special place." There may have been a short cut somewhere, but in his usual fashion, Mr. Goodson wanted to prove a point. "See son whenever you are going somewhere special there are no short cuts, no side paths. You must take the path of straight, so you will be fit and in condition to fully accept what is about to be revealed to you," his Godfather says with a twinkle in his eyes, as they move from one part of Ethiopia to the other.

They finally reached their destination after five hours. "Here we are" his Godfather says. Raymond looked at the so-called "special place" and it appeared to be a large house carved out of a rock.

"What is it?" Raymond asks.

"I'll tell you once we are inside," his Godfather says. When they entered he didn't have to tell Raymond anything as the structure and furnishings revealed its identity. The candles, rows of chairs and pulpit clearly indicated it was a church.

"Why did we have to come all the way up here to go to church, and it's not even Sunday," Raymond thought. "I hope he doesn't expect me drag Diamond up here to go to church, it's hard enough getting her to go to the 11:00 am service on Sundays at the church around the corner."

His Godfather interrupted Raymond's peevish thinking. "This is where I grew up, I went to school here," his Godfather says as he went into his hiking bag to pull out his bottle of water. "I learned how to play with my friends here, everything started from here for me. Everything has a starting point and this is where I began," his Godfather says and then sits down in the front row of the church. Raymond sits down beside him and they both drink their water, enjoying the coolness and peace that filled that place. "This is where I first believed. Do you remember when you first believed Raymond?" his Godfather asks.

"The summer of 94' in a revival at my father's church. It was good," Raymond says with a smile on his face.

"It's always good to believe, especially for the very first time, it's like you are invincible. If you believe or if someone believes in you, you can do the impossible," his Godfather says. His Godfather moved towards the pulpit and took a seat in the pastor's chair and began to look around the church. "This is the oldest church in the world," his Godfather explains.

"I read about this church and we talked much about it in Sunday school," Raymond says and then pauses as to suggest a thought just came to mind. "Oh, this is why my father was so fascinated with this place," Raymond says.

"What do you know?" his Godfather asks. "How Solomon and the Queen of Sheba had a son, and when he became king he established the way Israel worshipped the living God in his kingdom. Then when Philip the Evangelist met an Ethiopian eunuch coming from Jerusalem after attending worship, he taught him the way of Christ. So I imagine this church is a part of that specific branch of African Christianity," Raymond says.

"You prove to be a very spiritual person Raymond," his Godfather says.

"I wouldn't say that."

"I didn't say you know you are. I said you prove to be. You have proved it to me, to others, but most importantly to yourself," his Godfather says. Then he stands behind the pulpit and says, "Most spiritual people are the last people to recognize they are no longer operating in the natural. Believing in the promise is only the beginning. If you are going to complete this mission you must believe in miracles. Do you?" his Godfather asks.

"I don't know," Raymond answers.

"Raymond I am a spiritual person and most people here in Africa respect me and my family, but they think I'm crazy because I built all that you've seen. My family and I built it from nothing and they think it's for nothing. They don't believe anyone will live here and our vision and all of our time and money will have been in vain. I continue to believe in a miracle that will cause many to come from far and near to live in the New Nation," his Godfather says. He then comes down from the pulpit and walks over to Raymond and stands in front of him to say, "I want to thank you for helping to make my miracle come true. Maybe when others see the New Nation filled up with happy people living their lives to the fullest this will help them to believe in miracles."

His Godfather then pulls Raymond to his feet, looks him in the eyes and says, "Tonight, son you will create a miracle. I know Diamond can't conceive, but tonight she will conceive a son who will be the first President of the New Nation. Don't speak, you can prevent it from coming to pass by speaking doubt. Just believe my son, just like you believed in the promise. Tonight will you believe?"

Raymond shakes his head "Yes."

"I brought you here to teach you your final lesson before the departure day. The reason I chose this place is because you remind me so much of Solomon's son who was conceived in one place, but ruled a Nation in another. We both believe in each other and we both will see our miracles come into existence. Go home and teach your wife. Make this miracle happen" his Godfather instructs.

Picture 51: *Conceiving a Miracle*

The quality time Raymond and his Godfather spent together was very much needed. His Godfather came into his life abruptly, and changed and rearranged things overnight, always commanding and demanding, never suggesting or asking. Now Raymond has a better understanding of his behavior and reasoning, because these last few days he has seen a gentler, more relaxed man who really cares about people. Raymond discovered this philanthropist would literally take the shirt off of his back if you were in need of it. After their spiritual discourse in the church of Ethiopia -- the oldest church in the world -- Raymond and his Godfather made their journey back; it seemed as if they returned faster than it took them to get to the church. Raymond credited it to be the energy provided by the spiritual conversation they were having on the return trip; it was so good they lost all sense of time. Once back in the city his Godfather invites him to his mansion to clean himself up and to put on some fresh clothes. This also gave his Godfather a chance to show him pictures of his family and other precious mementos. Raymond was just as impressed with his Godfather's mansion and household management as he was with the operating structure of the New Nation.

Raymond reached outer boundary of his new estate and heard music like there was a party going on somewhere. He followed the music to the other side of the estate and he noticed his B2B staff and his new household staff dancing to a song that was playing in the CD player. When Raymond got closer Louise noticed him and said, "Come on Raymond and show us what you got."

"No you don't want me to do that," Raymond warned, but the partiers would not take no for an answer. Two of the staffers -- one male and one female -- pull him into the center of the circle and begin to dance with Raymond. Raymond refused at first, but then gives in, moving in his own funny way. He moves in front of each one of his staff members, takes them by the hand and dances with them. It appears to be more of a smooth jumping up and down then anything. Everyone begins to cheer him on, "Go Raymond, go Raymond, go

Raymond." This was indeed a wonderful sight; Raymond was completely relaxed and happy, dancing and smiling with his staff members. They had worked so hard for the last six months, that Raymond hadn't had the time to show this lighter and lighthearted side of himself. Just as his Godfather had recently opened up to him, he also felt compelled to do the same for his staff. This was also more than a time to laugh and dance; it could just as well be a victory dance for them all. All of their individual efforts had brought them to this point in the project. Millions had already registered and the majority of the campaign objectives had been covered. Many of the African American leaders and professionals had embraced the New Nation idea. Polls showed the majority of African Americans approved of the New Nation project. A lot of people are planning to leave now and others years from now, but at least they are considering the move. The only thing left to coordinate was the departure day details, and a very important meeting his Godfather scheduled to have with the international community of Africa the day before they returned to the States.

So in spite of the false accusations, the court proceedings, the assassination attempt, and his father's death, the New Nation Project was a big success. Why not dance a victory dance to let all of the forces that tried to stop them know that they hadn't given up. They have made great progress and no one could take that from them.

The others began to dance with each other and Raymond faded out of the picture to head to his new home, but something tells him to look back. As he does he notices the household staff teaching his B2B staff some of the African dances and his B2B staff teaching the New Nation citizens some African American dance moves. This was the global demonstration Raymond had been preaching all over America in living color, two different cultures of the same race meeting in the middle of the dance floor of Africa to exchange lessons in creating, celebrating and cherishing life to the fullest.

⚐ ⚐ ⚐

Raymond walks into his mansion and Ellen the Chief of staff meets him at the door. "Can I help you sir?"

"No thank you, I'm going to call it a night," Raymond

"Do you approve of the party sir?" Ellen asks.

"Yes, very much so, God knows they need it."

"I'm sorry about your father."

"Thank you for your concern. He is in a better place now," Raymond says.

"Yes sir. Your wife wanted me to ask you to come to the back of the mansion. Right through those doors and make a right," Ellen says.

"Thank you, I shouldn't need anything else tonight," Raymond says.

"Yes sir, goodnight sir."

"Goodnight...," Raymond pauses to remember her name.

"Ellen," she says and they both laugh.

"Right, Ellen," Raymond says. Raymond walks a few steps then Ellen says as though she just remembered something important to tell Mr. Jackson. "Oh sir," she says.

"Yes Ellen," Raymond answers.

"Welcome Home," Ellen says, smiling broadly.

Raymond was about to give a usual response, but paused because he realized that she was talking about Africa and not the mansion. "Thank you, it feels good to be home," Raymond says.

Ellen the mother figure and Chief of his household staff has pointed out the importance of knowing the true value of home. Raymond has accumulated a lot of material wealth for himself in his political career, he now has access to a private jet and a mansion that comes along with the position, but these "things" mean nothing compared to the feeling of being home. Somehow, without his knowledge, he had a treasure unseen that pulled him like gravity to the motherland. Ellen -- a mother figure -- welcomed Raymond back to the motherland. Could this be what every African American has been wanting, an Ellen saying to each and every one, "Welcome Home"?

Ellen wakes Raymond out of his brief reverie. "Now go, don't keep your lovely wife waiting," she says.

Picture 52: *Daring to Believe*

When Raymond reaches the back of the mansion, Diamond is lighting the last candle for their candlelight supper. "What are you up to Mrs. Jackson?" Raymond asks.

"I'm trying to surprise my husband with a romantic supper," Diamond says.

Raymond pulls his chair out and takes a seat at the table. "You did all of this?"

"Well, I can't take all of the credit, Ms. Ellen helped. She is really nice," Diamond says.

"Yeah, I think so too," Raymond says. Raymond looks around and says, "So this is our backyard. It's an entire beach."

"I know. Isn't it magnificent?" Diamond says and then comes over with a bowl of grapes and sits on his lap. She feeds him a grape and says, "I want to apologize for not believing in you from the very start. I never knew it was going to be like this," she gives him another grape and continues, "Here I was worrying about loosing the status that comes with being the wife of the first male African American Vice President, and you wanted to make me the first lady of a Nation. I am very proud to be your wife right now and everything we've been through has all been worth it, because I can see your vision, I can touch it, I can smell it, and it's beautiful," she says as she places a grape in Raymond's mouth then kisses him.

"It makes me feel good when you talk like that. Let's make a baby tonight," Raymond says.

"Why would you say something like that," Diamond stiffens as she starts to get off of Raymond's lap.

Raymond gently puts his arms around her stopping her from getting up. "I'm not making fun, I am not trying to upset you, baby," Raymond says.

"But you know I can't..." Diamond begins to say. Raymond interrupts her by placing his finger on her lips and says, "Not tonight, don't say it tonight," Raymond softly pleads.

"I don't understand Raymond."

"I don't either, but I think it's time for us to believe in a miracle," Raymond says and then kisses Diamond, but she pulls away looking for an explanation. "My Godfather showed me how far believing in a promise has gotten us, but what if we start believing in a miracle? If…" Raymond pauses, "No, not *if*, but *when* we conceive, our son he will be the first President of the New Nation of Africa," Raymond says.

"Raymond please don't talk like this. There is nothing more I want in the world than to give you a child."

"Baby can't you feel it in the air? It's the right time to believe. Look at where we are, look how far we've come in a short amount of time. It's time for us to believe in miracles."

"I never believed in one before," Diamond considers.

"And I've been in the church all my life, but I have never believed in one," Raymond says.

Diamond puts both hands on Raymond's face, looks him right in the eyes and tears trickle out of the corners of both of her eyes as she says, "I don't want to disappoint you again."

"You won't honey, because we are going to believe together, OK." Diamond shakes her head "Yes."

They begin to kiss, remove each other's clothes, and make tender love under the open sky, where a full moon and thousands of brilliant stars witnessed that they dared to believe they could conceive a miracle.

Picture 53: *What Do You Have to Offer?*

His Godfather arranged for Raymond to be introduced to the international community of Africa the day before they left for America. He scheduled it that way so he could prolong getting back to work as long as possible. A wonderful week of dancing, hiking, music, laughing, touring, boat riding, sleeping, eating by candlelight and just relaxing came to a close.

Raymond and his Godfather found themselves sitting at a big conference table with leaders of African nations, with their seconds-in-command, and top aides sitting behind them. On the table in front of them was a placard with their name, the name of their country, and their nation's flag, along with a microphone. This was not only a time for them to meet Raymond, but a time for Raymond to meet them as well.

"Let us begin our meeting by announcing your name, the name of your country and the name of the products your country produces," the chairman says. "I will begin. My name is Matunde Sassou of South Africa my products are gold, platinum and diamonds."

Each leader in turn announces his name, his country's name, and their products.

"My name is Lisimba Mbeki of Cape Verde. My product is fishing."

"Good morning. I am Lungile Bouteflika of the Republic of the Congo. My product is oil."

"My name is Lutalo Ahmad of Gabon. My products are oil, natural gas, iron and gold."

"My name is Kumi Hadj of Algeria. My products are oil and natural gas."

"My name is Kantigi Gloagbo of Angola. My products are oil, gold and diamonds."

"My name is Kimoni Mogae of Guinea- Bissau and my product is oil."

"Good day. My name is Nyamekye Abdoulaye of Nigeria. My products are oil, coal and tin."

"My name is Nkosi Mwanawasa of Egypt and my products are oil and tourism."

"My name is Ngozi Pires of Kenya. My product is tourism."

"My name is Nassor Kabila of Ghana and my products are tourism and fishing."

"My name is Minkah Obasanjo of Sudan. My product is oil."

"My name is Mopati Abidine of Libya. My products are oil, iron and steel."

"My name is Malik Qadhafi of Tunisia. My products are oil and tourism."

"My name is Bomani Guinea of Ethiopia and my product is airlines."

"My name is Abasi Santos of the Democratic Republic of Congo and my products are diamonds, gold, copper, iron and zinc."

"Good day. My name is Amari Mubarak of Zambia. My products are copper, magnesium and cobalt."

"My name is Abayomi Kufuor of Botswana. My products are diamonds, copper and nickel."

"Good morning. My name is Adjatay Bashir of Senegal. My product is fishing."

"We are here today to welcome Mr. Paul Goodson, Mr. Raymond Jackson and the New Nation to the African international community." the chairman says. The leader of Cape Verde raises his hand to be acknowledged. "Yes Mr. Mbeki," the chairman says.

"Chairman if I may interject, I believe it is only fair to the absent parties to place on record why they refuse to attend this meeting," Mr. Mbeki says.

"Yes, I will place on the record that many other nations -- and the secretary will note their names -- will not be attending because they believe Mr. Goodson should not be considered as a part of this international community. I also will go on record by saying their absence is offensive to this community, but should only be taken as an open protest to our candidate," the chairman says. The leader of Botswana raises his hand. "Yes Mr. Kufuor," the chairman acknowledges him.

"We all have known Mr. Goodson and his family and his great contributions to the welfare of our continent. He should be welcomed with open arms," Mr. Kufuor says.

"Yes Mr. Bashir," the chairman says acknowledging the hand of the leader of Senegal.

"I too would like to go on record as saying I believe the other countries' protest is an insult to everyone here, because Mr. Goodson has helped our countries in many ways, and therefore he has helped the entire continent of Africa. Now it's time for us to return the favor," Mr. Bashir says.

The young boisterous leader of Kenya has a tendency not to follow the rules of the community that dictates everyone must be acknowledged before they speak. He has ignored the rules so often that the chairman doesn't even warn him anymore. It can be perceived as a sign of weakness on their part, or a sign of strength on his. "This is exactly how our ancestors were sold into slavery -- by exchanging favors. If we are not going to repeat the same historical tragedy we must do away with these favors and stand by our principles and procedures," Mr. Pires says. Then he turns to Raymond and says, "Mr. Jackson, what do you bring to the international table?"

"According to the international law, in order to be acknowledged as a country one must have the land; we have that. One must have the people; we have over two million registered African Americans as of today, and I am sure that number has increased. And finally one must be acknowledged by another Nation, and we have on record the President of the United States giving us a complete endorsement," Raymond says proudly.

But his Godfather shakes his head in warning. He understood the negative direction in which Mr. Pires was taking the meeting.

Mr. Pires laughs. "That's how the western world invites one into the international community and that is fine for them. I'm talking about what product do you bring to the international table? See I have heard about your African American way of life Mr. Jackson, and I want you to know there is no affirmative action in our communities. There is no welfare in our communities. If you don't bring anything to the table, sir, you don't eat," Mr. Pires says.

"I told you, that when the time is right we will present our national product," Mr. Goodson confidently interjects.

"With all due respect sir," the meeting chairman says, "As much as I want to, I can not accept you into this community until the product is made known to us. This meeting is officially closed."

Raymond's Godfather stands to leave, but Raymond is still sitting there as to say "Wait a minute. What happened?" His Godfather taps him on the shoulder to signal him that it's time to go. His Godfather knew what was on Raymond's mind; he didn't get a chance to practice his silver-tongued oratory. Raymond thought he could sweet-talk the distinguished leaders into admitting the New Nation into the international community with a smile, and a promise that they would reveal the product on a later date.

The reason his Godfather didn't allow him to appeal to them is because it didn't matter what they said, there was no getting around process, procedures and politics. This was not the western world politics where the rules can be bent, broken and adjusted.

Raymond had a major reality check and it was simple, but yet profound. There were some places you can't talk your way into; you either put up or shut up. In this part of the world it is not what you say, it is what you have that really matters.

STATION BREAK!!! This is an announcement from the New Nation Campaign Headquarters

IT IS NOW 80 DAYS UNTIL DEPARTURE GOT FAITH!

Log onto
www.newnation.org
to register today and see the layout of the New Nation of Africa.

Picture 54: *Going to Another Land*

The limo arrives at the New Nation airport at five am. There was an unspoken sadness during the ride to the airport. It was like going to school after summer vacation and you must get ready for another year of work. This is how Raymond, Diamond and the staff felt, a sadness that caused them to reflect in silence on the good times they had in the last seven days.

Mr. Goodson told the driver to park and give him a few minutes before he opened the door because he wanted to have a few words. "Alright my friends this is where the fun stops and the work begins again. When we enter the jet we must focus on going to another level. We have done all we can do on this level. Now it's time to go higher. We experienced some rain the last time we were in the States, but it's time to show the spiritual evil forces that the rain helps us to grow to another level."

"Our main focus will be on departure day -- the transportation, the events and all the particulars of that day. Over two million people will be leaving to come here and I want complete order during this transition from the old nation to the New Nation. Our government administration staff here has everything in place to receive all of the new emigrants, and nothing has been overlooked. It's our job to get the people here and this is our focus from this point on. We have approximately 2 months, 3 weeks, 6 days, 23 hours, 59 minutes and 59 seconds before departure day. Louise there is a green bag in the compartment next to you. Please get it and pass out the boxes," Mr. Goodson says. Louise retrieves the bag and immediately begins to pass out the boxes to everyone in the limo as Mr. Goodson continues, "These are watches that I had a friend make for this time. These watches are like most watches, they can tell time, etc. They aren't encrusted with diamonds, gold, or silver because they will serve a greater purpose than styling and profiling. This is a departure day watch. When the alarm goes off on this watch, you and over two million people…"

Louise interrupts and says, "I received the latest numbers this morning from headquarters in America, and three million have registered," she says.

"Thank you Louise, you and over three million people should be on planes, trains, jets, and boats on your way to our Promised Land, better known as the New Nation of Africa. Once you hear this alarm go off you will have done all you were assigned to do and the departure will have gone according to the plan. Then you will have officially completed your mission. As I stated before, the administration's operations team will take over from that point. Do you understand?" Mr. Goodson asks.

Everyone nods their head and says, "Yes."

"OK, take off the watch you have on now and put on the one you just received," Mr. Goodson instructs them.

Everyone does as they have been instructed. "Push that small button on the side just before getting out of the limo. We will now pray. *Heavenly Father, the one who made a promise to Abraham, Isaac and Jacob and who has fulfilled that promise through Christ the Lord, give us the power to redeem the time and bring into existence everything you have revealed to us through the one who sits by your right hand with all authority and power. Amen.*"

"Amen," everyone says. Then they all set their watches.

⚐ ⚐ ⚐

Diamond is going to be staying back in Africa in accordance with Mr. Goodson's instructions. Mr. Goodson walks past Diamond and says, "You are greater than what you think. Always remember the Bible verse your mother made you memorize when you were a child. *"Greater is he that is in you,"* Mr. Goodson says.

Diamond looks at him strangely as she completes the verse in a mumble, *"Than he that is in the world,* I John 4:4." Mr. Goodson gives her a hug and walks to the jet leaving Diamond wondering how did he know her mother's favorite Bible verse? Not even Raymond knew that. Was her responsibility to the power in her, or the baby his Godfather told Raymond they would conceive?

Raymond walks to Diamond who is standing by the limo door. "Are you sure you don't want me to go along with you?" Diamond asks as she puts her arms around his neck.

"I wish you could, but Godfather thinks it would be better for you to wait here. Besides you will be here to witness the first generation of African Americans come to the New Nation," Raymond says. "Remember what I said, take care of our son, keep believing in miracles and I will be right back," Raymond says.

"Then we can live happily ever after?" Diamond asks.

"Happily ever after baby," Raymond says. They kiss long and passionately.

"You know you are my hero, and I love you more now than ever," Diamond says as tears begin to well in her eyes.

"Come on baby, you said..." Raymond starts to say.

"I know, I know" Diamond says as she begins to wipe the tears from her face.

"Let me get that," Raymond says and begins to kiss Diamond's tears away, then continuing to softly kiss her cheeks, nose, eyes, forehead, chin, and ears until he covers every inch of her beautiful face. Diamond stands still enjoying every kiss.

"Thank you," she says sweetly.

"Sir," the driver said looking at his watch indicating the jet was ready to take off.

"All right here I come," Raymond says and kisses Diamond one last time and then hugs her. Diamond is holding him so tight she doesn't want to let him go. Raymond can feel the love, like an electricity, coursing through their bodies. "I'll be loving you lady," Raymond says.

"I'll be loving you man," Diamond says back to him.

Raymond pulls away and walks towards the jet. Something was telling him not to look back, so he moved forward. It took all of his willpower to get to the door of the jet. If he couldn't turn around he would yell the last words out, "I'll be loving you lady," Raymond shouted as he walked without missing a step. He wondered if she heard him.

"I'll be loving you man," Raymond heard as he reached the jet door.

Picture 55: *The Seed*

Raymond boarded the jet and took a seat across from his Godfather. His staff was already busy making calls, working on their laptops, reviewing and discussing all of the necessary paperwork. Everyone stops their work for a minute as the plane takes off, but once in the air, they were right back at it again. His Godfather pulled out his book and papers for the long trip.

Raymond takes out his laptop to work on his departure speech. This would be the last speech he gives in America and he wanted it to be the best he ever delivered. Mr. Goodson puts a marker in his page, closes his book and places it on the seat next to him. "You carried yourself well yesterday," his Godfather says.

"Do you think so?" Raymond asks as he continues to type the last few sentences of his speech.

His Godfather smiles and says, "No you were outstanding, like Bryant said, you are a natural, so why do you sound so surprised?"

"My father and I had this unspoken understanding that nothing was good enough," Raymond said.

"Well, son never let anything or anyone make you underestimate yourself. Laugh it off when they do it to you, but don't do it to yourself," his Godfather says.

"Yeah you're right." Raymond sees an opening that he can use to ask the question he has been looking to ask since he met his Godfather, so he must take it now or never he feels, but he didn't want the question to be so bold-faced, so he decides to disguise it in the form of another question. "Tell me how you are so sure of yourself; how did you become so confident," Raymond says.

"Well, sometimes it's a gift, sometimes it's from experience and other times it's the process of nature," his Godfather answers.

"Which was it when you selected me? Why were you so sure I was the one?" This was Raymond's real question.

"First of all son this is not the Matrix, I'm not Morpheus and you are not Neo. You are not the one," his Godfather says. They both laugh out loud.

"I mean how were you so sure I would be the man for the job, and how did you go about picking me?"

"Raymond look around you," his Godfather says. Raymond takes a couple of seconds to look around, and sees Louise, Bryant, and the other B2B staff all busy at work. "What do you see?" his Godfather asks.

Hardworking intelligent people," Raymond says.

"That's good, but I see seeds. Everyone in this jet was handpicked before they were born, except of course, your security men. So if everyone was picked before they were born, how could I have picked them based on their own abilities or merits? The same goes for you. I knew your father when he was a young man preaching from one church to another in Atlanta, I watched him mature into a serious spiritual man with purpose, and I knew his seed would be more advanced than his generation. I knew your father could not make this happen, but he was carrying the seed, and the potential to produce what was destined to be. So it was not you, but it was the source you came from, that was the decisive factor," his Godfather says.

Raymond was astonished, looking into his Godfather eyes and listening to every word.

"It's all about giving birth to the next great generation. Always remember son, the reason a true enemy wants to kill you, is not because you've been born, but because he wants to kill what's inside of you that is about to be born," his Godfather says.

Raymond needed to hear this. He thought it was all about him, but it was about his father who gave birth to him. To hear these wise, healing words at a time when he was about to complete a great task felt good, as if his father was right there with him, sharing in every moment of glory.

⚐ ⚐ ⚐

His Godfather looked at Raymond and said abruptly, "Fasten your seat beat and tell everyone else to do so."

"What's going on?" Raymond asks.

"Don't waste time," his Godfather says as he fastens his.

"Listen everyone I need you to fasten your seat belts," Raymond yells as he fastens his seat belt. Everyone is getting into their seats and fastening their seat belts.

The stewardess comes out with a confused look on her face. "Is there a problem sir?" she asks Mr. Goodson.

"Take a seat and fasten your seat belt," he says.

"The pilot didn't say…" before the stewardess could finish her sentence the jet dropped and the stewardess hits her head on the ceiling and then hits the floor. She began yelling and holding her head as she crawled to her jump seat.

The voice of the pilot came over the loudspeaker, "This is your pilot Doug Houston, and we are experiencing a little difficulty. Everyone fasten your seatbelts until this minor problem is resolved. Thank you."

Raymond looks at his Godfather who is looking out of the window. The jet drops again knocking everything off the tables. It feels like something more serious than air pockets. Everyone looks frightened except for Mr. Goodson who is gazing calmly out of the window. The pilot's voice comes over the loudspeaker ands says, "We have a serious situation here. I need everyone to get into the emergency landing position."

The stewardess is crying and the other passengers are looking worried. All passengers begin to put on their oxygen masks and place their heads between their legs, and Raymond does the same. After a few seconds, Raymond looked up to check on his Godfather, and noticed his Godfather with no oxygen mask on, calmly reclining in his chair, almost peacefully. When Raymond notices this, he pauses, then sits up, takes off his mask and reclines in his chair. Louise notices Raymond position and she sits up, removes the oxygen mask and leans back in her chair resting her head. Bryant, sitting next to her was wondering what she was doing until he noticed Mr. Goodson and Raymond so he followed suit. He tapped the next staff member and once they recognized what was going on, they all, one-by-one, began to rise up, take off their oxygen masks, leaned back in their chairs and rested their heads. It was a powerful sight to see, it appeared everyone was saying "If we are going down, we are going down with our heads held high; if we must die, we will die with dignity."

The stewardess was still huddled with her oxygen mask on, holding her hurting head between her legs, crying and saying, "Lord please don't let me die, please Lord."

For 15 seconds the jet drops straight down like a deep loop in a roller coaster ride. Then out of nowhere the jet halts its decent, smoothes out and begins to ride straight again. It was like it was floating on a big cloud and the cloud broke its fall and began to carry it forward. The jet ascended back to the level it was at before the problem occurred.

A few minutes later the co-pilot came out of the cockpit and said, "I believe we have everything under control. I can't explain what just happened here."

"Everyone OK?" Raymond hollers out.

Everyone responds in their own way.

"I'll go and check on the stewardess," Louise says.

Raymond looks at his Godfather who looks at him. "I remember what you said in the graveyard. Once you know your purpose you can't die until it's fulfilled."

His Godfather smiles and says while unfastening his seat belt, "Neither can the people around you." His Godfather picks up his book from the floor of the jet, opens it up and begins to read where he left off.

Picture 56: *Are You Going or Not?*

Excitement about departure day is mounting. Even for people who are not going, there is an unmistakable excitement in the air that everyone can feel. The subject is discussed everywhere. Everyone is talking about departure day. This news has had plenty of airtime on TV, radio, computer networks, in the newspapers, magazines and other publications, but now the word is out on the streets -- which means it's officially on, and it's 100% true. Departure day will take place.

Departure day, better known as D-Day, is not only the topic of everyone's conversation, it is also the password that starts off most conversations, "Are you going?" That's all one has to say and everyone in and out of the African American community knew exactly what you were referring to. This is a very exciting time, but it's also a very controversial time, because everyone wants to express their reasons why they are, or are not going. Everyone wants to express their views of one of the greatest moments in American and African American history.

⚐ ⚐ ⚐

The B2B project is also a hot topic among inmates in the Penal System on every level from the county to the federal penitentiary. In Atlanta Federal Penitentiary a young man by the name of Andrew (b.k.a. "Steal") is laying on his bunk listening to his outdated Walkman. His friend Safe comes to the door of his cell and calls him, "Steal, Steal," then Safe walks into the cell and hits Steal's feet. Steal jumps up and reaches for something under his pillow. "Whoa, whoa," Safe says.

"That's a real dangerous thing to do in a place like this boy," Steal sputters.

"You're always thinking the worst," Safe says.

"Look at where you are. Your environment tells you how you got to handle yourself."

"That's the problem: you have done so much time you have become a byproduct of your environment," Safe says.

"What's going on man? I'm trying to get back to my music?" Steal asks as he puts the earphones back in his ears and closes his eyes.

Safe pulls one earphone out, "You can't escape this reality, so face it like a man," he says and they both laugh. "Here check this out," Safe says and hands Steal a computer print out. "My people sent this to me yesterday," he says. Steal looks over the paper as Safe talks to him, "Remember the politician who withdrew from the Vice Presidency race?" Safe asks.

"Yeah, Mr. Dummy," Steal says sarcastically."

"Yeah, he did it to start a New Nation in Africa and he is asking all Americans of African descent to join him and change their citizenship," Safe informs him.

"Ain't happening," Steal says.

"He's already got over two million registered now," Safe says.

"What do this got to do with me man?"

"Read the fifth paragraph," Safe says. He gave Steal time to read it. He knew he reached the spot, because Steal sat up in his bunk.

"Do you know what this says?" Steal asks.

"Yeah, 'Any inmate who wants to exchange their American citizenship for a New Nation citizenship will be released in Africa, placed on five years probation, but cannot return to the USA for 10 years. After that there will be a screening process," Safe says.

"Is this for real?"

"Everybody is talking about it," Safe says. Hunter walks into the cell, "Let me hold 10 books of stamps, he says.

"What do you think about the New Nation Project, back to Africa?" Safe asks Hunter.

"It's not back to Africa, it's moving to Africa. It's true, but I'm not doing that," Hunter responds.

"Why not?" Steal asks.

"For many reasons. I'm not moving away from my family. The phone calls would be to the roof. This place is not developed, so you know the prisons are even worse. This country is the best country in the world even if they are wicked, and I don't know any of the honeys over there," Hunter says.

"What about your freedom? You won't have to finish the rest of your time," Safe says.

"But I can't come back into the US for years, and they say you have to go through a screening process after the 10 years. Do you know what that means? 'No ex-offenders allowed.' That is just like being locked up, just without the bars," Hunter reasons.

"Man it's a difference between being locked up and locked out," Safe says.

"You will only be locked out of America for 10 years," Steal says. "I'm going to do it. What about you Safe?" asks Steal.

"You really got me thinking," Safe says.

"Man do you have books or not?" Hunter asks Safe.

"See that's what you are going to be doing for the next 25 years, running after stamps and cigarettes, while I'll be laying on the sand of a beautiful Africa beach with a beautiful African honey," Safe says to Hunter.

"I'm telling you they got a trick bag for you, time when you put one foot on that African soil they are going to lock you up like they did Mandela," Hunter says.

Steal laughs out as he puts the earphones back in his ears and closes his eyes to meditate on the possibility of freedom by way of moving to Africa.

⚐ ⚐ ⚐

The students of Atlanta High are moving in the hallway, attempting to get to the next class before the bell rings. Keith is hanging by the lockers with a few of his boys when he spots Tee coming his way. "Hold, hold, slow down sexy," Keith says as he grabs Tee gently.

"What boy? I got to get to class," Tee says blushing from ear to ear.

"What, you don't have a minute for your man or something?" Keith asks.

"All depends," Tee responds.

"I have to talk to you later about something important," Keith says.

"Keith you know I hate that. What is it?" Tee insists.

"Later baby," Keith insists. Tee begins to kiss him on his neck. "I'll see you guys later," Keith says giving his boys the signal to roll out because he didn't want them to see him become like putty in Tee's hands.

"Are you trying to seduce me?" Keith asks Tee.

"No, just persuade you to change your mind."

"OK, OK, I think my father is going to Africa," Keith says. Tee immediately pulls away.

"What?"

"I believe my father is going to Africa on departure day," Keith repeats himself.

"He can't do that. Why would he do that?" Tee asks hysterically.

"He said it's a once in a lifetime business opportunity for his new construction company," Keith explains.

"No, I have to talk to him. No you have to talk to him, we have to talk... we've got to do something," Tee says.

"Calm down Tee, it's not a big deal," Keith says.

"Maybe you can stay with your grandmother or something," Tee suggests.

"That's not happening," Keith says.

"Well... maybe we can get married," Tee says.

"Tee, Tee, hold up for a minute. I'm not ready to get married and you're not ready to get married either."

"Keith what's going on, it's like you don't care. It's like you want to go or something," Tee says.

"I do care, but there's nothing we can do. My father wants to go and I can't change that," Keith says.

Tee walks up to Keith and puts her little finger in his face, "That night I gave you the best part of me. I gave you a piece of my soul and now you are going to walk over to the other side of the world like it's nothing. I thought we had a future together. I thought you loved me, Tee says.

"You know I do, but…" Keith says when Tee interrupts him.

"You know what Keith, go ahead to Africa. Say hi to Kunta and Kizzy for me. If you don't care, I don't care." Tee walks away from Keith just as the bell rings, leaving Keith standing in the hall.

⚐ ⚐ ⚐

Out of all of the professors in the country Professor Tiron DuBois has taken the most optimal advantage of the entire B2B New Nation Project. He has used Raymond's political career from the very beginning, as a teaching tool in his Political Science class. This great move in the Africa American community could not have come at a better time as far as Professor DuBois and his curriculum were concerned.

Even though Raymond pulled out of the Vice Presidency race the Professor still used as much as he could of the B2B campaign to inspire his class by showing it is possible for an African American to reach the White House and have a voice in national affairs.

The professor is also using this opportunity to teach his students how history in the African American community had a way of repeating itself. The class' last assignment was to research the life of Marcus Garvey to discover some similarities and differences to the B2B project. The class has decided that Mr. Garvey's move might have been premature. The time was not set for him to take a people to a land they knew nothing about, and to a people who knew nothing about them.

When speaking of the right time to move one can never be talking about the time in the hour sense of the word, because it's always a good time to move out of a bad situation into a better one. But in this case of the B2B New Nation project one must consider the provisions that were made to move African Americans from one side of the globe to the other, and the operation on the other side of the globe was ready to receive them. Also along with that fact another fact must be taken into consideration: how would the receiving party react even if the party being received are distant relatives? There is no indication in evidence that Mr. Garvey had given these important details any thought in order for the move in 1920 to be a success.

However, Raymond is living in a time when the world has gotten smaller and modern technology is more advanced. Raymond and his Godfather had the luxury of learning and building from other great men's mistakes. His Godfather knew that African Americans would not be accepted back into the motherland with open arms by every nation and culture on the continent. This is one of the main reasons he created the New Nation of Africa, so African Americans would have a country of their own on the land they originally came from.

African Americans can not deny their heritage is both African and American and would be divided if attempting to do so. The scriptures say, *"A house divided can not stand."* But if a God-sent person came who would teach people how to appreciate their total selves, using the good experiences with the bad, living with their complete being, they might find out what they could contribute to the world. This is what his Godfather and Raymond offered the African American community at a time they were looking for a greater purpose. The time was right and therefore this move could never be premature.

Professor DuBois noticed the excitement that built up in his class around this hot topic. But there was some extra tension between Tim and Scott, so much so he had no choice but to keep them after class to get to the bottom of their dispute.

"Most of you did well with your Marcus Garvey report. I will be passing the papers back on Tuesday. I have some good news for you: The University will be closed on departure day, so we will have a three-day weekend," Professor DuBois says.

The class claps and cheers. "Tim and Scott I want to see you after class," the Professor says. Just then the bell rings, "You all be safe," the Professor shouts. Tim and Scott walk to the front of the class and have a seat. "What's the problem with you two? These unnecessary comments you've been making to each other, especially you Tim,"

"I don't know what his problem is, every time I say something he wants to shoot it down, so I started firing back at him," Scott says.

"All right Tim what is going on?" Professor DuBois asks.

"It's nothing. I'm cool," Tim says.

"Well you are going to be cool and late for basketball practice if you don't tell me what's on your mind." Professor DuBois says.

"Alright it's like this. When I first came to this class I didn't even like it, I only was here to get the credit I needed for my degree. But then I started listening to Scott's comments about the African American political plight, he made a lot of sense so I changed my major to Political Science," Tim says.

"And all this time I thought I had something to do with it," Professor DuBois interrupts. They both give a little laugh.

"Yeah, you had a lot to do with it too, but he really gave me a fresh new look at politics as a young black man in the Hip-Hop culture," Tim says.

"OK then, what's the problem?" Professor DuBois asks.

"Well, ever since the B2B New Nation Project was announced I've been seeing another side of Scott. When it first came out everyone was skeptical, even me. But once the project was proven to be valid I was expecting him to be one of the first students who registered. But instead we keep hearing why he is not going, he is a hypocrite just like those fake politicians he's always putting down," Tim says.

There was a little silence in the class as Professor DuBois takes in all Tim just spilled out. Professor DuBois looks at Scott and says, "Well, Scott what do you have to say."

"Man I don't owe anybody an explanation. I don't come to school to be a role model. I am a student," Scott says as he gets up, walks out of the classroom and slams the door.

Professor DuBois turns to Tim and says, "Well, that went exactly the way I planned. But seriously Tim, something Scott said is true, he is not a role model, but a student, which means he is still developing and discovering who he really is. He might think he knows himself and something like the New Nation Project can come along and make him redefine and rethink his entire value system. Have you made the decision to register?" the Professor asks.

"Yes, I already registered."

"Congratulations Tim that is really a big move." This brought a big smile to Tim's face, hearing someone support his decision to go, especially coming from his male political science professor, who was the closest he had to a father figure in his life. "That's real good son, but you can't expect everyone to make a big move like you. As a matter of fact it can be a little disappointing to hear people for years say, 'We should go back to Africa, or we are not totally free.' But when the chance for them to leave arrive, leaving is the furthest thing from their mind, which suggests they were just talking, or they never thought this day would come. But the good news is a generation of young men and women like you are doing more than just talking. You are 'bringing the noise' as you would say," the Professor says.

Tim smiles and gives Professor DuBois a high-five, shakes his hand, and gives him a hug. "Thanks for your knowledge Professor DuBois, I'm going to do something big," Tim says.

"I'm expecting you to become Mayor or something boy," Professor DuBois says.

"I think I can pull that off," Tim says. They both laugh as Tim walks out the classroom and Professor DuBois erases the board.

⚐ ⚐ ⚐

The New Nation Project has made an impact, good and bad in every area of the country, but no area suffers more than the workplace. Many employees have given their employers a two-week notice in order to begin new careers in the New Nation, or to open up their own business in fields where they couldn't advance any further in America. This has a double-edged effect. It has motivated many people who feel their pension is in jeopardy to take a chance in the New Nation, where the companies and corporations are expanding, not downsizing. Employers and corporate leaders who are looking for ways not to pay these pensions, welcome the idea of certain employees quitting or making the move to the New Nation. On the other hand there are many bright African American employees who have contributed to the goals of the corporate world, whom employers hate to see go. They never thought in a million years that they would be gone, (not for another 10-20 years at least). Workplace relationships are also feeling the impact of the New Nation project. Aside from the usual water cooler debates that occur because of this emotional event, there is the very real pain one feels when a valued co-worker and friend leaves the organization. This is what is occurring with Kim and Whitney.

Whitney walks into the lunchroom over to Kim's table where she is enjoying a big salad, a bowl of soup and a soda. Whitney sits down in front of her and takes a fork and eats some of her salad. "Why don't you get your own?" Kim asks.

"Yours taste so much better."

"You'd better start spending that money or it's going to expire," Kim says.

"Then I'll use yours."

"You're doing that right now," Kim replies.

"Oh, yeah you're right," Whitney realizes. They both laugh out loud bringing attention to themselves.

"Girl they are going to run us out of here," Kim warns.

"If they are not used to us by now they should be ran out of here. We bring in the big accounts, so we deserve to have a big laugh," Whitney huffs, raising her voice and looking over her shoulders rolling her eyes.

"And you've got the big mouth for it too," Kim responds. They both laugh.

There is a silence between them only for a few seconds, long enough for Kim to get up the courage to say, "Whitney, I did it."

"Good," Whitney says as she drinks some of Kim's soda. "Did what?"

"I registered for citizenship of the New Nation," Kim says.

"That's not funny," Whitney stares at Kim as Kim stares back at her in silence. "Kim, please say you are playing," Whitney says.

"I went to Raymond's father's funeral the other day to pay my respects, and things started to happen so fast, the funeral turned into a registration rally and I found myself signing up," Kim explains.

"But what about us, I thought we were a team, you know, partners," Whitney says.

"You can go with me. We can start our own business to do what we do here all over the world," Kim says.

"I can't just drop everything and pack up and go to Africa because someone says it's a nice thing to do. Neither can you! You can undo this, you weren't thinking. He caught you in an emotional state of mind. I understand that. Don't shake your head 'No'," Whitney says.

"Don't blame Raymond. I wanted to do it, I was just looking for the place and time, that's all he provided and I did the rest," Kim says.

"But you promised me you would not leave me, like the other folks did. You said you would not hurt me or disappoint me, but you're just like all the rest," Whitney says with tears running down her face.

"I didn't see this coming," Whitney says. "I didn't mean to disappoint you. I only want better for myself," Kim says.

"Yeah, that's what they all say," Whitney says as she gets up and leaves.

Picture 57: *Strange Love*

Ever since Raymond's assassination attempt and his father's death there have been a lot of conspiracy theories. The authorities are doing their best to solve these serious crimes, but they haven't come up with any good leads. Right now Raymond is a moving target. The fact that the person who killed Bishop Jackson was heard by several witnesses to have said, "Give this message to Raymond!" is a clear indication the perpetrator wanted to discourage Raymond from completing his task. But this clue doesn't make the fact-finding process any easier since Raymond could be on any number of people's hit lists right now.

Raymond's security men thought they had a good idea of who tried to kill him and who killed his father. Max was certain the KKK or Aryan brotherhood was responsible for the incidents, and he would bet his last dollar on it. But that theory was blown out of the water one evening at the B2B headquarters after Raymond had arrived back in the states from Africa.

Raymond was in his office putting the finishing touches on his departure day speech. He heard a commotion coming from the reception area, but he didn't pay it any mind at first, he just went back to his work. "Sir we have a situation. I think you should come out here," Louise interrupts. Raymond gets up from his desk and walks to the front of the building complaining every step of the way. "I thought I told you all I needed peace and …" Raymond stops in the middle of his sentence and stares at three white men pointing shotguns at his security men, and his security men pointing their handguns at these three white men. Another young white male, who was dressed in a conservative suit and tie with an overcoat thrown over his shoulders, was standing in the middle of the three white men.

"Hold, hold everybody stay calm, we can work this out. What is going on here?" Raymond asks in a peaceable way.

The white male in the suit places a smile on his face and says very calmly, "It's just a little misunderstanding. Tell your men to lower their guns and I'll explain," he says.

"No you tell your men to lower their guns," Max says.

"What can I help you with sir?" Raymond asks to get to the bottom of the situation.

"My name is Darryl Shineck," he says as he hands Raymond his card. Raymond looks it over.

"Mr. Shineck is from the white supremacy group," Louise explains. "The group was founded in May 1866 in Pulaski, Tennessee."

"Excuse me, 'organization', Mr. Shineck corrects Louise.

"He came to offer us six million dollars to help with our efforts," Louise explains.

"You see sir, the way I see it, you and me have the same common goal. You want to leave this country and I want you to leave. Sometimes even enemies can find a common ground to stand on every once in a while. Wouldn't you agree?" Mr. Shineck says.

"Sir, let me blast his racist butt out of here," Max says. He cocks his gun back, causing his security staff to do the same forcing the white supremacy group to do the same.

"No stop!" Louise shouts.

Raymond steps in between the two groups, raises his hand and says, "Wait, wait everybody just wait a minute." This is the loudest anyone of Raymond's staff has ever heard him speak.

"We didn't come here for violence," Mr. Shineck says keeping his calm demeanor.

"That's what you are going to get if you don't get out of here," one of Raymond's younger security men yells.

"Let the man finish talking. As you were saying sir," Raymond says still trying to find a way to cool off a hot situation that was growing hotter by the second, because those young white racist boys holding those shotguns appeared to be itching to scratch their trigger finger. As far as Raymond could tell the leader may have been sincere in his insulting offer, but those immature boys he brought with him could spoil the fun at anytime by one sneeze or cough.

"Thank you sir, I only came here to extend my hand in helping you fulfill your purpose. Here is a certified check for six million dollars," Mr. Shineck says while handing Raymond the check.

Raymond takes it and examines it. "And once you reach Africa, if you have any financial problems we can help you with, don't hesitate to contact me at that office number on the card at anytime, day or night. We will cater to your every need," Mr. Shineck proclaims.

Raymond smiles and looks at his security men and shakes his head as does Louise. "Well, Mr. Shineck, I appreciate your offer and I'll be putting this money in an appropriate place," Raymond says as his security men look at him like he was out of his mind. Here they are about to start an all out war trying to defend him and the mission's honor only for him to receive money from these people who would kill him at the bat of an eyelash under any other circumstances. Raymond shakes Mr. Shineck's hand and thanks him once more. Shineck turns around and walks out the door, with his men behind him, walking backward, still pointing the guns at Raymond and his security men. Raymond's men continued to do the same until Shineck's crew was out of sight.

Louise makes a noticeable sigh of relief. Raymond looks at the check, shakes his head again then hands the check to Louise and says, "Put this in its appropriate place," and then walks towards his office and then yells, "Put those guns up," to his security men.

Louise walks over to her desk and puts the check in the shredder.

Bishop Jackson had taught Raymond a lesson years ago when Raymond was running for Congress, and a member of a big drug cartel family wanted to contribute to his political career. Bishop Jackson said, "Don't let your good be evil spoken of." It was a biblical term that always stuck with Raymond, which simply meant you can't do good by accepting bad help, because contrary to popular belief, the end never justifies the means. If you accept blood money or dirty money you must expect your hands to be bloody or dirty. If it is truly your purpose to fulfill a certain vision, God has a way of giving the provisions for completion of the vision. That's why Raymond couldn't see himself taking one penny from Mr. Shineck. As far as Raymond was concerned his money was just as bloody and dirty as the drug cartel's.

⚐⚐⚐

Raymond made up in his mind the only way he was going to be able to finish his speech was to eject his work-aholic top aide and his trigger-happy security men. "You all have got to get out. I know it's bad English, but it makes a lot of good sense. So get to stepping, one-two, one-two, left, right, left, right, Raymond says playfully holding the door open as everyone leaves. "Don't stay up too late. We have a jam-packed day tomorrow," Louise cautions walking out the door.

"Take your own medicine doctor," Raymond replies.

"You've got the cord I'll be here in no time if you need me," Max says.

"You just keep your gun up," Raymond says. Max notices someone walking towards the door.

"Hi Max," a voice says.

"Oh Nicky, how have you been, I haven't seen you in a while," Max says.

Nicky gives him a hug. "I've been OK, I've been keeping a low profile," Nicky says.

Max turns to Raymond, "Do you want me to stay to help you with that situation?" Max asks sending Raymond a subtle message.

"No, I believe I can handle it," Raymond says knowing he was referring to Nicky.

"All right, goodnight. It's good to see you again Nicky. You are looking good," Max says as he walks out. Raymond notices Nicky's friend Sue waiting in the car. She waves at Raymond and he waves back.

"May I come in Ray?" Nicky asks. Raymond opens the door wider, but doesn't say a word. Nicky walks in and looks around. "It's really different," Nicky says.

"I thought we had an agreement," Raymond says to Nicky not wasting any time with small talk, knowing her skills as a corporate lawyer, and knowing her purpose for coming was to give a closing argument on a case of default on a promise of politics and love.

"No Ray! We didn't have an agreement. That agreement was under duress and false pretense. They tricked me into thinking I was no longer seeing you for your political career in connection with the Vice Presidency," Nicky says.

"Did they say that?" Raymond asks.

"No, but your Godfather and father gave me that impression."

"OK, it's one and the same."

"No, it is not," Nicky states.

"What's the difference?"

"The difference is they are going to kill you like they killed Martin and Malcolm and all the rest of them. I would have never agreed to anything if I knew *this* is what they were referring to!" Nicky makes her case.

"It's over Nicky, it's over," Raymond says calmly. Nicky starts to cry shaking her head.

"Don't say that Ray," she says.

"Nicky don't cry," Raymond says as he moves towards her, then catches himself and backs up, not wanting to be tempted.

"You're making me cry Ray. For five years you never made me cry Ray, you never made me cry," Nicky says.

"This is bigger than us. I have to think about the future of our people."

"You are a hypocrite Ray."

"Don't say that," Raymond responds.

Nicky shakes her head yes firmly, "Yes, yes, you are a big hypocrite. You get on national TV and radio, talking about a promise, and keeping a promise when you have broken everyone of your promises you made to the American people. What about the promise you gave to make the schools a better place to learn? What about the promise you made to get the guns off of the streets? What about the promise you made to America Ray? And what about the promises you made to me? 'I will always love you. I'll get a divorce when the time is right.' What about that Ray? How can you break all of these promises you made with people you knew for a long time to make a promise to people you just met?" Nicky says putting the final touches on a very emotional closing argument.

"I'm a different person. I'm not the same person who made those promises. Nicky they were false promises made by a person, who had a false identity, who had a false sense of power. Everything I did was false, but now I'm doing what I was created to do. This is who I am."

"Well, this pain is real and it's not false, Nicky says as she raises her voice.

"Keep your voice down they are going to hear you outside."

"How can I keep my voice down when you are killing me Ray? You are driving me crazy. I can't eat. I can't sleep. I look at the TV hoping and praying the flash crawl doesn't appear, saying you've been killed. Then I would have to live with not knowing why you couldn't talk to me. I asked you in the room that night what was wrong and you told me 'Nothing'. Why couldn't you talk to me about this?" Nicky asks.

"So you could talk me out of it?"

"No, so I could talk some sense in you," Nicky responds.

"This is destiny Nicky, can't you see?"

"If it is Ray it's not fair," Nicky screams from the top of her lungs.

"Nicky you have to keep…" Raymond starts to say.

"It's not fair," Nicky screams and crumples the floor repeating herself. "It's not fair! It's not fair!"

Sue hears Nicky yelling from the outside and comes rushing in, she spots Nicky on the floor. "What did you do to her?" she asks. Raymond is shocked to see Nicky in this state, and he backs up from her and just stares. Sue helps her off the floor and walks her to the car.

"It's not fair. It's not," Nicky is mumbling on her way out.

Nicky was a clear representative of America in the life of Raymond Jackson. She could have just as well been speaking for all of America when it came to the promises the old Raymond made to them. Crushed by destiny, laying on the B2B headquarters floor, all of America's dreams that were designed for Raymond were in disarray, never to come to fruition, because he accepted a higher calling.

STATION BREAK!!! This is an announcement from the New Nation Campaign Headquarters

IT IS NOW 30 DAYS UNTIL DEPARTURE IT'S A MIRACLE!

Log onto

www.newnation.org

to register today and see the layout of the New Nation of Africa.

Picture 58: *How Does It Feel To Be Free?*

Paul Goodson lay in his bed looking up at the ceiling with his hands behind his head. He is awake a little earlier waiting for the alarm to go off. While in the waiting room of life he takes the time to reflect how he accomplished everything by the wisdom he was given from above.

When his grandfather and father sat him down to explain to him the promise and the important part he must play in the entire process, he was only eight years old, but somehow he understood everything they explained. He was disciplined, prepared, schooled and trained for this mission for as long as he could remember. Even his childhood toys centered around his purpose in life. For example, when Paul reflected on his childhood he could only recall playing school, where he auspiciously always played the role of the great professor. Now that he is a master teacher he understands his grandfather and father strategically arranged his playtime to prepare him for his purpose. This revelation brought a smile to him as he lay in his king-sized bed.

He also recalls the time when his grandfather passed, how he called him in the room and gave him power of attorney over the entire New Nation estate. He was only 24 years-old and still in graduate school in Europe. He always wondered why he didn't give the authority to his father, but he came to realize that his grandfather wanted him to experience the power of control while someone still had control over him just in case he wasn't ready for the responsibility. He may have had the power of attorney, but his father had the power of life and death in the social structure of the African nation in those days.

Paul knew what he had in his power was more than a great estate and corporation worth over one billion dollars. What was passed over to him was a promise, and that was worth more than what any estate or corporation could offer. Paul could never forget the time his father passed away. He got dressed in a suit and tie and they spent the whole day together, eating, talking, playing chess, cards, and watching TV. And all during this time his father was dying and he didn't have a clue. They later discovered from his physician that he had cancer for many years and it was amazing that he had lived so long. Paul is sure that his father had the power to hold back death until he knew his son was competently prepared to fulfill the promise. It appears their entire last day together, as peaceful and pleasant as it was, his father was giving him his final exam. He must have passed with flying colors because his father didn't wait to go home to pass away in his sleep, but went home to glory during a chess game.

Paul looked at the clock in his bedroom. He had at least another five minutes before the alarm rang, giving him a chance to recall another memory before he started his day.

He reflected on the time he met Louise's mother, Juanita Rhea, in South Africa during apartheid. She was working in a gold processing plant, but was barely earning enough to take care of herself, not to mention her sisters and brothers. When Paul met Juanita she was a virgin and a recent Christian convert. When he told her about the promise and the role her un-conceived daughter would play in the process, she thought he was crazy. Especially when he told her she was going to be married at age 28 to a white man, Coleman Witherspoon, who was a part of the administration that oppressed her people.

After spending some time with her, teaching her the power of forgiveness and the strength of true love, he saw impressive maturity in her spiritual development. So much so that Ms. Rhea could easily have been Mr. Goodson's official and unofficial first love. This too brought another brilliant smile to Paul's face as he stared at the ceiling, using it as a projector to play back the great moments of his life. He recalls the night Juanita believed he was who he said he was, in his gifts, his mission, his prophesy to her and the promise. This happened on the night they both became totally, uncontrollably, infallibly in love with each other. Paul remembers that night like it was yesterday: the stars shined extra bright, the moon was closer to the earth, and the wind blew softly through the trees providing a gentle summer breeze.

He also recounted how hard it was to tell her he must leave her life, never to see her again. He left, but not before giving her five million dollars to relocate to Europe, where her daughter would be educated and trained in international affairs for the mission. Years later she met the same man Mr. Goodson spoke to her about, the man who was once her oppressor. They fell in love, got married and had Louise. That was the first and only time Paul loved a women. He never got married, but Louise, Gwendolyn, Ethel, Harriet, Sadie, Patricia, Jesse, Bush, Hank, Quincy, Delbert, Bryant, and Raymond were his children, in addition to their spouses. Paul knew he had to sacrifice having a family of his own if he was going to be a father of the New Nation.

All of these memories and more strolled across the stage of Paul's mind, parading themselves to be moments that could never be forgotten.

The digital clock radio went off and the voice of the radio announcer was heard throughout the bedroom, "Good morning Atlanta. It's a very exciting time in the African American community. We are less than four days away from departure day. In light of that fact, there is a song that has been number one across the nation for the fifth consecutive week. This song has found itself on the world music chart among the top 10 songs. This song is the most requested song and has easily become the theme song for the move to the New Nation of Africa. Listen to this multi-talented creative artist known as NaCo singing, "Know How It Feels To Be Free."

♪*I woke up early this morning I had a lot on my mind.*
I didn't want to get out of bed,
Don't look at me that way you know you've been there.
But I said a little prayer to the one who's always there,
And these were the humble words I said♪.

Paul sits on the side of the bed and put his slippers on. He walks over to the corner of the room to get his robe off of the chair and puts it on. He begins to hum the chorus of the song.

♪*I want to know how it feels,*
I want to know that it's real,
I want to know how it feels,
Know how it feel to be free♪.

Paul goes into the kitchen, pours himself a cup of fresh coffee and begins to read his newspapers as he listens to the second verse of the song.

♪I read my morning news as I sipped on my morning coffee,
And I don't know about you,
But to me it seems like overnight,
The world has gotten more crazy.
But I saw a bird flying high in the sky,
Now that brings a good idea to my mind,
I got to know♪.

Paul walks into the bathroom, removes his clothes and gets into the shower. He turns on the shower radio and starts to sing along with the chorus.

♪I want to know how it feels,
I want to know that it's real,
I want to know how it feels,
Know how it feels to be free♪.

Every great political movement has a great song to inspire the people and the leaders to press on to their goal and triumph over any type of difficulties. The "Star Spangled Banner," was for the new Americans who were fighting for their sovereignty and "We Shall Overcome," was the hymn of the saints who placed their lives on the line during the civil rights movement. So when anyone hears "Know How It Feels to Be Free," they will associate it with the great move African Americans made to live in their own Nation.

This song has grown on Paul to the point where he knows all of the words. This is surprising because he is not the sort of person who spends a lot of time listening to the radio, but this particular song is an exception to the rule. He even has a favorite part, where the background repeats the end of the chorus and NaCo begins to adlib. It is as if NaCo is singing about freedom as a person. He turns up the radio a little and just listens.

♪Know what it means to be free,
Know what it mean to be free♪.

The background repeats itself then NaCo adlibs.

♪When I was a little boy – I heard so much about freedom – I heard freedom was so sweet – I heard freedom was so beautiful,

But every time I went to look for freedom,
I could not find freedom in material things.
I looked for freedom in gold, silver and bling and all the nice things.
I looked for freedom in houses, cars, and clothes.
I looked for freedom in relationships –
I even looked for freedom in the White House, the schoolhouse, the church house,
But could not find freedom to save my life.
So I came here tonight to ask you can you do me a favor –
If you see freedom would you tell freedom I have been looking for her?
Tell freedom I've been praying, waiting, running, standing, shouting, walking, talking, hoping, wishing and crying for her.
And freedom if you are somewhere out there listening,
Freedom if you can hear this song,
I want you to know I need you freedom.
Can't you see I'm miserable without you freedom?
I got to see you freedom.
If I can't have you, can I love you?
And if I can't love you can I kiss you?
If I can't kiss you can I hold you?
If I can't hold you can I hug you?
And if I can't hug you can I touch you?
And if I can't touch you can I hear you?
And if I can't hear you can I see you?
And if I can't see you can I feel you?
I have to feel you for myself.
I have to know you are not a myth;
I have to know you are not a game;
I have to know you are not a figment of my imagination;
I have to know this for myself♪.

NaCo concludes the spoken portion of "Know How It Feels To Be Free." The background singers continue to sing. Paul gets out of the shower singing as he shaves his face. He puts on one of his best suits, and a pair of his best shoes. He walks in front of the mirror and looks at himself. "You still look good, sharp from head to toe," he thinks to himself.

Paul then walks to the living room to sit on the couch. He is sitting as though he is waiting for someone, maybe his driver or another staff member to pick him up. He stares at the curtains that cover the picture windows in the center of the living room. He looks at his watch, stands up, walks toward the crimson curtains and opens them up. The warm sunshine hits his face and he smiles. An assassin's bullet from an AR15 strikes him, entering the forehead and exiting through the back of his skull cleanly. He was dead before he hit the floor, but it seemed as if it took forever for him to fall. It was as though time had stopped. Paul's body lay slain on his living room floor as the ending of his favorite song played.

♪*Who the Son set free is free indeed,*
Who the Son set free is free indeed,
Now I know how it feels,
Now I know that it's real,
Now I know how it feels,
I know how it feels to be free♪.

⚐ ⚐ ⚐

Raymond is at the funeral home where his Godfather's body is on display. Max and his security team have strict orders not to let anyone in so Raymond can spend some final moments with his Godfather's body. Raymond is sitting in front of the casket with his head down dealing with the mixed emotions caused by this untimely death. He is sad that the only person who had a chance to take his father's place was gone. Also, he is left with no guidance when he needs it the most. He feels so vulnerable, unprotected, unsure and insecure. There was once a time he didn't think a man had to have someone to answer to, but since he met his Godfather he had to redefine what a true man really was. Yes, his father had a great impact on him as well, as a matter of fact he saw a lot of his father in his Godfather and vice versa. But Raymond was so busy trying to impress his father that he never got the opportunity to enjoy his manhood and appreciate his protection. So when his Godfather came along he was like a coach providing wise counsel from the outside; he had a way of separating the trees from the forest, allowing Raymond to see everything his father had intended for him to be from the very beginning.

Raymond began to cry. He never had the chance to really grieve his father's death, a death he believes in his heart his actions somehow caused. Now his Godfather lay in front of him dead -- maybe for the same reason someone killed his father. As much as he wanted to hold it back he couldn't, it was too much. The two most important men in his life were gone, the tears of sorrow rolled down his face uncontrollably. They were also tears of anger, because he felt they left him before the mission was complete, leaving him in a position to fail himself and over three million African Americans.

Raymond put his head in his hands, shaking it because it felt so heavy and hurt so bad from his whirling thoughts. He just couldn't take anymore; no more deaths, no more broken promises, no more tears, no more proving himself to people, no more controversy, no more explanations, no more speeches, no more news cameras, no more questions, no more pain, no more problems -- no more!

He held his head and ran his hands through his hair. "Now what?" Raymond began to talk to his Godfather's dead body. "Where do we go from here? We have nothing now. We can't go backward and we can't go forward, we are stuck in the land of nowhere. I knew it. I knew it was too good to be true. I don't know what I was thinking, believing I could accomplish something that not even the great men who came before me could not do. It was impossible from the very beginning and what about all the people who gave up their citizenship for a place we can't even go to? If you know so much, if you call yourself a seer, why didn't you see this coming? Why didn't you know that you would die before you gave me what I needed to complete this mission," Raymond shouted. Then he says in a whisper, "Man you didn't even see my father's death coming."

It was clear that Raymond was venting, getting all the painful thoughts out of his head, and if Mr. Goodson was alive he would be just as silent as he was now to let Raymond get rid of all his negative feelings. It's like they say about a blabbering drunken person, a lot of truth comes out. So it is with Raymond right now.

He is right about the great dilemma he finds himself in. This dilemma is greater than his father and Godfather's death put together. Because Mr. Goodson didn't give Raymond the product the New Nation would bring to the international community of Africa, Raymond and the three million African Americans would not be allowed to enter the continent. The New Nation citizens would find themselves having to fight different nations of Africa, while still in an infant stage, just to stay in their new homeland. He and over three million emigrants can't go to Africa, but yet they can't stay in America because they already gave up their citizenship. After departure day they would have to apply for visas in order to stay in the United States. This is why Raymond says, "We are stuck in the land of nowhere," because that is exactly where they are -- nowhere.

The more Raymond thinks about it. He begins to pace back and forth in front of his Godfather's casket. "Why couldn't you just let me become Vice President, and everything may have worked itself out. Even if it didn't work itself out at least we would be secure in our place and future in the world. I know, I know what you would say, you couldn't be Vice President because it wasn't your destiny, but this is. What kind of destiny is this? We have nothing; no place, no future, and no more hope. See I did my part, you said all you wanted me to do was to convince them to go, but to where? A place that is nothing more than a figment of your imagination!" He starts to laugh loudly. "This has got to be the funniest thing ever in the world. I'm doing my thing -- no I wasn't perfect -- but I was the people's choice to put in the White House. Then you came along talking about 'It's time for African Americans to have their own country.' You made me give up everything for nothing. Now we are going to be the joke of the world. What? African Americans didn't suffer enough shame during slavery in this country? What? We didn't suffer enough during the Jim Crow era, during segregation and during the civil rights era? What about when others said they had the same plan, but nothing happened? Weren't all those shameful events enough for this country to look and point the finger at us in shame? Why did you have to come all the way from across the world to pull us 100 years back in time?" Raymond stops pacing and is now standing in front of the casket looking at his Godfather. "Didn't we suffer enough sorrow when Martin and Malcolm died? Why this? Why now? Why me? Why us?" Raymond asks and falls on his knees with his head bowed down in front of the casket and begins to cry. "Why? Why? Why?" he cried like a broken man at an altar call during church service.

Despite his justifiably dismal outlook Raymond is about to progress to a higher level of spiritual and personal power. Before you can elevate to another part of your life the old, useless material of your being must be broken. The more one is broken the easier it is for them to let go of the natural and accept the supernatural. Raymond asked for a miracle and now he is being introduced to the process of getting one. Unlike what he might have thought, miracles don't just appear. It's not something you find under the Christmas tree, it's not delivered by the Easter bunny and it can't be found at the end of the rainbow. Raymond is discovering the formula and ingredients miracles are made of and that is our messes. That is why he had to face the pain of losing the most important and powerful people in his life so he could no longer depend on man's power, but God's power, and thus obtain a genuine miracle.

Sobbing bitterly on the floor of the funeral home, the leader of the New Nation Project is learning what miracles are made of.

Suddenly Raymond jumps back from the casket and hits his leg on the chair. *He could have sworn he heard his Godfather's voice.* Maybe he was going crazy. After all he displayed all of the symptoms. He was sad, and then mad. He laughed, and then cried. He suffered two sudden deaths in his life, one right behind the other in a short amount of time. There was also the stress of his own assassination attempt, with the combination of the Nicky situation, all the pressure white and black protestors have placed on him, and now the humiliating fact that Raymond has mobilized three million people with no place to deliver them. Any therapist would tell you a lot of people have suffered insanity from less pressure than what Raymond was experiencing. If he is hearing a dead man's voice then maybe the dire straits Raymond finds himself in has brought him to Crazyville, where it's easy to get in, but sometimes next to impossible to get out.

Max and his security rush in the room, at first glance you would have thought it was because of the commotion of Raymond hitting his leg until Max says, "Who was that?" Raymond was still laying on the floor looking at his Godfather in shock, unsure he had heard what he thought he heard. The security men rushed over to Raymond and lifted him off the floor. "Are you OK? Who was that?" Max asks.

"Who was what?" Raymond asks hoping they would give the answer he wants to hear.

"We heard another voice in here," Max says.

Raymond looks at one of the young security agents. "What did you hear son?" Raymond asks.

"'In my place' or 'At my place', something like that. It sounded like your Godfather's voice," the young security man responds. Raymond thought he was going crazy, but his security men saved his sanity by acknowledging they heard the same words and the same voice.

There have been times when we have heard voices calling us by name and we responded by saying, "Yeah?" only to find out there was no one else there. Usually this voice sounds like people we know. The only problem with this reality is most people don't want to admit they heard the voice, because they don't want anyone to think they are crazy. What will truly drive one crazy is to keep denying a voice that is crystal clear to your consciousness. Sometimes God will place someone in your life to let you know 'I heard that too,' that the voice and message are real.

Raymond looks at his security men and without saying a word they all rush to the car and then over to his Godfather's place.

⚐ ⚐ ⚐

Raymond and his security are admitted into his Godfather's penthouse suite by the manager. "I'll get in trouble if word gets back to my supervisor, so try to keep this on the DL and leave everything the same way you found it. The police said this was a crime scene or something," the manager states.

"I won't disturb anything," Raymond says. He shakes the manager's hand.

"Sir I'm sorry about Mr. Goodson," the manager says.

"Thank you. Can we be alone for a minute?" Raymond asks.

"Oh sure, if you need anything I'll be in my office," the manager says as he walks out.

Raymond didn't waste anytime. He turned to his security and said, "OK guys, let's search this place top to bottom and bottom to top."

"What are we looking for?" Max asks.

"I'm not sure, something that has international value or could be used for trade in exchange for goods," Raymond says. "You get all of the closets, you get the kitchen, you get the bathroom and dining room and I'll get the bedroom and office," Raymond instructs them. Everyone scatters to rake through the penthouse thoroughly. They look in the kitchen pulling out pots, pans, plates and silverware. They look in the bedroom pulling out shoes, flipping the mattress, going through pillowcases. They look in the living room; moving furniture, lamps, the TV, and looking in the seat cushions. They look in the office; moving furniture, looking through the desk, and going through files and paperwork.

They were looking over the house, top to bottom for over three hours. What would really help the search process is if I knew what we were looking for, but all I heard is what everyone else heard, "In my place," Raymond thinks to himself. When he was driving over to his Godfather's place he started to realize that even if his Godfather didn't give him the information about of the New Nation's national product, (which is their passport into the international community), he was too wise to let that type of crucial information die with him. The product had to be somewhere in the penthouse. "But where?" Raymond says out loud as he slaps his fist on the desk that was covered with papers. "OK I have to start thinking like my Godfather," Raymond says to himself as he looks over the room, "Think like a spiritual man Raymond, not like a political one. Where would he put something of that level of importance?" Raymond walks over to the fireplace and looks inside, but finds nothing. "You are not thinking like your Godfather," Raymond says. Raymond takes a deep breath then it hits him. The problem is he is trying to *think* like his Godfather instead of *being* like him. But if he stopped thinking like him and began to emulate him by asking questions, then maybe he could find the product. So he asked himself, *"What would my Godfather do if he was in this situation? If he was in a situation where everything is dependent on a product that can't be found and time is running out, what would he do?"*

It suddenly comes to him. Raymond opens his mouth and says, "Lord of heaven and earth, the Lord who sees all and knows all, would you give me a sign that leads me to this product. So you can complete what you started in me according to your will and for your glory? In Christ's name, Amen."

Now that's what a spiritual man does when his back is against the wall and time is running out. He prays! This is exactly what his Godfather would have done under these circumstances.

The moment Raymond completes his prayer an old grandfather clock chimed, but to Raymond it seemed extremely loud. He followed the sound into the living room, where one of the security men was searching. Raymond looked at the clock, which read 7:00 pm. "What time do you have?" Raymond asks the security man.

"It's eight. That clock has the wrong time," he says. Raymond looks behind the clock, but finds nothing. Then he opens up the door on the clock and reaches his hand down inside it and pulls out a black box. Even though he didn't open it Raymond had a certainty that this was exactly what he had been looking for. He couldn't explain it, but he felt the spirit of his Godfather all over it. "No, it's the right time," Raymond replied.

⚐ ⚐ ⚐

Raymond immediately takes the box and places it on the coffee table that is in the center of the living room. "Is that it sir?" the security man asks. Raymond was so focused on the box that he didn't respond. To his security man that was a good enough answer for him. "Mr. Max, guys, I think we got something," he shouted. They all rushed into the living room. Raymond didn't want to disrespect the moment by rushing to open the box like a treasure hunter robbing an ancient grave, but on the other hand he didn't have any time to waste.

"What we got?" Max asks. "We're about to find out in a minute," Raymond says as he opens the box. Inside the box was a DVD with a note attached: *"To Raymond,"* written in his Godfather's handwriting.

"Here play this," Raymond says handing the DVD to one of his security men. Raymond continues to look through the box. He finds a business card with a physician's name, address and phone number on it. Raymond is reading the card when he hears his Godfather's voice, causing him to look up.

There he was on the TV, sitting behind a long conference table. "You did well son. This is what believing in miracles can do."

"Raymond I knew this day would come so I arranged this DVD ahead of time. I completed my purpose and my mission in life, so I had to go. As much as I wanted to stay I couldn't. See Raymond, whenever someone's purpose is fulfilled, but yet they are still around, they will become a distraction. This is the reason Moses had to pass on before the children of Israel could go into the Promised Land. If not, he would have been an obstacle to Joshua and the entire Nation. I could have prevented my death, but instead I welcomed it, because I knew I had completed my part. Now you must complete yours. Son we don't have a lot of time left so you must listen to what I have to say very carefully. Inside this box is a card and a small bottle containing something very valuable. This is what we are bringing to the international community of Africa."

Raymond takes a syringe and a small bottle out. He holds the bottle in the air with a confused look. "This looks like water," he says.

"I want to introduce you to someone," his Godfather DVD voice says. A dark-skinned African man comes into the frame and takes a seat beside his Godfather. *"This is Dr. Andrew Anaga. He is a world-renowned immunologist from Senegal. For the last ten years I have been financing his research to find a cure for AIDS. This is what we are bringing to the international community of Africa,"* his Godfather says from the DVD. Raymond sets the vial down as if it was very fragile. *"Dr. Anaga is waiting on you. Take him to the administration estate, and treat him above excellent. I built him a private hospital in the New Nation. I want you to accommodate him with anything else that he needs. Give Louise all the instructions I have given you about Dr. Anaga. Raymond we not*

only have a product that will help us be accepted by the entire continent of Africa, but the New Nation will have the solution to the world's medical crisis. Son I knew you could do it and you did, now complete the mission and I'll see you later. Raymond, before you go someone else wants to talk to you. Mr. Goodson and Dr. Anaga rise from the table and move out of the TV frame. Bishop Jackson comes into the frame and sits behind the table. Raymond can only stare wide-eyed and listen. His security men are just as surprised, but they don't utter one word.

Bishop Jackson has a big smile on his face. *"You did good son. I know you don't have a lot of time so I'm not going to say much. You did not cause my death. All of this was predestined. As you can see we made this DVD before any of our deaths occurred. All of this was a part of God's plan. You have always tried to please me and everything you've done has been good enough even when you didn't think so. Give your mother, Diamond and sister my love, some roses and a big hug for me. Finish the work son and I'll see you later."* The recording ends. Raymond and his security had to do everything in their power to fight back their tears and from falling apart in his Godfather's living room. They managed to keep their composure in order to focus and catch up with lost time. Raymond gets up from the couch and puts the vial of AIDS vaccine and the syringe in his pocket. "Get the DVD," Raymond orders as he moves towards the door, with his security following close behind him.

Picture 59: *The Healer*

Raymond and his security break into the hospital like gangbusters. They had the nurse's attention even before they reached her station. "I know you, you're Raymond Jackson," one of the nurses says, then she turns to her co-worker and says, "Where is your cell phone? Can we take a picture?"

"Can I get your autograph?" another nurse says.

"Sure, but before I do I need to see someone," Raymond says.

"It's after visiting hours," one of the nurses says.

"What is your name?" Raymond asks.

"Nurse Grace Sands," she says.

"Well, Nurse Grace, if you can look at this as a favor, I'll owe you one," Raymond says easily. The other nurses start to laugh.

Nurse Grace smiles and says, "That sounds fair." Nurse Grace goes to the computer and says, "OK, who do you want to see?"

"The sickest child AIDS patient you have here," Raymond says.

Nurse Grace gets up from the computer and starts walking down the hall. Raymond and his security begin to follow her. She acts as though she knew exactly who Raymond needed to see without any doubt. "Follow me, you want to see Dee. She is eight and the doctor says she will not see her 9th birthday, which is in less than 30 days. She is a sweetheart, always trying to stay strong for everybody and having a positive attitude about her sickness," she says.

Nurse Grace reaches Dee's room and eases the door open. Dee is asleep. "It's one thing for the adults to get AIDS because of their lifestyle, but it really tears your heart out when innocent kids are afflicted because of their parent's actions. Did you know that approximately 14,000 - 20,000 kids and youth here in America are infected with HIV? I'll be glad when they hurry up and find a cure, because I don't think I can handle seeing all of these innocent children die," Nurse Grace says.

Raymond's could not help but reflect upon the conversation his Godfather had with him after his assassination attempt in the graveyard, about dying before they know or fulfill their purpose. "So why don't you quit?" Raymond asks.

"I can't do that Mr. Jackson. I love these kids too much. Even though I don't like to see death in their little faces, it is my job to make them smile and give them the best time of their short lives. I love my job," Nurse Grace says.

"Can I spend a moment alone with her? Raymond asks.

"Oh sure take your time. She is the only child of a single parent and she can use as many visitors as she can handle." Then Nurse Grace walks out the room.

Raymond turns to his security men and say, "I want you to guard this door and don't let anyone in but Nurse Grace."

"Yes sir," Max says as he starts to move, but can't take his eyes off of Dee. She looked so innocent and so pretty, but you could also see her life draining away from her.

"Come on let's move," Raymond says to Max to snap him out of his trance. The security men leave the room. Raymond immediately removes the vial and the syringe and put them on the dresser. He prays over Dee for a few seconds before he wakes her up. "Dee, Dee," Raymond says.

Dee wakes up and assumes Raymond was another doctor. She is used to being examined by many different health care specialists. She asked, "Are you another Doctor?"

"No, I'm not. My name is Raymond Jackson. I'm a politician," Raymond says as he reaches out to gently shake Dee's hand.

"Like a mayor or governor or something?" Dee asks.

"Yes, you are right. You are a smart little girl aren't you?" Raymond says.

"So which are you?"

"Which what?"

"Are you a mayor or governor?" Dee asks.

"Well, I'm what they call a founder," Raymond says.

"What's that?" Dee asks, looking at Raymond strangely.

Raymond smiles and says, "It's not going to bite you. It's a person who starts their own business, corporation or country."

"You have your own country?" Dee asks, excited as she sits up in the bed. Raymond notices how the conversation was bringing life to her face.

"Yeah, I have my own country and it's beautiful."

"Does it have schools?" Dee asks.

Raymond smiles "Yes" with a big smile on his face.

"Does it have playgrounds with swings?" Dee asks. Raymond nods "Yes." "Do you have ice cream stores and toy stores?"

Raymond says, "Yes."

"I know what -- you don't have horses," Dee says.

"We not only have horses, but giraffes, big elephants, hippos, and zebras," Raymond states.

"Can you pet them?" Dee asks.

"All the time."

"Oh man that is a nice country!" Dee exclaims.

"And do you know what Dee, you can go to my country to live, and play with as many of the animals you want to," Raymond says.

Dee stops smiling, gets very quiet and says," I can't go to your country Mr., because I'm about to die. I have AIDS."

Raymond looks in her eyes and sees the strength and resignation that Nurse Grace described. Dee had accepted the fact she was going to die. Maybe it was because she had seen so many of her friends, other children and AIDS patients die. Or maybe it was because all the doctors didn't cure her. Her mother told her she was going to a better place and she promised her daughter she would see her again in the place where there would be no more AIDS or any other kind of diseases. She had come to grips with this, and now in her mind she was just waiting to die.

"Well, we are going to see about that," Raymond says as he takes the syringe and extracts the prescribed amount of medicine out of the bottle, and injects it into Dee's IV drip bottle.

"Will this make me better?" Dee asks.

"I pray in God's name, princess."

"Can you tell me more about your country?" Dee asks.

"Well, I'll tell you what. If you go back to sleep and dream about what you would like to do if you could come to my country," Raymond says.

"OK I like to dream. My mother said if you think about good things before you go to sleep you can have a good dream. I'll just think about being in your country and I'll dream about it," Dee says as she gets back under the covers and Raymond tucks her in.

"I'll be right here when you wake up."

"You promise?" Dee asks.

"I promise," Raymond says. Raymond looks around the room and pulls a chair next to Dee's bed and sits down. He looks at Dee who has her eyes closed and a big smile on her face, attempting to dream. This is the most wrenching sight he had ever witnessed. She is teaching Raymond a lesson. Just a few hours ago he was in the funeral home on the verge of insanity, because someone died and left him with the responsibility of getting the people to the New Nation. He thought all hope was gone. But here is a little girl who is about to die and not only is she not falling apart, but she is willing to settle for a dream about the New Nation while Raymond was about to give up on the reality of the New Nation. Her example takes his entire mission to a higher dimension. Raymond is no longer concerned about the cure for AIDS as a passport into the international community of Africa. Raymond is determined to make that happen even if he has to personally fight every nation in hand-to-hand combat. Right now Raymond is praying that Dr. Anaga's cure for the AIDS virus is effective, because of this brave little girl who dares to keep dreaming even though she is dying. If she can attempt to dream while dying, then he can die a little while attempting to dream.

⚐ ⚐ ⚐

All of the trauma and stress must have caught up with Raymond, because he too falls asleep while watching Dee dream about the New Nation. Ever since he returned to the states he hadn't had a chance to get any rest, but sometimes the Prince of Peace has a way of putting you in a place of rest. Sometimes it occurs in one of life's waiting rooms, while you are hoping for a miracle to manifest, that He says "Close your eyes and get some rest." At that moment you will discover the immense difference between sleep and rest. While Dee was in the bed getting some sleep dreaming about a better world, Raymond was in the chair getting some rest dreaming about a better tomorrow.

Raymond is awakened by the sound of Dee's voice. "Mr., Mr., Mr. Founder," Dee calls Raymond. Raymond snaps to alertness. Mr., look at me. I feel better." Dee is standing on the bed touching her toes, then she does some jumping jacks, then she puts both arms in the sky and waves them around, all of this with a smile on her face as if she can not believe her own new found strength.

Raymond stands up slowly and steps back to take a long look at her while praying, "Let this not be a dream. Let this be real." When it hits him that this is the same little girl who was dying just a few hours ago, a brilliant smile spreads across his face and heart that illuminates the entire room. Between their smiles that hospital room may have been the most radiant place on earth.

Dee became very creative like most children when they are happy; she is singing a song she just made up while jumping up and down on the bed.

♪*I feel better, I feel better, I feel better, I feel better*♪.

Max walks into the room to inform Raymond, "Sir a nurse wants to ..." but he stops in the middle of his statement when he notices Dee jumping on the bed. The same little girl who he couldn't stop staring at who had the mask of death on her face was now so full life it was unbelievable. "What? My Lord -- that stuff works fast!" Max declares.

"What time is it?" Raymond asks. "Its 5:05 am," Max replies while looking at his watch, but quickly turning back to Dee.

"What time did we get here last night?" Raymond asks while keeping his eyes on Dee as though taking his eyes off her would revoke her progress, or something would go wrong.

"It was a little after 9:00 pm," Max says.

"Eight hours this vaccine works faster than the doctor thought." Raymond calculated. A nurse enters of the room, saying to the security guards at the door, "I just need to check… Oh my Lord, what did you do to her? Dee get down from there!

"Look I feel better Ms. Sue! I feel better!" Dee says. The nurse presses the emergency button. Raymond's mind is revolving at warp speed, thinking how he can keep this situation under control, for one of the worst things you can have is a miracle out of control. Now that the vaccine proved effective, he must deliver it where it can do the greatest good.

Raymond also knew he would be in a lot of trouble if word got out that he gave a little girl the vaccine without going through the proper authorities, not to mention giving her medication that had not been FDA approved. "Go out there and find the nurse on duty. Ask her to contact Dee's mother. Tell her to get to the hospital right away," Raymond instructs Max. Max rushes out.

The nurse was trying to check Dee's vital signs, but the little girl was so excited she couldn't keep still. The other nurses came into the room expecting the worst, only to find Dee to be full of life and energy. Amazement was all on their faces. "Oh my Lord," most of them said. Most of these nurses had been praying for Dee, but still looking for the worst. That day their faith had been renewed.

Dr. Mead, Dee's doctor for the last four years, walked into the room expecting them to report the time of death. Instead he was told, "Dee is feeling much better Dr. Mead."

"What?" he said as he noticed the life in her little pretty face. Dr. Mead has been trying to help Dee since she was four and no one could convince him she would not be dead within the next 30 days. There was nothing he or anyone else could do. To see Dee in this state was a miracle.

"What are all those people doing outside? Somebody tell me what is going on in here?" Dr. Mead says as he walks over and joins the nurses in attempting to take Dee's vital signs. But Dee just wouldn't keep still.

"Look baby, you have to keep still," a nurse says.

"But I feel better," Dee says.

How did they expect a little girl who was suppose to die around this time next week, a little girl who was born with a disease she didn't have any control in getting, a little girl who lost out on her terrible twos, who never got a real chance to run and play because she was too weak before she every discovered her strength. How can they honestly expect her to keep still when everything in her very being is shouting "I'm alive! Death thought it had me, but somehow by the grace of God, I got away!"

"Is she all right?" Raymond asks Dr. Mead.

Dr. Mead looks up at Raymond while still trying to check Dee. He does a double take. "Wait I know you, you are the Vice President, back to Africa guy."

Raymond smiles and says, "Yeah, something like that. Is Dee all right sir? I don't mean to rush you, but I don't have a lot of time."

"What did you do to her?" Dr. Mead asks.

"I can't explain everything to you now, but I promise you this: if you can keep everything that happened in this room in confidence, once all of the procedures are taken care of, you will be the first physician and hospital to get the cure for AIDS in this country. But I have to know if she is fine or not."

Dr. Mead's eyes light up, "Well, I will have to run some more tests, but as far as her vital signs are concerned, she is in better health than anyone in this room, which is unbelievable!"

Two of Raymond's security men give each other high-fives.

Right then Dee's mother Barbara Edwards rushes in the room wailing, "Dee, Dee, where is my baby?" She too was expecting the worst and all of the security guards outside and in the room didn't ease her mind. "No, no, please," Dee's mother was screaming, not being able to come to grips with her child's death.

"Mommy, mommy, I feel better, I feel better," Dee assures her mother.

Her mother couldn't believe her eyes. She hugged Dee at first, then she touched her face and noticed the life in it. Then she hugged her again. Then she touched her head and hair. She noticed Dee's bright smile. Then she looked around the room at the smiles of all of the nurses and doctors. They were also nodding their heads to confirm what Dee was saying.

Then it happened for the first time in that hospital: a mother's tears of sorrow were transformed into tears of joy, right before their eyes. As Dee's mother hugged her tight, Dee said while pointing to Raymond, "That man, he healed me momma. He's the one."

Dee's mother looked at Raymond. Raymond walked over to Ms. Edwards and said, "Don't get up, please. This is my card. My name is Raymond Jackson."

"I know," Dee mother whispers.

"As I was telling Dr. Mead, I can't explain everything at this time, but once the doctor gets finished running tests on Dee I would like you and your daughter to move to the New Nation. There, some of the best doctors in the world will continue to monitor Dee's health. You will not need to be concerned about any medical expenses or any bills for that matter. If you agree, my security man will be here waiting for you and waiting on your every call, just tell him what you need. What do you say about that?" Raymond asks.

Barbara is crying more tears of joy as she says, "The Lord is good Mr. Jackson."

"All the time!" Raymond exhorts, confirming the miracle to himself also.

Barbara hugs him again and says, "Thank you very much."

Raymond turns to one of his security men and say, "I need you to stay with them. Don't let them out of your sight. Whatever they need, make sure they have it. Also, I want them on the stage with me tomorrow at 9:00 am sharp."

"Yes sir you can count on me sir," his security man says.

Raymond is about to walk out of the room when Dee calls him, "Mr. Founder" she runs to him and hugs him as if she's been knowing him all of her short life. "I dreamt about your country, there was a big house and there was lots of water in the back, and I was playing in the water. *"Could she be talking about the administration estate where there was a beach in the back of the mansion?"* Raymond thought to himself.

"Well, your dream is about to come true because you are coming to my country and you will be able to play as much as you want," Raymond says.

"Okay!" Dee hollers as she claps her hands then gives Raymond another hug and Raymond hugs her back.

"Sir we have to go," Max says.

"You're right," Raymond says as he puts Dee down, walks out of the room and moves towards the exit.

"Mr. Jackson," a voice calls. Raymond stops, turns around and notices Nurse Grace. She catches up with him, "Can I have that picture now?" she asks.

"Oh that's right. Sure you can," Raymond says. As he stands beside her, she takes out the cell phone, put it in front of them and takes the picture. Raymond takes out his card and signs the back, and hands it to her. "Dee is going to need a private nurse for awhile. If you want that job it comes with an excellent pay and a promotion. The promotion will consist of running an AIDS recovery therapy center. There will be many of them soon. Give that some thought, then give me a call and we will take it from there," Raymond says.

Nurse Grace smiles, "I will think about it," she promises. Raymond didn't realize she started the thinking process right then, and the truth of the matter was, there was really nothing to think about. Grace Sands had been an unwilling but constant witness to the devastation brought by AIDS. But now she is being offered a job that would allow her to see AIDS being destroyed once and for all. Nurse Grace really didn't need to think about working in an AIDS recovery therapy center, because that would be the therapy she needed as well.

Raymond walked towards the limo while humming a tune he couldn't seem to get out of his head.

♪*I feel better, I feel better*♪.

Those three words effortlessly described the turn of events that took place in Raymond's life in the last nine hours. He came into the hospital feeling bitter and left feeling better. And he wasn't even the one who took the medicine, but the one who gave it.

⚐ ⚐ ⚐

In the limo Raymond is more excited than Dee; he could barely sit still. He was looking for his phone and Dr. Anaga's card at the same time. He doesn't know who to call first, Diamond, or his mother and sister to give them the message his father gave to them.

Or should he call Louise who is probably going out of her mind right now trying to locate him. From the time Raymond was in the funeral home viewing his Godfather's body his cell phone was turned off, and now that he thinks about it he need to call Louise first, to inform her about everything, "Get Louise on the speakerphone," Raymond tells Max.

"Where is she?" Max asks.

"Check the headquarters or her cell," Raymond replies. Raymond gets on his cell phone and attempts to call Diamond, but the signal keeps dropping.

"Hello," Louise's voice comes over the speakerphone in the limo.

"Louise," Raymond says putting away his cell phone.

"Raymond? Where have you been? I have been calling all over for you!"

"Well, I have been to hell and back. I hope I didn't take too long," Raymond says.

"Well, welcome back since you put it that way."

"I'm about to give you some very important information, I need you to write these instructions down. Are you ready?" Raymond asks.

"Let me get a pen. OK go," Louise says.

"Dr. Andrew Anaga," Raymond says.

"I know him. He used to do AIDS research. He had to be in his early 20s when they started the research. I heard he was expelled from their research team because he was taking too many risks," Louise says.

"Well, he must have taken all the right ones because he found the cure for AIDS," Raymond says.

"What? No!"

"Yes. And that is what my Godfather arranged for us to bring to the International Community of Africa," Raymond says.

"Brilliant!"

"Yeah, that's what I said. Now look you need to get the jet, get Dr. Anaga and take him to the New Nation estate. The operation's administration is going to show you his private hospital and research team. Louise I need you to take care of him to the fullest, treat him above excellent. Everything has already been prearranged and he knows what to do. Oh Louise, tell my wife I'll see her on Saturday morning," Raymond adds.

"I'll take care of this sir and everything is set for tomorrow; the transportation operations, the event at Atlanta arena and we have close to four million people registered to leave, some tomorrow and some later," Louise says.

"Give your assistant all the information you think I'll need and tell Bryant to come with my driver in the morning," Raymond says.

"What are you going to do now sir?"

"I'm going to sleep until tomorrow morning."

"I was going to suggest that very thing."

"Louise we did it! It's done! I'll see you on the other side of the world," Raymond says.

"Yes sir, I'll see you there," Louise answers.

Raymond lays his head back with a smile on his face and says in a whisper, *"You thought of everything."*

STATION BREAK!!! This is an announcement from the New Nation Campaign Headquarters

IT IS NOW 1 DAY UNTIL DEPARTURE IT'S OUR TIME!

Log onto

www.newnation.org

to register today and see the layout of the New Nation of Africa.

Picture 60: *Departure Day*

This day has been highly anticipated by African Americans all over the country. African American students, teachers, businesspersons, corporate leaders, professionals, religious leaders, entertainers, athletes and the small and the great alike have been looking forward to Departure Day.

Even some of the mainstream white Americans have high expectations when it comes to D-Day. There are many white Americans who see the B2B move for African Americans as an example of progress and democracy. To them this proves the American system works; a system that is built on immigrants and people from different cultures finding liberty and the pursuit of happiness in order to make the American dream a reality. Part of that American dream is to grow and achieve one's highest potential. The white Americans who see this move this way are more excited about this day than some African Americans.

But others in the mainstream believe this move is racist and has a malevolent intent. Some of these groups, whether they are right or left wing, suggest that African Americans can only achieve greatness within the America's borders. This is the 21st century manifestation of Jim Crowism. That is, it's OK for African Americans to achieve great awards under the umbrella of mainstream American life. But to suggest that African Americans can not take their achievements and accomplishments to a global level is to revive the same old Jim Crow attitude "Separate but equal." African Americans are equal in America but separated when it comes to events of international importance.

The white American mainstream are not the only ones who feel this way about the move to Africa. There are many African Americans who think as long as they are on American soil they can be productive, prosperous and problem-free. But if they decide to move into the global territory they will not be able to survive. Looking from a historical perspective one might assign the roots of this problem to low self-esteem or a "plantation" mentality. Raymond's projection is that African Americans have achieved getting a voice in every area

America have to offer and now it's time to reach an international level to be heard in the world at large. For African Americans to say this can't be done is to suggest their self-esteem will not allow them to look at themselves as worthy to compete in world trade, international sports, global entertainment, world education, global technology, or social and political development. This is a similar situation to the slaves at the time of emancipation proclamation, when they were told they could leave the plantation; some opted to stay and to simply change their identity from slave to sharecropper, because they didn't think they could survive off of the plantation. When African Americans side with some of the mainstream by saying the B2B move can't be done, they are mentally living on a political plantation, because they will always be sharecroppers and will be cheated out of their glorious destiny.

There is another group who could hardly wait for the departure day to come -- the haters. They have no reason why they are not going or staying, and if they are white Americans they have no reason why they want the African Americans to stay or go. They are only excited to see this day come in order to say, "I told you so." They are looking for something to go wrong so they can be a witness that it didn't work out.

Finally, there are hate groups, people like Shineck who prayed for this day to come in order to get rid of the so-called 'less desirables." So many people are finding this to be a very exciting time for many different reasons.

President Lyman authorized anyone who wanted to support the D-Day events to take the day off work and school, even if they haven't registered to depart. There were some families, friends, co-workers and classmates who are departing and Mr. Lyman has provided a time of support and goodbyes.

In the African American community it is a time for a great celebration even if most are not departing. Just the very fact that they had reached this point in history given where they started in this country, was a reason for joy. The move to Africa gave some an opportunity to celebrate, while others saw a perfect opportunity to get away. Get away from the injustice, crime, systemic racism, hate groups, unfairness, and poverty.

Ms. Gaither, the high school teacher, came in a little early to prepare her lesson plans for next week's assignments, so she could take the rest of the day to enjoy the D-Day festivities and begin her three-day weekend. The young gang member Tar runs into the classroom all out of breath. "Boy you startled me, slow down," Ms. Gaither says.

"I can't Ms. G somebody is after me," Tar says as he looks out of the window.

"Tar stop moving around and tell me what is going on."

Tar gets on the side of the wall to peep out the window at one of the gang members who was chasing him. "All right, something happened a month ago with the gang I'm hanging out with," Tar says still peeping out of the window.

"I told you not to ..."

Tar interrupts and says, "Ms. G, this is not the time to be telling me..." What was that?" Tar asks as he walks over to the door, but notices it is just the principal walking down the hall. "Oh it's just him," Tar says and then goes back to the window and spots two gang members. "To make a long drama short, we just had a shoot out with the Eastside gang," Tar says.

"Did you kill somebody boy?" Ms. Gaither asks as she stands up.

"No, but somebody got shot."

Ms. Gaither looks out the window. "Ms. G, I think you should get away from that window," Tar says.

"They are looking for you not me. Besides why did you bring them over here?" Ms. Gaither asks.

"It's not like I passed out invitations or something, I was running for my life."

"Look we've got to get out of here," Ms. Gaither insists.

"I was thinking the same thing," Tar says.

They both walk to the door. Tar pulls out his gun. "What are you doing with a gun?"

"That's a dumb question," Tar responds.

"Put that up and don't take it out unless our lives are in danger. Now come on." They both walk out into the school hallway. "It is a good thing school is closed," Ms. Gaither thinks to herself as she pulls Tar towards the employee parking lot. As they are walking down the hallway they pass the principal, Mr. Owens.

"Good day Ms. Gaither," Mr. Owens says.

"Good day Principal Owens." After walking a few steps Ms. Gaither stops. "Oh Principal Owens," she calls.

"Yes Ms. Gaither?"

"Wait right here," Ms. Gaither tells Tar. Ms. Gaither walks to where Principal Owens was standing. "I just wanted to inform you that you are a big fat liar. I know what kind of recommendation you gave me to stop my promotion. After all I have done for this school and your career, you are a backstabbing, sneaky, cheating piece of trash scum on the side of a dirt road. I hope you never get someone as good as me to work for a low life like yourself again. And don't even think about blackballing me any more, because, where I'm going you don't have any blackballing power. Oh, by the way, I quit!" Ms. Gaither shouts. She walks back to Tar who is shocked about what he overheard.

"What was that all about?" Tar asks as they walk swiftly down the hall.

"Just some baggage I couldn't take with me," Ms. Gaither says.

"You alright?" Tar asks.

"Better, much better," Ms. Gaither says.

⚐ ⚐ ⚐

Make no mistake about it, November 3, 2008 will go down in history as one of African Americans' biggest celebrations. Everywhere in the African American community someone is having a party. There are cars with B2B stickers, private businesses with B2B flags and banners, and people are wearing B2B T-shirts, hats and buttons. Raymond's staff already had New Nation departure brunches in the 25 largest cities where African Americans live and also in the other states. Now they have gone all out for D-Day by giving away B2B stickers, banners, hats, T-shirts, buttons, coffee mugs, pens and anything that B2B can be plastered on. The street and promotional teams have set up parties in every city around the country where free food and non-alcoholic drinks are dispensed. Some of these parties are cookouts, and others are being held indoors. Media coverage is high so everyone will know there is a party going on. Singers, rappers and other entertainers have been hired to put on a free B2B concerts in some of the major cities. All of these parties have motivated others to throw their own gatherings in light of what D-Day means to them. This is exactly what the New Nation staff wants to happen, because this will help them reach areas they could not. This great celebration is the Emancipation Proclamation party of the 21st century. This was the mother of all parties. No other party would ever outdo this major celebration. It was as though any and every form of progress that took place in the African American community, that enhanced the betterment of America and its citizens was being celebrated all at one time, once and for all.

Raymond was scheduled to give his departure speech at 10:00 am. The arena is packed to capacity. Many people from different races and cultures have come to celebrate together on this great day.

The people are wearing many different T-shirts and hats. Some read: "Happy D-Day, B2B (Back to the Beginning)", and others read, "It's not a Movement, it's a Major Move." Everyone was in high spirits as though their favorite candidate just won the election. The media was all over the place, interviewing people, and asking them what this day meant to them. Freedom Jones, an anchor from the largest black TV network is interviewing three ladies who happen to be best friends -- an African American, a white American, and a Hispanic American. All three of them are very attractive and in their early 20's. You can tell they are enjoying themselves with their party hats on, noisemakers and big bright smiles. "Are you all having fun yet?" Freedom asks trying to raise her voice above the party noise.

"Yes, yes, man yeah," they all answered.

"I'm going to ask you three the question I have been asking everyone here. What does this day mean to each of you? I'm going to start from my right," Freedom says.

The African American female, Coretta Phillips who has B2B painted on the side of her face speaks into the microphone, "This is an exciting time for my race, culture and family. A lot of people didn't think this day would ever come in our time, but I'm glad to be able to see history in the making. I'm going to finish my education in the New Nation and receive my Masters in Theology and Psychology.

"All right do it big then sister," Freedom says.

The white American female, Jane Wright says, "This day means a lot to me because it represents progress. The statue of liberty engraving states, 'Give me your tired, your poor, your huddled masses yearning to breathe free, The wretched refuse of your teeming shore, Send these, the homeless, tempest-tossed, to me: I lift my lamp beside the golden door.' Well, today is a picture of what can happen when destiny truly is at work. All dreams can come true, inside and outside of the American dream for the betterment of all humanity."

"Lady, you sound like a politician yourself," Freedom says.

"I'm studying Political Science and I worked as an intern in the governor's office," she says.

"And you Miss Lady what does this day mean to you?" Freedom asks the Latina female, Carlita Garzon who has a T-shirt on that reads, "Let's Take It Back."

"I love this celebration because it lets me know that all things are possible, and if you have faith in God you can do anything," she says.

"And what do you do?" Freedom asks.

"I work for my mother," she says.

"That's good, keeping it all in the family. Well, there you have it America, three different races and cultures explain what this day means to them. You can't get any better than that," Freedom says to the camera. "Before I let you three pretty ladies go, let me ask you one more question. Is Raymond fine or what?" The girls start screaming, shouting and laughing.

"Yeah, yes, he is the finest," the three reply.

Freedom starts to laugh, "I shouldn't have gotten them started," Freedom says and starts moving throughout the arena interviewing many others. Freedom finds an African American male o interview. "You know I have been interviewing people for the last several months about the B2B. Most of them were celebrities, stars or professional experts. You will be the first average African American male I ask this question to: What does this all mean to you Michael Bailey?"

"Well, I have been in and out of prison since childhood. I have a trade now and I want a change. I want to start completely over and I believe the New Nation will give me that chance to change. I'm taking my son and we are going to make something happen in a positive way," he says.

"That's major, real major," Freedom says as she gives him a hug. "It's close to 10:00 am and we are going to get ready for Raymond's departure speech and we'll be right back after that. Peace," Freedom says.

⚐ ⚐ ⚐

Raymond, his staff, his security, Dee and her mother, Ms. Edwards all walk on the stage. Everyone stands in front of their seats except Raymond who walks straight to the podium. One of Raymond's security men is positioned on his right, one on his left and the others behind him. As soon as the crowd notices Raymond they go wild. They are clapping, cheering, blowing whistles, using noisemakers, waving and screaming. Raymond stands behind the podium impeccably attired in a stylish suit, custom made shirt with matching tie and pocket square, and a pair of laced, cap-toe shoes. He looks like a million bucks and is feeling priceless. Raymond takes his time to scan the arena, while smiling broadly. The crowd of about 100 thousand gives him a standing ovation that seems like it has been going on for hours.

"To the President of these United States, to every government and city official in this Nation, to every leader of every organization, corporation and company, to my family, staff and security and last but not least, to every lady, gentleman, boy and girl in this fine country of ours, I give honor to you. Allow me to begin my departure address by saying, "We did it!" The crowd erupts into a cheer.

"We did what most people said couldn't be done. We moved obstacles that seemed unmovable. We overcame odds that seemed impossible and we faced oppositions that were unbearable, we dreamed the impossible dream," Raymond says. The crowd claps and cheers. Nicky is seating in the upper seat in the back of the arena, tears are streaming down her face as she is clapping and saying, "You did it baby, you did it." It's uncertain if these are tears of pain because she hasn't come to grips that she and Raymond will never be together again, or if these are tears of joy, believing Raymond would have been dead by now. But she sees him looking so good in the spotlight of triumph, saying to the Nation, the world and all of its citizens, "We made it."

"We had to face a lot of difficulties. Many people had to die on this mission; I lost my father, Bishop Jackson and my Godfather Paul Goodson, who was the architect of this move. But when I realize the amount of progress we made in such a short amount of time, when I see how we have redefined the word progress, when I notice the smile that comes along with adding another chapter to American History and African American History at the same time, I can say without a shadow of doubt, if I had to do it all over again I wouldn't change one thing," Raymond says. The crowd applauds and fills the arena once more with smiles for miles.

"We have men and women all across this country watching via TV, radio, satellite and computer. They are witnessing something they never saw before and something they may never see again. I want you to help me make it clear what they are witnessing. I have been going all over this Nation telling everyone this is not a movement, but it is...," Raymond pauses.

"A major move," the crowd shouts back at Raymond. "That's right a major move and whenever a people dare to dream the impossible dream of making a major move there will be pain, there will be problems and there will be perplexities. The Bible speaks of a time when two people will be in the field, one will be taken and the other will not. Well, my friends we have experienced just a glimpse of that revelation today. We have felt the pain of progression separation. There will always be pain when one person wants to progress into greatness and the other person wants to stay in the place of the familiar. There will also be problems whenever there is someone who has a strong desire to pull them into a brighter tomorrow and the other person only has a desire to stay in yesterday's past and talk about yesterday's possibilities. There will always be conflict when one is on the launching pad of faith about to blast off into the highest orbit of opportunity, while the other person has settled for the downward path of procrastination."

"This major move has brought a necessary pain to many households," (Dr. Williams is sitting in the arena looking at Raymond while her husband is watching Raymond from his Judge's chambers), "pain to many relationships," (Michele is sitting in the arena while Kevin is listening at home), "pain to many business partnerships," (Whitney is watching Raymond on TV in her office, while Kim is watching him on a large screen TV at the boat dock), "pain to many friends," (Tee is listening to Raymond in her car, while Keith is viewing the speech at the airport), "and deep pain to many families." (Raymond's mother and sister, Julia and Cristal, are watching from an enclosed area nearby). This movement has caused many to sacrifice relationships that were priceless. I must inform you this is exactly what a great move consists of. I had to learn the hard way my friends, a great move does not consist of lights, camera, and action. Hollywood can't produce a great move. Church can't preach a great move. Corporations can't manufacture a great move. A major move consists of giving up everything that will hinder you from making the move," Raymond says. Applause erupts throughout the arena once again. It was as though Raymond had confirmed why they felt positive about the pain they were feeling. It was also a great explanation to others who didn't understand if something was so good why it felt so bad. The applause was a language that said, "Now I understand."

"Would you help me get this message across by telling three people, 'It's your move'," Raymond says. Everyone in the crowd excitedly finds three people to tell them, "It's your move." This brought a ruffle of sound throughout the arena.

"That's right, the first thing you must do in order to make a major move is embrace the reality that there will be a painful sacrifice that needs to be made to start the move. The second thing you must know within your heart of hearts is it's your move. No one can make it for you and no one can take it from you. It's your move, no one can encourage you and no one can discourage you. It's your move, no one can convince you and no one can dissuade you. It's your God given..." "Move!" the crowd shouts before Raymond had a chance to complete his statement. The crowd claps and cheers. It appears they'd had a good idea Raymond was going to give the best speech he could give, because this might be the last time he would speak in the United States. They were all on the edge of their seats and he was living up to their expectations and more.

"We announced this move on national news, we celebrated this move on ZET, we gossiped about this move in barbershops and beauty salons. We debated about this move on political forums. We taught about this move in our schools and even prayed about this move in our churches. Well, it's time to stop all this talking and it's time to make our move. I have done all I can do, I laid out the blueprints of the foundation my Godfather and his ancestors have built, and now it's time for you to make your move. My sisters, my brothers you can no longer blame the white man, and you can no longer blame the government, because they have already given us the green light to make our move. You can't even use the excuse of what lies ahead in Africa, because the red carpet of greatness has been laid out for us to walk the path of destiny and claim our identity in the international community of humanity. It's time to make your move," Raymond says. The crowd roars in agreement. "I want to take this time to thank the President of these United States. I want to thank all the Presidents from Mr. Washington to Mr. Lyman. I want to thank all the grand leaders who have enforced the law of the land. Some of those laws hurt us and some helped us. I want to thank the slave masters of my ancestors. I must thank everyone who had anything to do with segregation, Jim Crow and any type of race hate crime. I realize that might sound bold, but in light of everything we've been through as a race and everything we are about to receive, our past experiences have prepared us to make the move we are about to take today," Raymond says. The crowd could not wait to applause and they did it in a big way.

"Which brings us to the third fact we must understand clearly, and that is, this major move is a strong move. That is, there are some who think we should leave bitter, but no we are leaving better. And make no mistake about this, every fortune and misfortune we have gained being citizens of this great country directly or indirectly has made us better movers and shakers for the opportunities of tomorrow," Raymond says.

The crowd stands up and gives him another ovation. "That's right my friends we are moving better. Our posture is better. Our stride is better. Our motion is better. Our step is better. Ladies, (I tell you) even your switch is better! Our direction is better. Our outlook is better. Our focus is better. Our objectives are better. Our aim is better. And 50 percent of the credit for all of this betterment goes to the good and bad, the ups and downs, the yes's and the no's and the help and the hindrances we experienced in this country. So therefore we are not only prepared to sit in the seat of brotherhood, but now we are prepared to sit at the international table of the world and contribute on an international level. I want to say thank you America, for making us *move* better than ever!"

"Preach son," Raymond's mother Julia says as she watches from a VIP area.

"He sounds just like daddy when he says that," Cristal replies.

"Finally my brothers and sisters, after we accept the fact that this is our move and after we recognize we are moving better than ever, there's only one thing left to do, and that is, move out!" Raymond says.

"Take your time son," a man shouts from the crowd.

"Talk to us," another shouts out.

"Most adults here can identify with growing up in your parents' home. When you were a baby it was nice. When you were a child it was cute. When you were a teenager there were changes. When you were a young adult there was conflict. When you became an adult it was time to go," Raymond says. The crowd laughs, and then claps. "It was time for you to go -- for their sake and yours. The place was getting too small and you needed more room to do what you needed to do. Well, America the African American community has nursed on the breast of lady liberty for a long time. We have matured from the cradle of slavery to be offered a position in the White House. We have achieved and accomplished as much as we can in this house, and we feel it is in the best interest of both parties that one of the children pack their bags and moves out."

President Lyman is watching Raymond from the Oval Office with his cabinet members when he says, "Good riddance, and I hope I never see you again."

The crowd is on their feet clapping. Raymond has taken them to a higher level with the revelation and wisdom he is sharing, and it seems the more he gives them the more they want. Raised hands, clapping, pumped fists, cheering, whistling, noisemakers, and screaming are telling Raymond "Take us higher if you can." *If he can?* There's nothing more that he wants to do than take them to a place mentally and spiritually they have never been before.

"Well, maybe somebody didn't like that example, so allow me to give you another one. Whenever you stay at one place too long you can wear out your welcome. Sometimes the person who put you up for a few days, that somehow turned into months, can start leaving suggestions that it is time for you to leave. If you don't get any of these hints, others can become more obvious as time goes on. Well, I don't know about you, but I got all of the hints. Now for those who are a little socially and politically slow I'm going to remind you with these obvious hints." "Black males are overpopulating the prison system is a hint. The high rate of African American youths from ages 15-35 who are infected with AIDS or HIV is a hint. Drug addiction at an all time high in the community, that's a hint. Illegal immigrants being hired, before African Americans is a hint. All of these facts are just a few hints that send the message, it's time to move out. It's time to move out of crack houses, move out of fear, move out of the ghetto, move out of greed, move out of violence and move into a place of possibilities." The crowd is still on their feet, no one is in their seat – Raymond has taken them to a higher spiritual level in no time at all.

"For many months I spoke to you as a politician who became a spiritual motivator on the way to fulfilling my purpose. But right at this very minute I'm changing my tune. I'm speaking to you as a drill sergeant commanding every true soldier to prepare to move out. Prepare to move out by trains, planes, boats, and jets. And while we are moving out please don't forget the spirits of Frederick Douglass, George Washington Carver, Carter G. Woodson, WEB DuBois, Edward M. Bannister, Joe Louis, Simon Bolivian, Joan Baez, Marcus Garvey, Langston Hughes, Jesse Owens, Booker T. Washington, Malcolm X, Martin Luther King, Ethel Waters, Sojourner Truth, Adam Clayton Powell, Biggie Smalls, TuPac Shakur, Jam Master J, and Left Eye Lisa Lopes, and all of our ancestors who saw this day approaching over the horizon."

A lion running, is projected over the large screens all around the arena, and the crowd loves it. They clap and cheer, some just stare at the focus and determination of the lion as he runs, fast and furious. "It's time for us to move in the pace of that great lion. It's time to move to the place of destiny, and I need somebody to do me a favor as I prepare to get on my jet to catch the first flight to Africa. Would somebody get on the international phone and tell the Europeans in Europe we are on the move. Tell the Australians in Australia we are on the move. Tell the Chinese in China we are on the move. Tell the Egyptians in Egypt we are on the move. Tell the Germans in Germany we are on the move. Tell the Indians in India we are on the move. Tell the Ethiopians in Ethiopia we are on the move. Don't forget about the Spaniards in Spain, we are on the move. Tell the British in the United Kingdom we are on the move. Tell the New Zealanders in New Zealand we are on the move. Tell the Japanese in Japan we are on the move. Man, tell the whole wide world there is a people who are on the move, and they have purpose in their heart, possibilities in their mind, the power of God in their hands, persistence in their feet, and the promise of a divine possession in their eyes. You'd better tell them because when they see us coming in the words of Ludacris, they better move and get out of the way," Raymond says. The crowd cheers, claps, some are crying, waving their hands, jumping and screaming. This was undoubtedly the best speech Raymond had given since he left for spiritual rehabilitation. He was speaking with an ultimate power. He spoke for himself and for the people. This is what they came to hear. Those who had been following Raymond knew if there was ever going to be a time they would hear Raymond give his all, it would be now. Raymond gave them everything they were looking for and much more. The fire that came from his words and voice felt like the spirit of the living God was speaking through him to a people who needed to be inspired and motivated before they made the major move to the New Nation. They had been inspired, motivated and uplifted, if anyone had any doubt about whether they should move or why should they move, those doubts had been completely erased by the power of Raymond's words. Raymond lifted up his right hand and waved to the crowd. He walked off the stage with his staff and his security following him.

Picture 61: *How Do We Say Goodbye?*

Departure Day has been taking place for three days. If you are not at a party you might be saying your goodbyes to someone who is leaving or someone who is staying. This great time in history contains many contradictions. People are reluctant to part. Divided souls always cause pain in the tenderest parts of the heart. The mind says, "I must go but I hate to leave." Emotion says, "I want you to stay but I know you must go." This will cause any poor soul to struggle to find words to express one of the simplest terms that has been used for centuries, "Goodbye."

Many people are moving around on the boat docks. People are saying their goodbyes, waving to one another, both coming and going. Kim is walking with her bags in hand towards the vast ocean liner, but before she can reach the entrance she hears someone calling out her name, "Kim, Kim." Kim turns around and it's Whitney. "No you weren't going to leave without saying goodbye."

Kim is smiling from ear to ear. "I knew I couldn't get away from you. How did you know…?" Kim asks.

"Well, you always talked about going on a cruise so knowing you like I do, I thought you would try to accomplish two things at once," Whitney says.

"You know me too well sister, too well." Whitney and Kim hug.

"I'm going to really miss you Kim."

"I'm going to miss you too. Maybe you can come once I get everything established." "Maybe, we'll see. It's not going to be the same without you," Whitney says still holding Kim in her arms. "Don't say stuff like that. I'm going to start crying all over you," Kim says. "Well, we will just be crying on each other!" Whitney replies. Kim pulls away from Whitney, "I have to go," Kim says and then they both kiss each other. "You know I'm going to run your phone bill up don't you," Kim says. "Oh you finally found a way to get back at me for my mooching," Whitney says. They both laugh out loud to the point where everyone around them stares and smiles a little. It was the only way these two could have said goodbye.

⚐ ⚐ ⚐

Tim is sitting in the waiting area of the ATL Airport reading a book. A young lady sits beside him. "What are you reading?" she asks.

"A drama," Tim says.

"I love dramas," she replies.

"My name is Tim," he says reaching out his hand.

"My name is Tyre," she says as they shake hands.

"Are you going to the New Nation of Africa?"

"Yes, yes I am," Tim says. "Me too,"

"Good, I'll have someone to talk with on the way," Tim says.

Tim turns to get something out of his bag and spots Scott. "Excuse me for a second I'll be right back. Here you can read this if you like," Tim says and hands Tyre the book.

Tim walks over to where Scott is standing, "What are you doing here?" Tim asks. "Man you don't have to play hard with me. I wanted to talk to you before you left," Scott says. Speak your mind." "Look man I felt what you were saying about being fake. I didn't at first, but now I get it, but I wanted to explain something," Scott says. "I'm listening." "I was like you a few years ago coming to college looking for something or someone to believe in. So I ran across these brothers who sounded like they had it all thought out and all together. They put me down with blacks having their own businesses, corporations and even their own Nation one day. Well, when the B2B move happened, they started coming up with excuses not to go," Scott said. "So you followed your leaders?" Tim asks. "Yeah, until you made me look at myself and I didn't like what I saw. They are just talkers and I'm a doer. I like making things happen. So I got myself together and I handled my business," Scott said pulling out his ticket and passport. Tim smiled and gave him a hug. "Man that's big. What time is your flight? "4:15 pm. What about yours?" Scott asked.

"Mine is at 2:00 pm," Tim said looking at his watch. "They are about to call me in a few minutes. Look, let me get my bag and I want to introduce you to someone," Tim says. They both walked over to where Tyre was sitting.

"Scott this is the lovely Tyre and Tyre this is my boy Scott," Tim says. "Nice to meet you," they both say. "Flight 112 is boarding at gate 15," the stewardess announces over the loud speaker. "Well, my man, we'll see you later, this is our flight." Tyre doesn't move, "This is not my flight. I don't leave until 4:15 pm," she says.

"Well, look what we have here," Scott says as he sits down in Tim's seat next to Tyre. Tim just looks at Tyre and then realizes she only mentioned she was going, but not what time she was departing. "Man you'd better get to stepping if you don't want to miss your flight. We'll catch up with you in the New Nation," Scott says teasing Tim. Tim walks past them while saying to Scott, "You make me sick," then to Tyre, "Give me my book." Tim takes his book and leaves. Scott laughs.

⚐ ⚐ ⚐

At another airport gate Keith and his father are waiting for their flight to be called when Keith's father notices a couple running through the airport. "See what I mean son, all these people rushing because they started at the last minute. "Yeah, getting up at four in the morning to be here on time was a good idea," Keith says while shaking his head. Keith notices his father looking around the airport, "Who are you looking for Dad?" Keith asks. "A friend who is suppose to be seeing us off." Keith takes out his cell phone and begins to play a game. "Did you talk to your girl friend lately?" his father asks. "I've been calling her, but I think she is not trying to talk to me since I told her about me leaving for Africa." "Son I feel bad about us dropping everything and leaving. It's hard to compete with the illegal immigrant labor market in this country, and I heard it's going to get worse. The wages they are working for are not allowing me to get a fair bid on the contracts. So I look at this move as a once-in-a-lifetime chance," Keith's father says. "I understand, it's a chance for us to come up in the world," Keith says.

"That's right, and once you get out of college you will be working full time," his father says. "Yeah, I'm going to find a way to take the business to an international level. Maybe issue an IPO on Wall Street or something," Keith says. "Now you are thinking," his father says. Keith returns back to playing his game. "Look son I'm going to get something to drink. Do you want anything?"

"Yeah, a soda please," Keith says without looking up.

"You got it," his dad says as he walks away.

While Keith is into the game his cell phone rings. "Hello," Keith says.

"You don't know how to call a sister," Keith recognizes Tee's voice.

"Man I have been trying to call you for days," Keith says.

"I know that's why I'm here."

"What?" Keith says as Tee walks in front of him. "Oh that's how you do," Keith says with a big smile on his face. Keith stares and then gives her a big hug. "How did you find me?"

"I called your father to talk to him about the situation and he took time out to explain to me how important this was to your family. Then he made me promise I would come to see you off," Tee says.

"That's my dad," Keith says.

"Yeah, he is cool. I wish my dad were like that," Tee says. Keith takes Tee by both hands, looks into her eyes and says, "I thought I really loved you, but I'm still discovering what love and life really are. I knew I should have thought of all of this that night, but it took this move to help me to realize it." "Yeah, it was my fault too. I wanted us to share something special without thinking about what could take place in the future," Tee admits. "Look, I want us to keep in touch, and maybe during the summer I can come to America to chill with you, and you can come to Africa to hang out with me, it will be like our vacation spots," Keith suggests.

"Sounds good to me," Tee replies. Keith's father returns with three drinks. "Hey dad I found the friend you were looking for," Keith says. "Why Tee, what are *you* doing here?" his dad acts surprised. "Yeah right," Keith says and they all laugh.

⚐⚐⚐

Ms. Gaither and Tar get out of the cab and head into the train station. "Give me the gun," Ms. Gaither says.

"No, I got it," Tar says.

"Do you think you are going to make it through here with that in your pocket?" Ms. Gaither asks.

"I guess you got a point."

"Come on, hand it over," Ms. Gaither says. Tar pulls the gun out while Ms. Gaither pulls out a bag, "Put it in here," Ms. Gaither says. Tar places the gun in the bag and they both walk into the station. Ms. Gaither slips the bag into the trashcan on their way to the ticket counter. "I need two tickets to Los Angeles," Ms. Gaither says.

"Where are we going?" Tar asks, not sure of what he heard.

"Well, we will get two tickets to LA, and when we get there you can get a passport to go to the New Nation of Africa from there," Ms. Gaither responds.

"Hold, hold I don't want to go to Africa." "Hold, hold you should have thought of that when you were gang banging," Ms. Gaither says. "Man can't we go to somewhere close, like Jersey or something?" Tar asks. "Yes we can, but I'm not on my way to Jersey, I'm on my way to Africa. Do you want to go or do you want to stay here and shoot it out with your gang friends?" Ms. Gaither says as she hands the attendant her credit card. "How long do I have to stay?" Tar asks.

"I'll tell you what, let things cool down over here for a while and if you don't like it you can come back," Ms. Gaither says. "Is that a deal?" Tar asks. "Word," Ms. Gaither says Tar smiles and says, "You know that is played out don't you?" Ms. Gaither puts her credit card in her purse and they begin to walk towards the trains.

"I will need to stop by the bank to get some cash," Ms. Gaither says. "I got some cash." "Yeah right, I need a little more than what you have," Ms. Gaither says. "More than this?" Tar asks as he opens his book bag and shows Ms. Gaither ten thousand dollars. "Boy, put that up," Ms. Gaither says as she closes the bag and looks around to see if anyone saw what she can't believe she just saw. "What are you doing with… where did you get that … you know what, don't even tell me, I don't even want to know," she says and then takes Tar by the arm and walk towards the trains. "That will come in handy where we are going," Ms. Gaither says.

Picture 62: *I Fought A Good Fight*

Raymond, his staff, his security, Dee and Ms. Edwards get out of the limos and walk towards the jets. Max thought it would be a good idea for Raymond to be alone in order to get some rest on his way to the New Nation, so he asked Bryant to arrange for two jets instead of one. "Come with me sir, you will be flying in this jet, this way you can get some much needed rest," Max says.

"Man that sounds too good to be true," Raymond says. Raymond turns to Bryant, "Look, I want you to take good care of Dee and her mother. Explain everything I told you about them to Louise. They are your responsibility," Raymond says. Raymond and Max walked toward the other jet.

"Sir, sir," a young man's voice called out making Raymond stop and turn around. It was his young security man. When he caught up to them he said, "Sir, I just wanted to say it has been an honor to guard you during these events. You are a great inspiration to me. You have taught me a lot and I'll never forget you," he said.

"Are you leaving me son?" Raymond asks.

"Yes sir, I'm going to my next assignment," he says.

Raymond shakes his hand, "Thank you for being there for me at all times and God bless you and your family." Raymond steps into the jet. The young agent now addresses Max. "Sir thank you for an opportunity to watch Mr. Jackson. Thanks for picking me for your team." "You did a good job son. Take care," Max says. "We did it sir," the young security man says. "Excuse me?" Max says. "We didn't let him die before his mission was completed," the young man says with a big smile on his face. "Yeah, we sure did son. You'd better go and say your goodbyes to the others," Max says as he steps up into the jet and the young man runs to catch the other B2B staff before their jet door closes. Inside the jet Raymond is fastening his seat belt. After Max does the same the jet is released for take off. Once in the air Max makes Raymond a drink and gives it to him.

"Here sir, drink this, it will help you relax," Max says. Raymond takes the glass and eagerly gulps most of it.

"We did it Max," Raymond says.

"No sir you did it," Max says.

"You know I couldn't have done it without you," Raymond says. "I don't know about that sir, you had one hell of a team," Max says. "Heaven of a team," Raymond corrects Max. They both laugh. Raymond puts the glass to his mouth and finishes the fruity drink.

Max takes the glass and says, "I'm talking about your Godfather, your father and you, now that's a dream team. Three men on a mission," Max says.

"I still can't believe over three million people decided to move to Africa in that short amount of time," Raymond says.

"The power of persuasion. I see why they call you the three M's in one. Raymond smiles and takes off his shoes. "I tell you Max it's a power greater than myself. A power I can't explain, ever since my Godfather touched me that night in his suite…" Raymond says. "Oh man that was wild," Max agrees. "From that time on, every time I began to speak it was like I could communicate to the soul of the people," Raymond says. Raymond begins to undo his tie and unbutton his top button on his shirt. "I'm getting hot, is it hot in here?" Raymond asks. "Sir you did a big thing. You made history. You will never be forgotten," Max says avoiding Raymond's question.

"Man I feel so great right now. I never felt this way, I feel complete. I have to call Diamond and my mother. I want them to share this with me," Raymond says as he reaches for his phone.

"Raymond put the phone down. As a matter of fact throw it over there," Max says with his gun pointed at Raymond. Raymond does as Max orders. "So it was you all this time," Raymond says. "Not quite. I was hired by your old campaign partner John Newton. All he wanted me to do was to stop you from going on that B2B Tour and get you to come back to be the Vice President, so he could be President," Max says as he grabs the phone off the jet floor. "But you just didn't stop. We arranged to scare you by the assassination attempt the first time, but you didn't stop. Then we had your father killed, but you didn't stop. And then we killed your Godfather, but you still didn't stop. Everyone was telling you to stop, but no, you are truly unstoppable," Max says.

"Why did you poison me? It's over. It's done," Raymond says.

"My orders were if I couldn't stop you after today, then kill you like the others," Max says.

"You let them use you to destroy me and my family?" Raymond asks.

"No Raymond you destroyed your own family, you destroyed the American family Raymond. This country is made of many cultures and many different people, it was created for that reason Raymond. You know the constitution. Immigrants come from all over to live together in this country, that's the plan. The plan is not for someone to start a New Nation and take one of the main threads from the fabric of this country. That is what you did Raymond, and when you did that, you divided a Nation," Max says.

"So that's what you are going to tell yourself to justify killing my father, my Godfather, and now me? What about the fact that most of the immigrants that come over here were coming of their own free will, and if they decide to go back they have a place to go back to. We were forced over here by people who enslaved our ancestors, but that was not the bad part. The bad part was up until now we didn't have a place to call our own country, because of what slavery has done," Raymond says. "You are so selfish Raymond. What gives you or your Godfather the right to decide to create a Nation for African Americans? Who died and made you the boss of history, giving you the authority to do something that hasn't been done before? Man I don't think anybody was thinking on this level until your Godfather came along. Everybody was happy the way things were."

"People were into music videos, rap, sports, DVD's, fashion, mega churches, big cars, big houses, and nice jobs. No body was talking about, "Back to the Beginning" until you started this crazy mess. You got my little girl asking me, 'Why can't we go the New Nation'?" Raymond can't you at least admit you were wrong for bringing division to homes, jobs, schools, and relationships?" Max says.

"If causing a people to think beyond their scars and their present condition, inspiring them to want more for themselves and for the future generation, if that's what you call division, then yes I caused division, but a good division," Raymond says.

"There's no such a thing as 'Good division'," Max says.

"We are just as American as most Caucasian people. Our race help build this Nation. Our ancestors nourished the Presidents of this country on their breasts. Our ancestors made companies millions of dollars, and we are still doing it today in one way or another. We are all related, because the black slaves had the babies of the white slave owner," Raymond says.

"Look at you Raymond, you've got some white in you. You went to the all-white schools. You were brought up in a predominately white community and you love your white girls too. Why? Because you got white all up in you. That is why they were going to put you in the White House, because they know you got white all up in there. When you try to divide this country you are only dividing yourself," Max says.

"This had nothing to do with black or white, it was only based on progress. If our ancestors nourished the Presidents of this country on their breasts, don't you think it's only fair for the children of those ancestors to one day become President of their own Nation? I could have easily played the race card, especially after the false sexual assault charges. You and I both know white interests were behind that, but I didn't mention race, and you know why? Because I didn't want all white Americans to suffer because of what one dirty politician did. This move was destiny, it was time for this to happen," Raymond says.

"I don't want to hear that destiny mess! You know what was destiny, you becoming Vice President. Everything was prepared well in advance. As a matter of fact around this time tomorrow you would have been America's first male black Vice President. You would have been sitting pretty in the White House instead of sitting here dying. But that wasn't good enough for Mr. Raymond Jackson. You had to go and start your own Nation. Look at yourself, you are an ingrate and don't even know it. The greatest country in the world offered you the highest position in history and you turned it down. I feel sorry for you, you are so divided within yourself, you couldn't help but to divide a Nation with your dreams," Max says.

"Was it just a dream Max? You saw it for yourself. You saw the buildings, homes, schools, streets, the universities, the government structure, the public transportation, the restaurants, hotels, TV and media outlets. You witnessed the modern technology, businesses and government operations to be just as good as in the US, or maybe even better. You've seen the New Nation before its own citizens saw it. I know you saw the potential that lies ahead. In five years Max we will be the wealthiest Nation in the world because of our cure for AIDS. Every nation will be beating a path to our door to get medicine, we will be known as the Healing Hospital of the World. In ten years Max we would have trained the best in sports, music, drama, business, corporate leadership, inventors, education, world politics, economics, construction, architects, sociology, psychology, theology, medicine, writers, singers - every area of creative and intellectual endeavor. Everything we accomplished in America we are going to accomplish again but for ourselves and for the world. In 20 years Max my son will be the first President of the New Nation of Africa and he is going to take the country to a stratospheric level you could never fathom." Raymond pauses, his voice becomes weaker and there is a slight rasp to his breathing. "So you see Max, it wasn't just a dream, it's a beautiful reality. A reality that will live on forever in spite of my death," Raymond says and then begins to cough.

"Raymond I wish I could go back and forth with you, but you don't have much longer," Max says as he looks at his watch. "The poison should be in its final stage in a minute, just enough time for me to go check on the pilots. When I come back out you should be dead and I can act surprised and then call for help," Max says. Then he turns around and walks down the aisle into the cockpit and locks the door. Raymond thought to run behind Max, grab his gun from him, and tell the pilot to fly to the nearest hospital and get the poison out of his system. But knowing how Max, along with John Newton had arranged the murder of his father and Godfather, he would have no reservation shooting him and the pilots on the spot. Raymond was more concerned about the pilots. He thought to himself that enough people have died and suffered for this mission already.

Raymond couldn't believe it was Max, an employee he has known for five years, who ate with him at his family's table, who slept in the same room and went across the country with him. The very man who was hired to protect him and had done so perfectly for five faithful years, is the very one who's been hired to kill him by a slow death. So Raymond sits in his seat cruising 45,000 feet in the air, going 577 miles per hour, 5,000 miles away from America and 5,000 miles from Africa.

The most powerful sign and symbol of Raymond's mission is his dying between two great nations. As the poison takes its toll on Raymond's body his mind begins to go back to a time when he was a college student home for the summer break. He could never forget one Sunday at the 8:00 am service where his father preached a sermon he continued to replay in his mind. Raymond is frustrated, because he knows he is dying and he would like to take a minute to reflect on his mother, sister, wife and other good memories, but instead he can't shake this one particular sermon. The text was where the Apostle Paul was writing to his young student Timothy during the time he was preparing to be executed, and he penned these farewell words, *"I fought a good fight. I kept the faith. I finished the course."* Out of all the thousands of sermons Raymond had heard his father preach it was that one that found a resting place in the corner of his mind, and now it was very clear why. It would be these exact words that summed up Raymond's own life and mission in connection to the New Nation. Raymond recalls his father saying in a sermon, "A good fight is a fight that brings the best out of you." If this indeed is the case then Raymond fought a good fight. Because he started out as a passionate politician, full of self-interested dreams and ideas, a person who could not control his desires and surrounded himself with people who pampered him, never pushing him to be all he was created to be. But during the good fight he transformed into a compassionate visionary who sacrificed himself to fulfill a purpose that would benefit the entire world.

Raymond also remembered his father saying, "Whatever you do, don't let go of your faith. You can let your enemies take your car, house, clothes and business, but whatever you do, hold onto your faith. If you can hold onto your faith you can manage to get back what you lost and some." Now he understands why his Godfather locked him up in a room for 40 days with nothing but bread, water and a Bible. He wanted Raymond to get steeped in his faith, the kind of faith that Abraham needed in order to give birth to nation. The same faith Moses needed to lead a nation. The same faith Joshua needed to inspire a nation. The same faith Samson needed to rescue a nation. The same faith David needed to rule a nation. The same faith the prophets needed to speak to a nation. The same faith Mary needed to give birth to the Savior of a nation. The same faith Christ needed to save a nation. The same faith George Washington and the forefathers needed to fight for a nation. The same faith African American slaves had to have to face a nation. The same faith civil right leaders had to desegregate a nation. It was the same faith Raymond had to have to be a founder of the New Nation. Now it was clear why the Caretaker's last words to him were, "Keep the faith." And in spite of the false accusations, an assassination attempt, being misunderstood, talked about, rejected, heart broken, underestimated, depressed, and oppressed, by the passion of a promise, in spite of accidents and incidents, in spite of his father's and Godfather's deaths, Raymond can honestly say in these crucial final moments of his life, "I still have my faith."

Finally Raymond had finished his course. Most of us have problems with finishing. We are great starters, but we can't finish our projects. Broken relationships are a clear sign that we can start something but can't finish, especially when there are objects and oppositions in our way. From the time Bishop Jackson was approached by Mr. Goodson, to the time Raymond drank the poison, Raymond was on a specific course. Even when he fought against the very idea of giving up the race of the Vice Presidency he was on his course. Every pain, problem, and perplexity was part of his course. He wouldn't change anything if he could, because only this course led him to his intended destiny. Any other course would have taken him in political circles around people who were saying all the right things, but doing nothing and going no where. It was a pleasure for Raymond to be offered a position in the White House as the first male African American Vice President. But it was a privilege and an honor to change the course of time by becoming the founder of the New Nation of Africa.

Raymond would never get to see the New Nation full to capacity with its citizens coming from all over the world. But what he saw already was more than enough. To Raymond the New Nation of Africa has become the Promised Land of the 21st century. Could this be the land Martin Luther King, Jr. was referring to when he said, *"I've been to the mountain top and I looked over and seen the Promise Land. I may not get there with you, but we as a people will get to the Promise Land."*

"Beep-beep-beep-beep-beep-beep-beep-beep-beep-beep-beep-beep-beep-beep," The alarm Raymond's Godfather had given him and the B2B staff while departing Africa went off, indicating the mission was completed.

"I finished," Raymond says then closes his eyes and passes from this world to the next.

Picture 63: *Carrying the Future*

Six months after Raymond's death, Diamond was appointed as the CEO of the New Nation of Africa. Mr. Goodson had left behind a handwritten will with explicit instructions naming Diamond Jackson sole proprietor of his entire estate including the New Nation, with specific instructions on preparing and training Raymond, Jr. to be the Nation's first President in the next 20 years.

Diamond is six months pregnant, standing in the executive administration conference room before her cabinet. She is dealing with the final issues to bring a long meeting to a close. "As I stated before, everything has been laid out before you as to how the New Nation is to be ran for the next 20 years. At that time my son will be installed as the first President," Diamond says.

"I want to announce today that I have decided to add to my staff a young lady who I have known for years. She was my husband's top aide in his political career before the New Nation Project, I believe she can be a great help to me and to this Nation. I would like you to welcome Ms. Tarisha Holiday and I would like for her to have a few words with you. The staff gives her a standing ovation

"Thank you all for your warm welcome. Please be seated. I want you to know I'm proud to be a part of this country and this administration. I'm prepared to work closely with Mrs. Jackson and you all to make this the greatest Nation on God's green earth. Thank you," Tarisha says. The staff gives her another round of applause.

"The very last matter before this meeting is adjourned is an announcement that the International community of Africa has officially accepted the New Nation as a member of the international counsel with unanimous support."

The staff gives another standing ovation. "This meeting is adjourned. Thank you very much." Everyone leaves but not before shaking the hand of their new founding leader. Once everyone has left the room, Diamond sits down, picks up the remote control, pushes a button and a projector descends. She pushes another button and a montage of pictures of Raymond, Bishop Jackson, the Godfather and the two men who were best friends in Africa long ago appear on the screen. Raymond, Jr. begins to kick and move around in her belly.

"Hold little man. Do you recognize them?" Diamond says as she laughs a little. "Well, it's time for me to tell you the story again," Diamond says rubbing her stomach. "It all started with a promise..."

To be continued...
Divided Nation
Part II
"Growing Pains"

Outro

It has been revealed to me something great will take place in the African American community. Apostles, prophets, evangelists, teachers, pastors, bishops, and elders are going to come together with their gifts, and insight, to do something that will impact the entire world in a glorious way.

Please believe me!
The Author

Acknowledgements

To my wife Vanassa, thank you for everything.
You keep my world running together smoothly.

I would also like to thank Judith C. Allen who did an outstanding job in editing this work.

About the Author:

NaCo has been blessed by the Most High God and his Son Christ Jesus to be able to discover his tremendous gifts. As a songwriter, singer, scriptwriter, inspirational speaker, founder of Divine Royalty Ministry and Divine Royalty Publishing. He recently released a spiritual self-help book entitled, Wife Material: Preparing Every Female For Marriage. This book gives single females hope to get married and stay married.

The author is part of a generation that has faced many conflicts, challenges and confrontations that have prepared them to be escorted into the presence of kings and queens and to share with them the solutions to the problem of the people. A new spiritual wine is about to be poured into a new generation. Get ready for the Joseph generation.

CPSIA information can be obtained
at www.ICGtesting.com
Printed in the USA
LVHW051036070623
749110LV00024B/76